What Happened to Him?

By Roger Neumaier

This book is dedicated to the memories of two of my teachers: Erling Larsen and Harriet Sheridan.

Prologue: News Story – March 15, 1993

President Clinton Commends Mayor Oleson

Story by Jeff Washington, *Saint Paul Daily Journal*

Thursday, after addressing the American Federation of Teachers Leadership Council, President Bill Clinton visited Saint Paul's North End Childcare Center. The childcare center has been lauded nationally for its innovative approach to teaching children from lower-income communities in the Greater Saint Paul area. Saint Paul's Mayor Douglas Oleson accompanied the president throughout the visit.

As he left the center, Clinton was asked if he felt there were lessons to be learned for the rest of the country from how the daycare center was managed. "Yes, certainly. The rest of the country should look closely at what this city under the leadership of Mayor Douglas Oleson is doing to innovate how government can work with diverse communities of need and the private sector. Oleson's approach to innovative government has been an effective laboratory showing the rest of the country how communities can bridge the gap between systemic poverty and economic growth."

Clinton was asked by a reporter if he had considered bringing Oleson into his cabinet. "Thought about it? I begged the young man to join my administration. Seems he's too committed to whatever has been started here in Saint Paul. But mark my words, friend, Douglas Oleson will be an important player in the future of the Democratic Party. He will have an influential future role in governing this country."

After departing from the daycare center, Clinton's motorcade

(See Clinton's Visit - Page A6)

Chapter 1 –My Name is Paul Newton

My name is Paul Newton. I was the undistinguished child of two highly successful and motivated parents. In September of 1995, I departed from my hometown of Chicago to pursue an undergraduate education at Carleton College in Northfield Minnesota.

My father, a successful corporate attorney, gave me advice as he chauffeured me to Chicago's Union Train Station, "Get your undergraduate degree in political science, son. Then knock off a law degree at Yale. Unlimited opportunities for success will follow."

The previous day, after hearing from me that I did not know what I wanted to study in college, my mother, a highly-regarded psychologist, had sharply responded, "Paul, when are you going to grow up?"

There I was, between the proverbial rock and two hard places. I had no interest in the law and if growing up meant being like my parents, I had no desire to reach my twenty-first birthday.

I didn't know what I wanted to study at Carleton. I had no aptitude in science or math. Studio art and art history seemed exciting. But my parents would accuse me of treating my education as entertainment. Economics was out. I quickly discovered in a high school economics course that I was interested in neither guns nor butter. So, the only areas I could figure out that were left were history and English literature. I would enjoy either of them. But for the life of me, I had no idea what I would do with those degrees after graduation.

I finally chose the obvious course of study. I would become a philosophy major. While I didn't know how I would use the degree, it seemed like learning about truth (which I anticipated must be the focus of philosophy) might be a good start for my adult life.

During my freshman year, I took two introductory philosophy courses. My conclusion was? Studying philosophy didn't lead to truth. It led to other philosophy courses and word games. Being a philosopher seemed like it would be similar to being a dog that continually chased its tail.

*****

The day after deciding to abandon philosophy, I knocked on the office door of my academic adviser. My advisor, Dr. Sharon Harris, was an English literature professor. After I knocked, she called out, "Come on in. The door doesn't have a bolt on it."

I entered Dr. Harris' office. She looked the part of a Chaucer scholar with a grey-buster-brown haircut and large, plastic-rimmed, thick-lensed eyeglasses. Her old-school wooden desk faced a large window and was surrounded from floor to ceiling with an array of well-worn hard-cover literature classics.

Dr. Harris said, "Paul, this is a nice surprise. Come on in. How are things?"

I sat down on the oak chair next to her desk and said, "I'm doing well, Dr. Harris. That's defining *doing well* as passing all of my courses. But I have an issue."

I paused, took a deep breath, and spit out, "I have had it with philosophy—I mean as my major."

Harris gave a soft laugh. "What took you so long, Paul? You never seemed like the sort of person who would be stimulated by Immanuel Kant."

Then, still with a smile, she added, "What have you decided to study?"

I was relieved she wasn't going to try to talk me into continuing as a philosophy major.

"That's the problem, Dr. Harris. I don't know."

Harris chuckled, took a drink of coffee from a large purple ceramic mug, turned back toward her window and looked out across the campus.

She was silent for a couple of minutes. I wondered what she was thinking.

When she looked back at me, she said, "Well Mr. Newton, I have two questions for you. Number one, what interests you? Whatever you study should grab your imagination—it should inspire you."

I was going to respond to the inquiry with an *I don't know*. But she continued. "My second question—probably the more important one—is what do you want to do when you grow up?"

Dr. Harris waited with a wry smile on her face while she studied my reaction. I felt uncomfortable. Harris had asked the right questions. I just didn't have the right answers. The silence made me uncomfortable but I realized I had to say something. She was going to make me respond.

"Good questions," I said as I stifled a nervous laugh. "I'll answer your second question first—because I know the answer to that one. I have no idea what I want to do when I grow up. My dad wants me to become an attorney—you know—make him proud—practice in front of the Supreme Court—like Oliver Wendell Holmes and all. My mom, well, she has much milder expectations. My mom hopes I graduate in four years. She told me it would be nice if I could support myself. Me, you want to know what my expectations are?"

She nodded and said, "Yes, that is why I asked."

I paused, trying to figure out what I could say. Finally, I just blurted out, "I don't have a clue."

Dr. Harris gave a kind smile. "OK. I'll accept that. But it's not a strong basis for me to give you a lot of advice. Many students don't know what they want to do. But often they don't recognize that important fact until after they have received their bachelor of arts diploma. You're way ahead of them. Those students, out of desperation, end up going back to school for a master's or PhD—or worse yet—they become teachers because they have no idea what else to do. The real tragedy is that they make terrible teachers—and there is such a need for teachers who care."

She smiled at me as she said, "Now, why don't you take a shot at my first question? What interests you?"

I figured I better come up with something a little better than *I don't know* and gave it a shot. "What interests me, huh? Well, everything interests me. I get turned on by a lot of stuff. I mean, I like to read—all sorts of fiction. I even got a kick out of reading *The Canterbury Tales* in your course."

I felt my cheeks turning red and quickly added, "I mean, I enjoyed the course—a lot. You taught it well. And I also enjoyed some of my other courses. I loved learning about history. And I read the *New York Times* every day. And I like sports—I played football in high school—but I didn't start."

I was quiet for a moment, then said, "You see, Dr. Harris, I like a lot of things—but I'm not too good at anything. That's why this is so darned hard."

I was thinking *what a stupid response* and added, "I don't know if what I'm saying means I shouldn't be in college. Maybe, I need to go out and, you know, do some grunt work for a couple of years before I try to get an education. Maybe…"

I stopped speaking. I had no idea how I could finish that thought.

Harris rescued me. "I understand, Paul. Go ahead and drop the philosophy major. I agree. Philosophy isn't for you. The breadth of your interests is wonderful. You enjoy a lot but you haven't closed in on what you want—and you shouldn't have to decide that—not now anyway. Go ahead and keep your options open. Become a history or English literature major for now. Enjoy an array of courses. In a year or so, we can sit down and repeat this conversation. I bet you'll find it easier to tell me what you want to study—and what you want to do with your life. Then we can talk about your major."

I gave it a minute's thought. What she said made a lot of sense.

Five minutes later, I was walking across the campus. with a big grin on my face. What a load off my shoulders! I liked everything about delaying that decision.

*****

Almost exactly a year later, I returned to Dr. Harris's office.

Harris had a smirk on her face as she said, "Well if it isn't the former philosopher. I have been looking forward to hearing how the muses have inspired you."

5

I couldn't help but laugh. "It's good to see you too, Dr. Harris. It's been a great year and I am glad to announce I am returning to your office today with a plan. A year ago, you suggested I tread water. You said that in a year, I might be ready to select a major. I come to you today with a plan. It's going to take a little help from you, but I think you're going to like it."

"Let me decide that," she said with a smirk.

"I want to become a journalism major. Last term, I took a course called *Joe McCarthy and Red-Baiting in the 1950s*. Learning about right-wing activism after World War II was an eye-opener for me. And Edward R. Murrow inspired me. By the end of the course, I realized I wanted to become a journalist. That, Dr. Harris, is why I am here today. I have decided to major in journalism."

It felt so good to tell her about my plan. I had a big smile plastered on my face as I waited for a response. But I had to wait for a couple of minutes. Harris had turned away from me and was looking out her window across the campus. As I watched the back of her head, I got insecure. I wondered what she was thinking.

She finally let me know. "First of all, I understand why you're impressed with Murrow. Every time I see the film *Point of Order* and am reminded of how Murrow took on Senator Joe McCarthy, I get inspired. Murrow was a great American—a real live hero. So, I understand why you are inspired."

Then she gave a look that wasn't so encouraging and I began to worry.

"Has it crossed your mind that Carleton does not offer a journalism degree? Doesn't that sort of create a sizeable roadblock?"

I took a deep breath and put it out there. "I considered that. But I think I've got it worked out. I plan to put together an interdisciplinary major in journalism. And you, Dr. Harris, can be my sponsor."

Once Dr. Harris had stopped laughing, she said, "Paul, this isn't exactly like being asked to the prom. I'm flattered, yes. A special major in journalism—that's a novel idea—I'll give you that. But I am not sure I have much to offer you in regards to journalism and I sincerely doubt that the college's academic curriculum committee is going be excited about someone who hasn't exactly been a stellar student creating a whole new department."

After taking a drink from her coffee mug, she turned away from me one more time and looked out that window across the campus. I waited nervously. I was relieved that at least I had been able to explain my plan.

Still looking away from me, she shook her head slowly from side to side before saying, "I remember when I was younger, Paul. I was quite the radical. I was angry at the establishment, passionate about getting the U.S. out of Viet Nam and not very focused upon my studies."

While she sat there looking away from me, I waited, wondering where this was going. And she made me wait at least a couple more minutes.

Finally, she sighed and said, "OK, Paul. I'll consider it. You put together a syllabus for your dream journalism program. I'll go over it. Then we can talk. But don't hold your breath—and keep trying to identify other options. All that I'm willing to commit to today is that if you put together a syllabus, I'll try to review it with an open mind."

Then the tone of her voice changed. "I do have a couple of suggestions, however. Instead of calling your special major *Journalism*, you need to give it an edge—call it something like *Modern Media in the United States*. You can pull in all of the things you spoke about. But you don't want to make your special major seem like you just want to learn to write a news story. You want to raise the stakes. Make it seem like you intend to analyze the cheesiness of our time. Maybe even include a couple of sociology courses in your study plan? And perhaps a few political science courses as well? Make your focus be that you want to analyze how journalism can investigate and address the challenges of modern life in America."

As I listened, I realized that Dr. Harris understood what I wanted to do even more than I did.

"On a practical level, give a call to the University of Minnesota's School of Journalism. Learn about their requirements for a major. You might want to ask to speak to their program's director, Dean Chambers. I went to school with Dean. He's a good chap. Tell him I suggested you contact him. Explain what you are trying to do. Ask him for advice in putting together your proposal."

*****

I thanked Dr. Harris and was about to leave when she added, "By the way, I do not consider your ideas to be lamebrained in any way. Your ideas are the product of a bright mind trying to do the right thing. I don't want you to ever hesitate to drop in and run ideas past me. I will let you know when I see landmines in your dreams."

I said, "Thanks, Dr. Harris. You'll be hearing from me."

As I left her office, Dr. Harris was looking down at the floor, chuckling.

*****

A few days before spring break, my syllabus for a special major was complete. I gave it the title *Journalism in Modern America.* The courses I proposed included:

- Three modern American history courses;
- A political science course entitled *The Elements of Democracy;*
- An English Department seminar on the history of story-telling;
- Another English Department seminar entitled *American Twentieth Century Biographies;*
- An information technology course—*Technology as a Research Tool;*
- A philosophy seminar with the promising title *Truth, Deception and Ethics;*
- Two original independent studies. I named the first one *The Development of Media in America* and the second, *The Role of the Press in a Free Society;*

And I threw in that I would find a summer internship between my Junior and Senior years with an as-yet-unknown newspaper. I also topped it off with a senior thesis that would require researching and writing a series of mock newspaper articles about some famous or notorious person.

I was so proud of my plan.

Two days after I submitted my final draft to Dr. Harris, she gave me a call and said, "I've read your proposal and I like it, Paul. Go ahead and submit it to the registrar."

I was so proud.

On the first day of the spring term of my sophomore year, I hand-delivered my request for a special major to the office of the college registrar.

*****

Four weeks later, Dr. Harris sent me a note asking if I would come to her home for tea. That Sunday morning as I walked to her two-story arts and crafts home, I was worried that the purpose of the meeting might be to inform me that my proposal had been rejected. Dr. Harris answered the door. A moment later, we were sitting at her elegant dining table, drinking from delicately flowered teacups while munching on scrumptious butter pecan cookies.

Dr. Harris gave me a thoughtful look. I wasn't sure where that look would lead. Then she gave a great big smile and said, "Congratulations, Paul. The curriculum committee loved your proposal. It's a go. Now, you've got some serious work to do."

Without much hesitation, she added, "And we can make one edit in your plan right away. I ran into an old friend of mine from college, Webster Pedersen. Pedersen publishes a weekly newspaper in the Minneapolis suburb of Bloomington. I told him about your special major. He told me he could use an intern this summer. I know that's a year ahead of your plan, but...."

She gave a big smile and completed her thought, "Are you interested?"

Chapter 2 –The Internship

I accepted the intern position at the *Bloomington Weekly Dispatch.*

A few weeks later, the school year was over and I rented a room near the newspaper's office. I had no doubt my parents were relieved that I would not be returning to Chicago for the summer.

I was ready to become the next Edward R. Murrow.

*****

Upon arrival at the *Bloomington Weekly Dispatch* for my first day of work, Webster Pedersen, the *Dispatch's* owner, publisher and primary reporter, invited me into his small office. Webster motioned for me to take a seat and called out, "Dolly, get in here."

A woman whose desk was outside of Pedersen's office joined us. Dolly, who must have been in her mid-50s, gave me a big smile. She had short white hair and was casually dressed in blue jeans and a Minnesota Twins T-shirt.

Webster took a drag from a lit cigarette and said, "Dolly is my only employee—other than you. She is part secretary, part business manager, part reporter and chief attempter to keep me out of trouble. Dolly has worked here since shortly after I bought the paper. If you have any questions and want an intelligent answer, don't ask me. Ask Dolly."

Dolly smiled, welcomed me and went back to her desk. Webster got up and went to a percolator that sat on a table in the corner of his office. He poured a full mug of coffee, returned to his desk and handed me the cup of steaming hot coffee. Then I listened to Webster for the next quarter of an hour as he reminisced about his days as a reporter with the Minneapolis Star. This was the first of many interesting sessions in which my new boss described the world of journalism. During the chat, Webster made clear that I should always address him by his first name.

Webster had short grey hair and a Hercule Poirot mustache. He always arrived at work in a black and white houndstooth sportscoat (even on hot days) but would take the jacket off and roll up the sleeves of his white button-down-collar shirt before sitting down at his desk.

During our conversations, Webster always chain-smoked Benson & Hedges cigarettes. After taking a puff, he would focus much of his attention on the ash of the cigarette, holding the lit cigarette at an angle while pointing it towards the ceiling. It almost seemed like some sort of personal contest—how long could he leave that ash undisturbed on the burning cigarette? As the cigarette burned and the ash extended, the angle at which he pointed the cigarette toward the ceiling increased. Despite Webster's intense efforts, after a cigarette was half-smoked, the cylinder of ash invariably separated from the rest of the cigarette almost like a rocket stage falling from a space capsule. The ash would land on his desk or shirtsleeve and once that had occurred, Webster would pause, scowl for a moment, then continue with whatever he was saying.

*****

At that first meeting, Webster asked me to write a story about Bloomington's two high school football teams and get to know the Bloomington city government structure and its leaders. He informed me that he and his wife would be taking a cross-country road trip the following week and expected me to make a lot of progress on those projects in his absence.

So, I had to hit the ground running. That week, I met with each high school's coach and listened to their ambitious plans for improving their team's record during the coming season. The coaches each made positive statements like, "We got a bunch of juniors who are ready to turn things around;" and "This year's quarterback could very well become all-state. He's matured."

The following week while Webster was out of the office, I sat down with Bloomington's mayor and each city council member. Every one of them spoke enthusiastically about economic development, bragged about reduction in auto-theft crimes and shared their hope for new innovative programs in the upcoming budget. They also provided a steady undercurrent of subtle sniping at one another. These interviews were an education in how bureaucrats try to raise themselves by drawing down their listener's perception of their colleague's worth.

I also met with the city's chief administrative officer. She characterized Bloomington as *a fantastic place to live, do business and raise a family*. Then she took me on a quick tour of the city showing me parks, schools and the Mall of America—the city's major economic engine. She bought me a chocolate milkshake at the mall and, with a cute smirk on her face, told me not to consider the milkshake a bribe.

I promised her I wouldn't.

*****

After he returned from his road trip, I gave Webster the first draft of my story about the high school football teams.

Webster laughed and said, "I like the story. But be honest with me, Paul. Do you think either of those football teams will do any better than they have in the past?"

It had been obvious that both football programs had been awful forever. Nothing that the coaches had said had led me to believe things were going to get any better. I blushed but said nothing.

"Anyway, good job," Webster said. "Have Dolly put it in next week's edition."

I walked out of the office saying to myself, "Whoa! Maybe I'm better than I thought."

Webster called out after me that he wanted to meet with me the following day about the Bloomington city government story. He added that he would give me an investigative report assignment. I stepped back into his office and asked what he meant by an *investigative report assignment.*

He smiled coyly and said, "You'll have to wait until tomorrow. But trust me, it will be interesting."

*****

The following morning, I knocked on Webster's closed office door as soon as I got to the office.

"Enter, oh wise intern."

"How did you know it was me?" I asked.

"Dolly doesn't bother to knock and you're the only other person here. Come on in. I assume you want to find out what your new assignment is going to be?"

I gave an *I-could-care-less* shrug *and said,* "Uh, yeah, I guess so."

"But before we get into that," Webster chuckled, "I want to chat about your interviews with the city politicians.

I'm pleased you met with that gang of fools. Use those interviews for your next story."

Uncertain of how to approach the story on the council and mayor, I asked, "What sort of approach were you—uhm—thinking I should take?"

Pedersen silently watched his cigarette smoke curl toward the ceiling while he carefully balanced its delicate ash. After a moment, he looked back to me and said, "You're writing the story, my boy. You figure it out. I'm not paying you nothing for nothing—or wait," he chuckled, "I guess I am. Anyway, you figure it out."

Then Webster Pedersen handed me a manila folder stuffed with newspaper clippings and said, "I promised Dr. Harris that I'd give you an interesting potential project. Read over these articles. We'll discuss them in a day or two."

Then Webster stood up. "I've got to hustle on over to the Chamber now. They're serving chicken and rice for lunch today. I certainly don't want to miss that!"

He paused and winked as he squashed his cigarette into an already overflowing ashtray. Then he walked out the door.

*****

I went back to my cubicle and opened the manila folder. In it were about forty news articles about a politician named Douglas Oleson. I'd heard of him. He had been mayor of Saint Paul when I started at Carleton. The articles were primarily from *The Saint Paul Daily Journal* and *The Minneapolis News Chronicle*. Each article was hand-marked with its date of publication. I recognized the handwriting. It was Webster's.

Chapter 3 – The Assignment

Webster was out of the office. His friend, a pastor at a local Lutheran church, had passed away. Dolly told me Webster was staying home to write his friend's obituary.

I spent the day reviewing the articles Webster had shared about Saint Paul's former mayor. The clippings traced Oleson's rise to success, his battles with other Minnesota bureaucrats and the scandals that brought him down. One of the articles described his career as "a meteoric rise and an even more rapid and remarkable fall."

*****

The following morning, when Webster walked into his office, he called out, "Heh intern! Grab a cup of java and get in here. It's time to talk."

I got this sinking feeling. Had I done, said or written something that pissed Webster off? Was I about to get dumped on—or dumped? I grabbed my cup of coffee and hustled into his office. Webster gestured for me to take a chair, then took a long drag from his Benson and Hedges. I waited and watched. After blowing smoke out toward the ceiling and completing his focused act of balancing the cigarette's ash, Webster asked, "Well, what did you think?"

I wasn't sure what he was talking about. The possibilities that raced through my head included his obituary for the pastor had been in the morning's Saint Paul *Daily Journal*; The Bloomington city council's squabble from the previous evening; or maybe, he was wondering about how badly the Minnesota Twins were tanking. (Webster was quite the baseball fan).

I'm afraid my response was just a blank stare.

"I see you are befuddled," he said. "I'm asking about that young idiot politician who imploded—the one who was the subject of the articles that are sitting on your desk. What are your thoughts, oh wise and insightful intern?"

I thought about his question for a moment, took a gulp of coffee and responded. "I read the articles. The guy had it all—wife, career, charm. But for some reason, he screwed it all up. I have no idea why he did that. Maybe he was just a fraud in the first place?"

Webster appeared satisfied with my response. "I don't know either. I've heard a variety of different theories. Wouldn't a case study that explored his career, one that touched bases with the people he knew and worked with— those he impacted—wouldn't that be something fantastic? Putting together those facts could turn into a fascinating opportunity for you to write something compelling."

Webster took a sip of coffee and then a drag from his Benson and Hedges. After the cigarette smoke had melted into the ceiling and the ash on his cigarette had been inspected (making sure it was still intact), he continued to speak. "I'm sorry you have to put up with all of this smoke, Paul. But I don't enjoy my coffee unless I accompany it with a cigarette. And once I light a cigarette, after I inhale, I have to exhale. Then, well, smoke enters the room."

"No problem," I said.

"You're wrong Paul. It is a problem—a big one. These damn cancer sticks will eventually take my life. But I just don't enjoy my coffee without them—and I couldn't live without my coffee."

Webster took another long drag from his cigarette and studied the smoke as it disappeared above his desk.

He gave a pensive look and asked, "What do you think motivated Oleson? Why do you think he screwed everything up?" He paused, then asked, "Would you like to work on a project that attempted to answer those questions?"

"It would be interesting," I responded. "The guy had the world by the balls. Then he messed everything up. What do you think happened?"

Webster laughed while shaking his head. "I'm asking you, rookie."

"I'm not sure," I said. "I'll have to think about it for a little while."

"Well, I'm willing to give you the time. If you're interested, it could be a fascinating project. You'll need to start with a foundation of what has already been written about him—what's already known. Over the next week, I want you to write a compilation of what you found in those articles I gave you—I mean doing that in addition to knocking off whatever other hot journalistic assignments I give you."

I asked, "Is there anything special about this guy—I mean anything beyond what's in the articles?"

"That's the question, Paul. I don't know. Investigative journalism is about exploring what you don't know—not about confirming what's already known. I've always wondered what made that guy tick. Where did he come from? Where did he go? Why? Those are the things you'll need to find out."

Webster paused, taking another long drag from his cigarette. Then he coughed heavily. After the ash from his cigarette fell onto his sleeve, he brushed it off with his free hand and said, "Dr. Harris told me you are bright but that you need some sort of challenge to start your engines. She asked me to throw something challenging at you, something you can work on after you return to school. Voila! This story about Douglas Oleson is my proposal. Pull it together. Talk to the people who knew Oleson—whose lives he impacted—the ones who worked for him—those who judged him—maybe some who looked up to him as well as others who thought he was a creep."

He took a sip of coffee and added, "If you're not interested, you can just give me my file back. But if this draws your attention, hold onto it. Do something creative with it. I'll continue giving you assignments during the rest of the summer. But you also can be working on this. And, as I said, you might want to use this assignment as the cornerstone for doing something bigger when you get back to school."

The wheels were turning in my mind. This could be my senior thesis!

"Thanks, Webster. This sounds like the project I needed."

Pedersen was silent for a moment; his attention having turned to extinguishing a cigarette in his ashtray.

Then he looked up with a smile and a twinkle in his eye and said, "Good. I like your attitude, boy. Now, I have a second assignment for you. You need to get to work on that article about Bloomington's leadership. You've met all the players in this little suburban empire. Tie them together. Take some chances on the story. I'll review your draft—making sure we don't print anything that will get me sued. But the city's mayor and council are a bunch of dufuses. Someone has to point that out. You've been anointed."

Feeling like a real reporter, I gave a confident nod and said, "You got it, boss."

As I began to head out of his office, Webster asked, "Can you get me a draft on the dufus article in a couple of weeks?"

Webster had thrown me off by first speaking about Oleson and then jumping to Bloomington's city government. I wasn't sure what angle I should take on the story about the city. But I thought of some of the newspaper reporters I'd seen in Hollywood movies and responded, "I'll get it done."

"Thanks, Paul." Have a good day. I have to take off—got a close friend to whom I need to bid *au revoir*. I've got a funeral to attend."

Chapter 4 –Summarizing the Oleson Articles

Over the next few days, I reread the Oleson newspaper articles and started to draft the paper about Oleson Webster had requested. The clippings included information about Oleson's background, the history of his runs for office, his political successes as well as the controversies that brought an end to his tenure as mayor of Saint Paul. But they didn't tell me anything about him as a person. Who was Douglas Oleson anyway?

Rather than repeating the entire compilation I wrote for Webster, I've condensed what I put together. It is included below.

*****

Douglas Oleson was born in 1960, the only child of Millie Oleson. The newspaper articles gave no information about his father or any other living relatives. During his youth, the mother and son moved often, living in a variety of apartments, rented houses and trailer homes in the Minneapolis-Saint Paul area. After graduating from high school, Oleson attended St. Cloud State University, a public college an hour's drive from the Twin Cities of Minneapolis-Saint Paul. At St. Cloud State, Oleson earned a bachelor's degree in political science.

After graduating, Oleson married his college girlfriend, Miki. They moved back to Saint Paul where he went to work for Minnesota's Democratic Farmer Labor political party.

Miki's parents lived in the Twin Cities area. The articles didn't say much more about Miki except that both sets of her grandparents had been incarcerated in a California relocation center during World War Two.

Four years after gaining his college degree, Oleson was elected to a seat in the Minnesota House of Representatives. His legislative district included most of the City of Saint Paul. In 1989, Oleson became a candidate for the position of mayor of Saint Paul against a one-term incumbent. He ran a brutal campaign accusing his opponent of incompetency. He promised to cut fees and taxes through better management of the budget and increased revenues that would come from economic growth. Oleson's campaign for mayor was heavily funded by Saint Paul's property development community and the city's employee labor unions.

Once elected mayor, Oleson appointed a cabinet that was young, bright and ambitious. Its star was Debbie Perth who became his deputy-mayor. Perth had been Oleson's legislative assistant when he served in the State House of Representatives. During his first term, Oleson made many organizational changes throughout the city while continually battling with the Saint Paul City Council on a litany of issues. In the 1991 city council election, he sponsored three council candidates, two of whom defeated incumbent council members who had blocked some of his initiatives. In this way, Oleson sent out a message to the remaining incumbents—don't mess with me.

Oleson was gaining regional recognition. A Minneapolis News Chronicle article quoted unnamed party insiders that Oleson might become the state's next governor. A 1993 story compared him to John F. Kennedy.

It was accompanied by a photograph showing Oleson holding his three-month-old son, Douglas Jr. In the photo, his wife Miki looks on proudly at husband and son.

In 1992, Douglas Oleson led Minnesotans for Clinton for President. A nationally syndicated columnist predicted that Oleson would be appointed Clinton's Secretary of Labor. One story from The Saint Paul Daily Journal included a photo showing Douglas and Miki Oleson with Bill and Hillary Clinton, champagne glasses in hand, at Clinton's inaugural ball.

President Clinton visited the Twin Cities in March of 1993. An article quoted Clinton as saying, "Douglas Oleson will be an important player in the future of the Democratic Party. He will have an influential future role in governing this country."

A January 1993 article in The Daily Journal reported that an organization called The Saint Paul Minority Coalition awarded Mayor Oleson the title of 1992 Community Champion for his administration's outreach programs that promoted citywide services for preschool children and low-income single-parent families.

Oleson ran for a second term in 1993 against a weak opponent. He won with 65% of the vote. He described his landslide victory as a mandate for change. However, Oleson's glowing fortunes began to change during his second term. In early 1994, a Daily Journal editorial was entitled, Change? Change from What to What? The story mocked Oleson's constant promises for the future and criticized a perceived lack of success in implementing anything of substance.

Several Minneapolis News Chronicle articles in 1994 documented Oleson's questionable campaign practices. In both of Oleson's mayoral victories, one contributor had skirted Minnesota campaign finance laws and had coordinated the contribution of at least two hundred thousand dollars to each campaign. That contributor was the owner of a property development firm which later benefitted from some questionable zoning decisions. Another article documented major contributions from the Saint Paul Police Officer's Guild to Oleson. It included a summary of the union's contractual achievements that resulted from negotiations with the city after the election.

In June of 1994, Oleson and his wife spent a week at a Mexican resort. The trip was financed by the Minnesota State Contractors Association. After the article was printed, Oleson immediately reimbursed the contractors. Another 1994 article highlighted Oleson's multiple political trips to the East Coast. It referenced rumors about a purported love relationship between Oleson and his chief of staff. Oleson's response to critics was that "tawdry accusations are the price of success."

In October of 1995, The Daily Journal added detail to the allegations that Oleson was having an affair with vice-mayor Debbie Perth. It identified publicly financed trips that Oleson and Perth had taken together to Atlanta and San Francisco as well as a weeklong trip to Europe investigating opportunities for public-private partnerships. The article included photographs of Oleson and Perth dancing at a San Francisco nightclub. Two weeks later, Ms. Perth resigned, moved to Washington DC and took a position with the Democratic National Committee.

Later in 1995, the Minnesota State Attorney General began an investigation into quid-pro-quo contributions and zoning decisions that occurred during Oleson's first term. The city's planning director who had been implicated in the investigation, resigned and took a position with a California construction company.

In January of 1996, a brief article from The Daily Journal reported that Miki Oleson filed for divorce. It implied that the action had been driven by rumors about her husband reportedly having a new love interest.

In April of 1996, Oleson abruptly resigned.

The final article in Webster's manila file folder was dated April 30, 1996. The article, taken from the Ramsey County Register, is included on the following page in its entirety.

Mayor Oleson Resigns

Douglas Oleson, Saint Paul's embattled mayor, resigned on April 24. In a letter submitted to City Council President Dave Dickens, Oleson stated his resignation was effective immediately. The action represents the culmination of months of battles between Mayor Oleson and the City Council. It also may have been driven by a year-long Ramsey County Attorney's Office investigation into possible Oleson campaign violations.

Oleson's resignation followed a tumultuous year in which battles with the city council, allegations of a romantic liaison with his deputy mayor and the County Attorney's investigation dominated municipal public attention.

City Council President Dave Dickens said in a written statement that Oleson's action "would allow the city to move beyond the acrimony and controversy that had dominated Oleson's administration. Saint Paul deserves better than the controversy it has faced under Oleson's leadership. Hopefully, the next mayor will be able to create an environment that is more conducive to teamwork."

When asked if he would be a candidate for mayor in an upcoming special election to replace Oleson, Dickens indicated it was too soon to say but that he would consider that option carefully in the coming weeks.

Douglas Oleson had been elected as Saint Paul's 49th Mayor in November of 1989 becoming the youngest mayor in the city's history. The energetic Democratic Farmer Labor candidate had run on traditional Republican themes promising no new taxes, fiscal responsibility, innovation and accountability. During his first term in office, multiple local pundits predicted great things for him including roles as the state's governor and the nation's president. Oleson made no secret that both of these positions attracted his attention.

Oleson recently separated from his wife. The couple has one small child. His wife has refused comment.

Chapter 5 – The Project Plan

After summarizing the Oleson articles, I began to focus on Bloomington's city leaders. I was uncomfortable addressing their political disagreements. But Webster had made it clear he wanted me to speak directly to their conflicts.

A week later, I handed Webster a draft of my Bloomington city leadership story. I had entitled it *City Leaders Can't See Eye-to-Eye.*

Webster took a drag from a newly lighted cigarette and pointed at the chair in front of his desk. I sat down and watched him as he digested my draft. He looked up at me once and nodded. Then he took a deep breath, picked up a sharp pencil and I watched him edit the hell out of my article. He drew a line through one sentence after another, occasionally slashing whole paragraphs. For ten minutes, the only sound in the room was Webster's pencil scratching through my submission. Halfway through the markup, he turned around and reached for an electric pencil sharpener on the credenza behind his desk. After his pencil had been sharpened, he returned to his task—dismantling the product of my hard work.

When he stopped crossing out my work, he looked up, gave me a grim smile and said, "I congratulate you on taking my directions literally. You left no politician unwounded. That being said, you should never listen to any boss too literally. This boss intends to stay in business in this little burg. My edits have hopefully reduced the number of traumas your article will afflict on these clueless nincompoops. The possibility that I will be lynched or tarred and feathered in the next week has been significantly reduced."

He handed me the edited story. Less than half of it remained.

Then Webster changed the subject. "I read your background piece on Oleson. Nice job, Paul. Looks like you thoroughly absorbed the articles I shared and did some extra research to boot."

"Thanks, Webster. I found a few articles at the library. The whole story is, as you put it, fascinating."

He took a drag from his cigarette, followed by his ritual attention to the disappearing smoke and the remaining ash on the lit cigarette.

Then he continued. "My big question is whether you want to hang on to that folder of clippings? Do you want to work on the Douglas Oleson project when you return to school?"

I had thought a lot about it and responded, "I badly needed a project to work on for my senior thesis. Douglas Oleson's saga fits the bill. But the thing I keep wondering about as I put this all together is that there was nothing—no follow-up articles about what happened to Oleson after he resigned. What did happen to him?"

"Hmmm," Webster gave me a thoughtful look as he crushed the remaining stub of his cigarette into his ashtray. "That's the mystery, my friend. The bugger left Saint Paul and no one has heard from him since."

Webster lit another cigarette, inhaling deeply and sighing as he blew the smoke toward the ceiling. "No one knows, Paul. That's the ten-million-dollar question. No one knows. What happened to him?"

There was silence in the room for a couple of minutes.

Finally, Webster said, "Go ahead. Put together a project plan. The plan should state what you are trying to find out, learn or prove and how you're gonna prove it. Include who you think you'll want to interview and what questions you might ask. Bring the project plan back to me. I'll give it a once over and share my ten cents worth. But I'm sure that when you get back to school, Sharon—er, Dr. Harris will scrub the hell out of it."

Grinning, I said, "Sure, Webster. This is going to be exciting. I'm about to become Sherlock Holmes."

Webster chortled, took a sip of coffee and responded, "I am not sure that's such a good thing, boy. I heard that Holmes turned into a drug addict. Stay away from the cocaine—he didn't."

*****

I returned to my cubicle and stared at my computer terminal. I was wondering, "What was I going to investigate? What was I trying to prove? What would I write?"

After fifteen minutes of meditating on a blank computer display without even touching my keyboard, I arrived at a decision. I needed to go for a walk.

*****

After trudging through muggy, oppressive heat for an hour, I found myself at a neighborhood schoolyard. I sat down on a bench at the side of the playground and watched some kids playing some sort of ballgame.

Their orange soccer-sized rubber ball bounced up to me. I picked it up and a girl ran up to me—her long blond ponytail swinging behind her. The girl was maybe ten years old and was wearing blue jeans, a T-shirt and a baseball cap.

She said, "Thanks for catching the ball, mister. Can I have it back?"

"Sure," I said. "But I have a question, first. What game are you playing?"

"Well," the girl said, "we're sort of making it up as we go. It's sort of a combination of kickball and boomerang—and soccer. It's a whole lot of fun."

"How do you win the game?"

"Uhm," she paused, then said, I don't know that yet. But we're having a whole lot of fun—so who cares?"

She grabbed the ball out of my hands and dribbled it (like a basketball) back toward a half-dozen other boys and girls who chased her—now carrying it like a football—until she kicked the ball to the far corner of the playground. There, a boy in red shorts and a white T-shirt caught the ball, turned and tossed it up hitting the backboard of a basketball basket."

I stood up and started on my way back toward the *Dispatch*. As I walked, I thought about those kids in the playground. They sure were having a lot of fun. Their object seemed to be to follow the ball and let whatever happened happen. They were making up their rules as they went.

Maybe, that's what I needed to do.

*****

A few minutes later, sitting down in my cubicle, I typed: *What happened to Douglas Oleson?*

I paused, evaluating what I had just written, then, continued to type.

- *Where did Oleson come from?*
- *What drove him?*

- *What was he trying to achieve?*
- *Why did he screw it up?*
- *Where did he go?*

That was it. I had described my project! Those were the questions which I would address in my senior paper. But what was I trying to prove? I had no clue. I stared at my computer display.

After I few minutes, I shrugged and decided, once again, that I needed to act like those kids on the playground. I would have to let the game evolve rather than establish rules before beginning. I realized I'd have to defend the vagueness of the project to both Webster and Dr. Harris. I couldn't tell them I was copying a ten-year-old girl from a playground who had a long blonde ponytail that dangled out of her baseball hat. I'd have to put together a more profound defense. But I knew I was copying that little girl. And, I was certain that this was the right approach.

But now I needed to turn that approach into a plan. That meant putting together a list of the bureaucrats I proposed to interview.

Suddenly, I realized I had found an enthusiasm for the project. I worked with an uninhibited zeal—sort of similar to what that little girl had demonstrated when she took the ball out of my hands and ran off with it.

I typed a list of names of those I should interview.

- Miki Oleson;
- Oleson's mother Millie;
- Saint Paul's current mayor, Mayor Dickens;
- Oleson's deputy mayor, Debbie Perth;
- Jim Jolly, Saint Paul's previous mayor;
- Some of the reporters who had written the articles for which I had clippings;

- Whoever was the second love interest referenced in one of the articles; and
- Some childhood friends or teachers

Minutes later, I was done. Sure, the list would change. But it was a start.

I took my plan to Webster. He was on a phone call but gestured for me to take a seat. He pressed a button and suddenly his caller was on the speakerphone. The woman was angry that the city had not accepted her request to rezone her home from residential to business. She was explaining to Webster how corrupt Bloomington's city government really was. She wanted *The Dispatch* to run an expose on the city's planning department.

Webster kept saying things like, "Uh huh—yeah. Yes. I certainly do understand. Gee, that must be awfully frustrating."

Webster saw my typewritten project outline, reached out and took it from me. While the caller droned on with complaints about the city, Webster scanned the plan. A moment later, he picked up a pencil from his desk, circled interviewee #3, the current mayor and penciled onto my plan,

> *Good start, I'm going to see Mayor Dickens later this evening at a fundraiser. I'll tell him about your project and ask him if he'll give you an interview.*
>
> *Oh yeah, by the way, drop the idea of interviewing Jim Jolly, the incumbent Douglas beat to become mayor. Jolly took losing hard, started drinking and died a couple of years after his defeat. It was a good idea and Jolly would have been a*

good interview. Unfortunately, reality has intervened.

*****

The next day when I arrived at my cubicle, a brief handwritten note sat in the middle of my desk.

> *I have an all-day meeting today. However, I did ask Dickens about the interview. He's expecting you to call to schedule it today. Dolly has his secretary's phone number.*
>
> *Rotsa Ruck —Webster*

Chapter 6 –Interview with the Mayor

Webster's note about setting up an interview with Saint Paul's mayor caught me off guard.

Sure, I'd put together a list of people I might interview. But I wasn't ready to actually interview anyone—certainly not the mayor of a large city. While I wasn't a total neophyte—I had already interviewed the city officials of Bloomington—in interviewing Mayor Dickens, I was stepping up to a higher level of the political fray.

That being said, the die was cast. Webster had committed me. One positive was that if Saint Paul's mayor was at all like the Bloomington officials, I wouldn't need an exhaustive list of questions. Bloomington officials just liked to talk. I would introduce myself to Dickens, tell him about my project, ask him a few general questions and hope he would run with it from there.

Dolly gave me the phone number of the mayor's administrative assistant. I dialed it and was immediately greeted by a cheerful voice who informed me that the mayor was eager to make my acquaintance. We agreed I would come to the Saint Paul City Hall at two that Friday afternoon.

*****

That Friday, when I arrived at the mayor's office, his administrative assistant explained, "The mayor has been pulled into an important meeting that's running late. Take a seat in the conference room over there. He'll join you as soon as he can. He is eager to meet you."

She pointed at a small conference room with a rectangular glass table and six beige plastic chairs. I entered the room and sat down. One wall of the conference room had a whiteboard and another had a large framed photo of F. Scott Fitzgerald.

I entertained myself by looking at that profile portrait of the famous writer. Fitzgerald's straight nose, stiff white collar and carefully combed hair made him look like an old-time movie star. I had known that Fitzgerald was originally from Saint Paul and I'd read three of his novels, particularly enjoying *The Great Gatsby*.

I spent time watching the conference room wall clock which was next to the Fitzgerald photograph. The second hand went round and round as minutes slowly passed. I began to wonder if I would even see the mayor that day.

But at about a quarter to three, a short trim man dressed in blue jeans, cowboy boots and a button-down plaid cowboy shirt walked up to the office assistant and chatted with her. She pointed at me. He turned, looked at me, said something to her and headed toward me.

After he entered the conference room, he walked up to me, stuck out his hand and firmly shook mine.

"Howdy. You must be Paul. I'm the mayor. You can call me Dave. Sorry about the blue jeans—it's casual Friday around here."

The mayor sat down at the head of the table and jumped right into it.

"So good to meet you," he started it off. "Webster told me you are a sharp cookie who could use some assistance on a project. I look forward to helping you in any way I can. I was sorry to make you wait but you know how it goes, I had an important meeting. Got to keep the city running. Why don't we start out by you telling me about yourself and your project."

I spent a few minutes telling him about my special major and how the internship with Webster fit into it. Then I described Webster's idea that I write a paper on the rise and fall of Douglas Oleson.

Dickens fought off a smile as I said *and fall.*

I kept going. "I didn't know anything about Oleson until Webster dropped a folder full of articles about him on my desk. You are my first project interview. So, what you share with me is going to shape much of my attitude out of the chute. The paper I write will end up being my senior thesis."

After pensively nodding ascent throughout my description of the project, Dickens smiled and said, "That sounds good. Let's go for it. What would you like me to tell you?"

"Could you let me know how you first met Douglas Oleson and about your relationship with him?"

Dickens looked up at the ceiling for a moment. He seemed to be seriously considering my question. After a deep sigh, he gave an odd, almost quizzical expression (which I didn't understand) and launched into a response.

"Well, It's like this, Paul. I met Douglas Oleson soon after he graduated from college. He was an intern working for the party. Seemed like a nice kid, obviously ambitious, but a nice kid. Later, he became a state representative. He stopped by my city council office a couple of times to introduce himself. He was working it hard—you know—trying to flatter me. He was my best friend and we were going to be best buddies."

Dickens gave another sigh, looked down and shook his head sadly from side to side before continuing. "When he decided to run for mayor, he visited me again—still my best buddy. He turned the charm on even more intensely telling me how competent our city council was—how much he respected my opinion. He promised to be the best team player the city council had ever known. I listened to him and thanked him for the visit. However, there was no doubt in my mind that he was utterly insincere."

I interjected, "But then you endorsed him, didn't you?"

Dickens looked up at the ceiling again before clearing his throat and saying, "I don't think it was really an endorsement, Paul. I think it was more like, have at it, Doug. Anyway, I was being cautious. You know, damned if you do and damned if you don't."

Dickens's face had turned a little red after my comment. I decided not to ask any more questions about the endorsement.

Dickens stood up, opened the conference room door and approached his administrative assistant. He spoke with her for a moment. After he returned, he said, "I asked my assistant to bring us a pitcher of water with a couple of glasses. I'm thirsty and figured you might be as well."

He sat down and said, "Of course, the moment Oleson got elected, he showed no spirit of teamwork. According to him, anything the city accomplished was his creation—even if he had nothing to do with it. On the other hand, anything that went wrong, well, that was the fault of the prior mayor or of the city council—take your pick. While I wasn't surprised, I didn't enjoy it. He came into a city government that was working pretty well and became the divider-in-chief."

Dickens's assistant entered the conference room and placed a glass tray with a pitcher of ice water and two glasses on the conference table. She quietly said, "I need to remind you, Mr. Mayor. You have an appointment with Councilman Reynolds in about five minutes in his office."

"Oh, yeah," Dickens responded. "Damn, Paul. I am sorry I was so delayed in getting here today. Let's push through your questions."

He poured a glass of water for each of us.

After taking a long drink from his glass, he checked his watch. Then he continued to speak. "You asked me about my relationship with Oleson? He had no respect for me. Douglas Oleson was a son of a bitch from the outset, manipulating people, using them, taking advantage of them—then discarding them. I saw the way he flirted with the female staff. To say it gently, the guy was always on the make. We were never friends."

Dickens had not minced words. He stopped speaking and his face turned from light red to crimson. I had planned on asking about Oleson's weaknesses and strengths, his achievements and mistakes. But Dickens had already given me his cold opinion on those factors.

I was trying to figure out what I should ask when Dickens said, "What you are trying to ask me is *Other than that how did I like the guy*? Right?"

We both laughed.

I tried a different tack. "Did Oleson accomplish anything during his terms that made the city a better place for its residents?"

Dickens looked at his watch again. "You're asking me if I can say anything positive about the creep. Hmm. Let me think. Oh, yes," he smiled as he said, "I know—he resigned—and left town—disappeared. Thank you, Doug."

The mayor's assistant peeked her head inside the door. "Mayor, Councilman Reynolds is waiting."

Dickens stood up and gave me a thoughtful look. "I know politicians have a bad name. But a lot of us go into this business because we want to make this world a better place. We spend our time and our energy working evenings and weekends, reaching out to constituents. We try to create change for the better, to improve our communities. But there are some people out there who are just out for themselves. And Oleson—he was such a person. Was he smart? Sure as hell—that is if smart is defined as being able to figure out how to manipulate people and get them to do things that they know are wrong. But did he produce anything of value? No. He didn't. Nada. Nothing. Zip."

Dickens looked at his watch again and said, "Look. I have another meeting to go to. Is there anything else you need to know? Because I think I've been pretty clear with you about my perception of the Douglas Oleson."

I asked, "Do you know what Oleson did after leaving Saint Paul?"

"Haven't a clue—and don't give a damn—unless he plans on returning."

The mayor was on his way out of the conference room. I picked up my notebook and followed. Before we got to the door, I asked, "Is there anyone else you would recommend for me to meet with—you know, to learn more about Oleson?"

As he opened the conference room door, Dickens turned his head back toward me and said, "I am sure you have lined up the usual suspects. But there is one person you might have missed. Why don't you check with that developer—you know, the guy who gave Oleson a couple hundred thousand bucks—a couple of times? Ask him what was so special about Douglas that would cause him and his friends to throw away that cash. And yeah, there was also that girl, the public information specialist. Oleson apparently liked to spend time with her. It would be interesting to find out what she felt was so damned special about Oleson. Maybe you should ask her what caused her to get a divorce a couple of months before she left the city—and to lose custody of her kid."

As he left the room, Dickens turned to me and said, "Anyway, pleasure meeting you, Paul. Sorry, we had to rush. Give my best to Webster. And good luck on your paper. It'll be interesting. You're certainly researching a piece of work. And oh, send me a copy of the final paper when it's done."

*****

As I left the mayor's office, I looked at my watch. Dickens had spent less than thirty minutes with me. My next step was to digest what had transpired in that short meeting. True, Dickens had responded to my questions. But what was behind all of that bitterness?

As I rode the bus home, I jotted down a couple of questions that the interview with Dickens had brought to the fore:

- Dickens obviously hated Oleson. Why?
- Who was the developer that Dickens said had contributed to Oleson's campaign? What was his story?

    o   Who was the public information specialist to whom Dickens had referred? What was her story? Was she the other love interest mentioned in that article in the Minneapolis paper?

*****

The following Monday, Webster took me out for lunch. He was curious about my meeting with Dickens. After I repeated Dickens's statements about Oleson, Webster laughed so hard that he ended up coughing for a couple of minutes.

"Dave Dickens didn't like Doug Oleson at all. But Dickens is his own amazing story. There's a lot more to it than he shared with you. Hopefully, you'll get some of those pieces filled in during your interviews with other players."

"Could you give me some insight into those pieces?"

Webster smiled with a twinkle in his eye.

"Sorry Paul, this is your project. I wouldn't want to deprive you of any of the excitement of the chase. But I can say this. You are going to be interviewing a lot of folks. They each will have their own perspective, their own interests. Your job as a reporter is to figure out when someone is giving you useful information and when they are trying to work you because of their personal biases. You are going to have to be able to smell the truth—as well as the lies. But enough philosophizing from an old man. Now that you've spoken with Dickens—who hated Oleson— you need to balance your perspective. It's time to meet one of the former mayor's unabashed supporters.

Chapter 7 –The Labor Federation

Later that afternoon, Webster handed me the business card for Chris Thompson of the Saint Paul Regional Labor Federation.

"I guarantee you," Webster said, "Thompson's perspectives on Oleson are different than Dickens'."

I walked over to the Bloomington Public Library and reviewed a variety of newspaper clippings related to Thompson that had been written during Oleson's tenure. Then, I put together a list of questions for the labor leader.

The following morning, I called Thompson's office.

"Labor Federation, Thompson here. How can I help you?"

I introduced myself and my project, then asked him, "Would you be willing to meet with me to respond to a few questions about Douglas Oleson's terms in office."

"Glad to," he responded. "Douglas Oleson, eh? You picked yourself a fun one there. Yeah, I'd be happy to sit down with you. When do you want to meet?"

After Thompson realized I didn't have a car, he offered to meet me at a coffee shop near the *Dispatch's* office.

*****

That Friday morning, as I walked into the coffee shop, someone called out, "Hey, you must be Paul."

The only other customer in the coffee shop was a middle-aged, slightly stout guy wearing blue jeans and a dark blue T-shirt that had *Give 'em Hell* printed on it.

I said, "Yeah, that's me. You must be Chris Thompson."

"Grab a cup of java and a pastry. Have 'em put it on my bill."

A couple of minutes later, I sat down next to Thompson with a coffee latte and fresh cinnamon roll.

"So, you're a Carleton student, eh? That's a pretty pricey school. Either your parents have a lot of money or you're really smart—probably both."

What could I say? *I'm dumb and they're rich?*

I just said, "Good to meet you."

Thompson moved right into it. "What do you want to know about Doug Oleson? Do you wanna talk about when he was taking off as the toast of the town—or about when he crash-landed like a wayward rocket from outer space? Because that guy did both—he went for one hell of a ride."

"I'd be interested in both."

"I met Oleson while he was still in college. He spent a summer working on a local congressional campaign. It was clear he was a smart cookie. You'd ask him a simple question and get back a thoughtful analysis. If he didn't know an answer, he'd tell you and then get back to you quickly—after he researched it. You could see he was capable of accomplishing a lot with his life."

Thompson was interrupted by a cell phone call. We were meeting back when most of us didn't have a cell phone. But Thompson had one and used it a lot. He took several incoming calls during our conversation.

This call was from a state legislator. I listened as Thompson said, "You can do whatever the hell you want. But you know, senator, you made a commitment to my organization, to my members. What you're doing now—

that's not what you promised. But go ahead, do your thing. We'll evaluate it all before the next election."

Thompson apologized for the interruption and continued. "Oleson understood labor, the pressures upon the workers at the City and how tough it is to make it if you're not part of the landed gentry. He also made it clear that his campaign needed money and valued the labor's ability to hit the street with door-to-door appeals."

Thompson took another call. He listened for a moment then said, "I'm sorry honey. I'm meeting with somebody right now. You'll have to ask someone else to do it."

He turned back to me, scratched his head and gave a philosophical look. "Oleson and I hit it off pretty good. After he got into the office, we went out for an occasional beer, sometimes dinner. I'd describe it as a cordial relationship that worked pretty well for both of our organizations. If you read the papers, you know that right after he became mayor, we completed negotiations on a bargaining agreement for most city workers. City rank and file had been working without a contract for several years. Oleson was criticized for caving in on the negotiations. However, the city was woefully behind in employee compensation levels. We provided the comparisons and Oleson realized the city needed to get with it. That didn't mean he didn't get roasted for settling with us. I get that. But the contract the employee union negotiated with Oleson also authorized the city to make significant organizational and classification changes they'd sought for years. Newspapers don't tend to cover both sides of those kinds of issues. And, young man, there are always two sides—to every story."

I asked, "Do you think that Oleson initiated changes that made a worthwhile difference in how the city operates?"

"The guy wanted to make some pretty radical changes in how the city worked. Many of his proposals were good but required employee support—legally and operationally. My members understood that changes needed to be made and, in many instances, my members strongly supported the operational improvements and streamlining Oleson was pushing. When employees are allowed to innovate, they are more productive—their work is more satisfying. The challenge that Oleson faced was not labor. It was the mid-level managers he had inherited. They didn't want change. The Peter principle had been happily at work in the city for decades. People were hired into the city as clerks and, if they didn't offend any of their higher-ups, they ended up as supervisors or managers and stayed until they retired. Turf was the rule. You know, you don't touch my program and I won't touch yours."

Thompson looked reflective for a moment. "You can't blame it all on the incumbent Mayor Jolly who Oleson defeated. Like most cities, Saint Paul had a long tradition of electing nice guys as mayor who were clueless about how to manage. They just sort of depended upon the mid-managers they inherited and presided over the mediocrity that was the unavoidable result."

Thompson's phone rang. He looked at the phone, apparently recognizing the caller, scowled and ignored the call.

"Oleson took on the mediocrity of existing mid-management. City rank-and-file workers applauded him for that. The changes that came out of his actions saved tons of money for the city and increased its effectiveness. If you want to get a sense of the deadwood that Doug took on, meet with one of those former mid-managers. The most obvious candidate for that might be the city's former finance director, Warren Daniels."

"How about the fact," I asked, "that property developers and labor unions gave generously to his campaign. Isn't that sort of like being in bed with the devil?"

Oleson chuckled, then shrugged his shoulders and said, "Nobody gets anywhere in city government unless the developers are happy. When the developers are making lots of money, they cooperate. They contribute to campaigns. That's the way it is—in every local government."

Thompson was interrupted by another phone call. This time, he took the call and listened for fifteen minutes saying very little. You could see he was aggravated. Finally, he angrily said, "Just tell them to go to hell."

After he snapped his flip-phone shut, Thompson said, "Sorry but I've got another meeting to run to in a couple of minutes.

I asked, "What do you think of deputy-mayor Debbie Perth?"

"That woman is a firecracker," he said with a smile. "If she isn't mayor someday, she's gonna be governor— maybe president. She's aggressive and intelligent. Hiring her was the smartest thing Doug did. Almost every good idea Oleson tried to implement was Debbie's—or else Debbie was the point person on implementing it. However, I think Oleson probably should have had a little more discretion in his relationship with her. Fucking his deputy-mayor—and getting caught—was not the most brilliant move."

"And what do you think of the new mayor— Dickens?

Thompson chuckled. "I'll give you an honest answer. But you're going to have to give me your word it's totally off the record."

"You've got it," I said.

Thompson broke into a big smile before saying, "I mentioned the Peter principle a little while ago. Dickens should just bite the bullet and change his first name to *Peter*. Just get it over with—accept the obvious. Dickens is in so far over his head he's ready to mow the city hall's lawn after a snowstorm in February. He is a little bureaucrat who has no clue about who's on first or what's on second. He'll be a one-term mayor if there ever was one and then he can go run some podunk water district in western North Dakota."

Thompson chuckled and looked down at his watch. "I gotta run in a minute. Sorry."

"One more question," I said. "I read in *The Daily Journal* that you called for Oleson's resignation toward the end of his regime. That doesn't sound too chummy."

"Well, it wasn't intended to sound chummy. Oleson knew that he'd lost control of his administration—as well as his personal life. He was a dead fish in the water. It was time for him to go. In calling for his resignation, I was just admitting the obvious."

Thompson stood up and reached out to shake my hand. "It was good to meet you, Paul. Send me a copy of the article when it's complete. And try not to screw labor in what you write. I need to say that because, well, screwing labor is something newspapers are prone to do."

And Chris Thompson was on his way out the door.

Chapter 8 – A Former Director

When I returned to the office, Webster was waiting to be briefed on my Thompson interview. He listened attentively and nodded as I read my notes that concluded with Thompson's recommendation that I meet with the former City of Saint Paul manager. I asked Webster what he thought of that suggestion.

Webster nodded and said, "Yeah, that's a good recommendation. I vaguely remember Daniels. He of slinked around in the background, making mistakes and correcting them whenever possible. If he couldn't correct a mistake, he'd blame it on his staff or someone higher up in the organization. He'd be a good one to interview. I don't have his phone number but anytime I run into a dead end on something like this, I just ask Dolly. She always finds a way to come up with whatever I need."

Webster lit a cigarette. Before drawing any smoke, he said, "Keep it up. You're going to turn into an ace reporter yet."

As I left Webster's office, I approached Dolly asking for her assistance. She told me she would try to locate Daniel's phone number.

*****

Monday morning, as I walked into the office, Dolly had a twinkle in her eye. When I asked her what was up, she handed me a slip of paper with Warren Daniels' phone number written on it.

I asked her how she got it.

"Well," she said looking like the cat that ate the canary, "I go to church for multiple reasons. One is that I know a lot of people there who have access to a lot of information."

*****

A little while later, I called the number she had given me. I asked the woman who answered my call if Warren Daniels was in.

"May I ask who is calling and why?"

I wanted to tell whoever was on the phone, *no you can't*, but instead, I stumbled through a brief explanation of my being an intern writing a paper about Saint Paul city government.

The woman paused before saying, "Well, all right. I'll get him."

She must have tried to cover the mouthpiece on the phone but I heard her holler, "I don't know who the hell it is, Warren. He says he's an intern. He's writing a paper about Douglas Oleson. He just asked to speak to you."

A moment later, a loud, gruff voice said, "Yeah, this is Daniels. What do you want?"

This time I delivered a more coherent description of who I was and what I wanted.

When I finished, the man said, "OK. I'm Daniels. I used to be the director of finance and information technology for the City of Saint Paul. That was until Douglas Oleson threw me out onto the street. Sure. I'll meet with you. Why don't you come over to my home tomorrow morning? We can have a cup of coffee and you can ask me your questions. Does that work?"

I agreed to be at Daniel's condo at ten the following morning. I wasn't looking forward to the interview, but it made a lot of sense to speak with him.

*****

The next morning, I got out of the elevator on the fourth floor of Daniel's Minneapolis condominium building and rapped on his door. An older man came to the door. Daniels was dressed in brown baggy pants, slippers and, even though it was a hot day, a fairly heavy cardigan sweater.

He yelled, "You're 15 minutes late," Then Daniels gave me a friendly smile. Based upon that smile, I decided I must be dealing with a guy who was yelling because he was hard of hearing rather than full of anger.

Daniels invited me into his living room. The room was warm and stuffy but smelled like something good had just come out of the oven.

I sat down on the couch in front of a coffee table. Warren Daniels sat across from me on a large, worn, stuffed chair. A moment later, his wife came into the living room with a tray that held three coffee cups, a matching coffee pot, three small plates, a cream and sugar set and a large plate loaded with thick cookies. Mrs. Daniels set the tray down on the coffee table and filled each cup with coffee before sitting down on a rocker next to her husband.

Warren yelled, "That's my wife, Betty. Hope you don't mind if she sits in with us. Sometimes I have a bit of trouble hearing. She helps me out. Have a cookie."

I placed a still hot cookie on the small plate Betty had set in front of me. The coffee was weak and without flavor but the warm oatmeal cookie was soft and brimming with nuts and raisins. As I describe that cookie today, I can still almost taste it.

50

"I didn't catch your name yesterday," Daniels started out. "Was it Peter?"

I quickly realized I would have a much more successful conversation if I spoke slowly and loudly. "My name is Paul. I'm a summer intern working for the *Bloomington Weekly Dispatch*. I'm working on a project that..."

He interrupted me. "No. You don't need to tell me that stuff. I got it on the phone. I just didn't catch your name. So, you want to know about the city, do you? Well, let me tell you, I worked for the City of Saint Paul for forty years. I was director of finance and information technology for fifteen of those years. I managed both areas at the same time. A lot of city employees just serve their time. But I tried to deliver quality. I introduced computers to the city and found people who knew how to make 'em work who could fix 'em when they broke down. I managed the accounting stuff too, got us audited every year, and whenever there were audit findings, we'd fix whatever needed fixing. City employees are not necessarily the best employees. But I ran a tight ship. When I said, *jump*, they asked, *how high?*"

Betty spoke up. "Paul, would you like another cookie?"

I was embarrassed but these cookies were so good. They seemed to include banana, cinnamon, raisins and walnuts along with the oatmeal. I felt I should say *no*, but I gratefully took another cookie.

"Go ahead, Peter," Warren said. "Ask me any questions you got."

"Thank you, Warren. What did you think of Mayor Oleson?"

"You mean," he angrily responded, "what do I think of that shit who put me out to pasture? What do I think of that egotistic moron who destroyed what I had spent so long building? What do I think of that ambitious son-of-a-bitch who ruined the city? Well, I guess I didn't consider him my best friend."

Warren looked at Betty and they both giggled. I realized I wasn't gonna get a lot more out of the interview. We spent the next hour talking about funny things that had happened over the years at the City of Saint Paul.

One woman who worked for Warren stood out in his memory. "This woman—uhm—her name was—well—I can't remember her name. Anyway, she used to take a nap every day. She'd get her work done and head over to the break room couch. Soon, she'd be snoring. Well, one day we had this fire alarm. Everybody cleared out of the building and gathered at our appointed street corner about a block away. When we took roll out there, she was missing. Anyway, when we returned to the building, she was there, in the breakroom, sleeping like a baby. But she did good work and boy, could man, could she ever make a great tuna casserole that she brought into our Friday potlucks."

Warren laughed as he finished this story.

*****

An hour later, as I headed out to catch a bus back to Bloomington, I decided to skip lunch. I had eaten four of Betty's huge scrumptious cookies.

As I waited for the bus, it occurred to me that it would be useful to have an objective measure of how well the city's finances were managed under Daniels.

In a high school basic accounting course, I'd learned that a well-managed business or government would rarely have audit findings and its audit opinions wouldn't be too harsh. Instead of returning to Bloomington, I took the bus to the Saint Paul Public Library. I planned to review the city's audited financial reports.

I found the city's annual audited reports for the years 1978 through 1989. Each of these reports had at least three audit findings. They spoke about inadequate controls on automated systems; weak internal controls; and poor cash management. In one year's financial statements, the state auditor had given the city a qualified opinion. It stated that that the financial statements might contain material misstatements or omissions—a big deal.

OK. That meant that during Daniel's tenure, finances weren't that well managed. But what was the reason? Did he have too few staff? Was he a poor manager? I wanted to find out. The other question was how well did the city do after Oleson became mayor.

That last question was the easiest to answer. I looked at the audit reports for the years 1990 to 1995, during Douglas Oleson's administration. There was one finding in 1990 and none in the following years.

But how about personnel levels?

By looking at staffing distributions in the annual reports, I was able to determine that during Oleson's administration, there had been decreases in staffing in the areas that Daniels had previously managed. There were 20% fewer staff in those areas between 1990 and 1995 than there had been at any point between 1978 and 1989.

I had pretty much confirmed Chris Thompson's comment about the improvements in quality. But I was curious. Was it Daniels's fault or was there a different reason? I decided to ask Thompson. As a labor leader, he would have contacts who could speak to what sort of manager Daniels had been.

Once I returned to the office, I gave Chris a call. Moments later, I was on the phone with Chris Thompson as he drove up to Duluth for a labor meeting.

I told Thompson that the financial statements confirmed finances at the city had improved after Oleson was elected even though finance staffing had been reduced. I asked, "Was the problem Warren Daniels' poor management style?"

Thompson laughed. "I congratulate you on determining that there was a change in the quality of the city's financial management under Oleson. What was Daniel's management style? Based on grievances that came through my office, I can tell you unequivocally that Warren was a bully. He bullied his staff and he bullied other department managers. Using the carrot and stick approach to allocating city resources, Warren Daniels was more powerful than the city's mayor."

Thompson paused, I heard a car horn and Thompson swearing under his breath.

A moment later he continued. "Sorry about that. Some fools shouldn't have a license. Anyway, if a department did not cooperate with Daniel's wishes, they lost some funding, their contracts weren't approved or their information system requests were ignored. What sort of manager was he? The guy was a little emperor. He hated Oleson for separating him from that power. But he didn't go down without a fight. He sued the city after Oleson fired him. I'll send you a clipping about that. In the hearing, one manager after another, one employee after another, testified that Daniels was an incompetent bully."

Thompson paused, then said, "I got another call I gotta take. Keep it up. You're doing a good job."

*****

I left work that night simply glowing. I really was turning into a reporter!

The following Tuesday, a photocopy of a news article from *The Daily Journal* was delivered to the *Weekly Dispatch*. The article was entitled, *Former City CFO/CIO's Suit Thrown Out*. The sub-heading for the article was *Fired City Manager Described as Bully*.

Thompson's description of Warren Daniels was confirmed in the article. Attached to the article was a handwritten note from Chris:

Paul, I should have anticipated that there'd be questions after you met with Warren. I came up with another way for you to get perspective on the changes that occurred after he was booted out. Spoke with someone I know, an accounts payable supervisor who worked for Warren. She still is with the city. If you want her insight into the changes that occurred, give her a call. Her name is Barbara Robbins.

Chris's note included a phone number. It made sense to speak with Robbins. I gave her a call. She told me she couldn't take time off from work during the week but offered to meet me on Saturday morning. We agreed to meet at the same Bloomington Coffee shop where I'd met Chris. She told me I could recognize her by the Minnesota Twins 1987 World Series Champions T-shirt she would wear.

*****

Saturday at ten, I was sitting in the coffee shop when a trim, friendly-looking woman in a Minnesota Twins World Championship T-shirt walked into the shop, up to me and said to me, "Be with you in a sec—gotta get myself a cup of java."

A couple of minutes later, Barbara Robbins was sitting across from me chatting like we were old buddies. Chris had told her about my project.

"It sounds interesting," she said. "Chris said you wanted to know what it was like to work in accounting before Oleson became mayor and how it changed after Oleson's team took over. I'll probably tell you more than you want to hear."

She took a bite from a jelly-filled glazed donut, a sip from her coffee (in a plastic Minnesota Twins cup) and continued. "Maybe Warren wasn't a bad person. But he certainly was a crappy manager. He didn't have a clue about accounting or information technology. He was hired by the city to throw mail in the mail room. He did that for almost a decade. Then he became the mailroom supervisor. A few years later, he was promoted to acting manager of accounting—then they just removed the word *acting*."

She took a sip of coffee. She gazed out the coffee shop window for a moment, then said, "Warren may not have known much about accounting—he let everybody else do the technical stuff—but he understood the power that comes from controlling peoples' budgets. That's what he spent his time on—not planning the budget or analyzing revenues and expenditures. His shtick was to use the budget to punish and reward. People began to fear him. If anyone treated him with disrespect, their budget was cut. Later, when he took over information services, he made sure that new equipment was installed only in areas that kissed his ass. What a creep."

She chuckled for a moment. "A few of us knew what we were doing. We tried as hard as we could to get things right. However, several employees were totally confused by any accounting entry. If they woke up from their naps and happened to make a general ledger entry, they made it backwards. Those people treated Warren like an absolute god and were rewarded for it. The same stuff went on in information services. Cute young women who had never touched a keyboard soon were supervisors. Anytime we got a really good programmer or technician, he or she stayed for six or seven months, then found a better job somewhere else. It was painful to watch. As a result, our systems were really awful."

She stopped speaking. I thought maybe she was done but a moment later, she sighed and said, "Warren retired from the city the day after Oleson took the oath of office. Information services and accounting became separately managed areas. Our new accounting manager had worked as a CPA in the private sector and had been an auditor. Our new accounting manager knew the difference between a debit and a credit and so did the people she hired. Incompetent staff started choosing to retire. We installed a new automated accounting system and before you knew it, we were proud of the quality of our work and morale shot up."

I asked, "Did productivity and morale go up elsewhere in the city?"

"I don't know," she said. "Some departments got smaller. Their staff were not happy. But Oleson told everybody to start measuring quality and productivity. That was an exciting change for some areas but it scared the shit out of others. My opinion? Productivity improved."

"What did staff think of the new mayor?"

"I don't know. Some people thought he was in love with himself. A lot of us figured he would only be around long enough to get a more important position. Some staff missed the good old days when there was less pressure to perform. With Oleson constantly promoting everything he claimed to have done, there was a whole lot more attention on all of us. If you did something really good, Oleson took credit for it. If you made a big mistake, someone would see that it ended up in *The Daily Journal*."

Barbara gave a big sigh, grinned and said, "There you have it."

She asked me what I had heard from the other people I'd interviewed. I told her I'd only met with the new mayor, Dave Dickens, Warren Daniels and Chris Thompson.

She responded, "Mayor Dickens—he's a royal idiot. While Oleson may have been a narcissist, at least he was a competent narcissist. Dickens doesn't know whether he's coming or going. I ignore him. Accounting ignores him. We are still being run well and I enjoy my job."

Barbara told me that she needed to get going. She had to do some shopping at the Mall of America.

After she left, I sat there for a while digesting the conversation and another doughnut. I realized Chris Thompson had been pretty accurate in all he had said to me.

Chapter 9 – Spin City

The following Monday morning, as I was putting together my notes from my meeting with Barbara, my phone rang. A pleasant-sounding woman said "Paul. My name is Mary Anne Swenson. I ran into Warren Daniels the other day—I used to work with him at the city. He mentioned you were working on a project related to Douglas Oleson. Warren said he had spent some time chatting with you about Oleson's administration."

I responded, "Yes, that's true."

Mary Anne Swenson waited to see if I would say more. When I didn't, she said, "It sounds like a really interesting project. Warren explained you're a student at Carleton who is doing this project during an internship with the *Bloomington Daily Dispatch*."

I was wondering where this was going and simply said, "Yes. I am."

"I thought you might want to sit down with me and my colleague. We worked with Warren. We might be able to answer some of your questions, you know supplement what Warren has already shared with you."

I now understood where this was going. Warren had told somebody I had interviewed him. Recognizing his communication skills—or lack thereof, they decided they needed to shine up his version of the past.

"Sure," I said. "That would be great. I'd enjoy sitting down with you. When would you like to meet?"

"Well, it just so happens, Paul, that my colleague and I were going out to lunch tomorrow. If you are available, we'd love for you to join us."

We quickly agreed that Mary Anne and her colleague would pick me up the following day at 11:45. They would take me out to lunch at Ciao Bella, a restaurant located in Edina, a prestigious Minneapolis suburb near Bloomington. Given that the restaurant was in Edina, I figured there was a good chance that Ciao Bella might be pretty pricey.

*****

I walked into Webster's office and told him about the conversation.

"Do you know what spin is?" He asked.

I nodded and said, "Uh-huh."

"Prepare yourself to become an expert."

*****

The following day at 11:45 on the nose, a shiny black Jeep Cherokee pulled up to the curb in front of the *Dispatch*. The man driving the car lowered his car window and said, "Paul? I'm Bill Jones and this is Mary Anne Swenson. Hop on in."

Jones looked to be in his mid-sixties. He was fine-boned, had a thin gray combover and was wearing a light blue open-collar button-down shirt. Sitting next to him in the front seat was a woman of about the same age. She had shoulder-length strawberry blonde hair, was wearing a yellow sleeveless summer dress and had a sheer pink silk scarf tied around her neck.

I got into the back seat of the Jeep and we were on our way.

Mary Anne turned to me and gave a warm smile. "Hi Paul, it was so nice of you to meet with us on such short notice. I was Jim Jolly's human resources director. Bill was Jim's deputy. We are both so pleased you can join us for lunch."

*****

While Ciao Bello was the fanciest restaurant I had dined at in Minnesota, I had often dined at elegant Chicago restaurants with my parents. So, dining at an expensive restaurant didn't intimidate or ingratiate me. But the fact we were going to such a nice place told me that Webster had nailed it. Bill and Mary Anne were intending to become my new best friends.

We were quickly seated in an elegant dining room. Mary Anne ordered a caprese salad and a glass of Chardonnay. Bill ordered the Bella Burger (a fancy hamburger) and a Miller light beer. I followed his lead on the burger but replaced the beer with a Pepsi. I continued to suffer from the unfortunate circumstance of being under the drinking age.

*****

Mary Anne started the conversation. "Warren Daniels was a loyal hard hard-working public servant. With Warren's hearing going and his advanced age taking its toll, I doubt you were too impressed after your meeting. We recognize Daniels wasn't the strongest accountant in the world, but he relied upon other skilled employees to do the technical work. His focus was making sure that crucial initiatives were funded."

They both waited for me to respond. I figured Mary Anne had told me something and asked nothing. So, I didn't need to say anything. Finally, to dissolve the discomfort of quiet that followed her statement, I said, "But boy, does his wife ever make good oatmeal cookies."

All three of us laughed. Any tension was erased.

Bill took over. "What Mary Anne said is the truth. Warren got a lot of things done. You should have seen accounting before he moved into the top position. It was awful. We never had been able to get a meaningful report from them. And Daniels created the information services department from nothing. But Mary Anne and I thought you might have questions about Jim Jolly and Douglas Oleson's administrations to which we could add a response."

I pulled out my notebook. I had written down a few questions just in case.

I started out. "I heard that Oleson was pretty hard on Jolly during that first election. What's your perspective on that?"

Bill Jones leaned forward, gave a reassuring look, and began to describe how Oleson tore into Jim Jolly. "It would be pretty hard to understate the vengeance of Oleson's campaign. Jim Jolly was the happy warrior—the community leader who always saw the bright side of things. His success was his ability to get people in the community to work together. He wasn't a technocrat and he didn't push. He inspired."

The waiter delivered our drinks and Bill took a sip of his beer. "The Reagan-Bush years had been pretty tough on the city's finances. But despite the financial challenges we faced, Jim kept his administration and the community focused on what needed to be done. During that campaign, Douglas Oleson picked at everything that didn't get done and blamed it on Jolly. Jolly took it hard. Oleson's criticisms weren't fair. Then, after Oleson got into office, he took credit for everything that Jim had accomplished. It made me sick."

Jones took another drink of beer and looked down, shaking his head. When he looked up, he had a bit of a smile on his face. "Oleson hired a bunch of young bureaucrats who were more skilled at public relations than at connecting with the community. He threw out the people who had worked for the city for years—people who had close relationships with Saint Paul's citizens. The new administration spent its energy manipulating information in order to find ways to declare themselves brilliant administrators without doing hardly anything new."

I asked, "Did Oleson accomplish anything of value?"

Jones responded, "Sure. I think he did a lot on parks. But he depended upon employees that Jolly had brought to the city in the first place. His programs for helping lower-income kids were great. But he never gave credit to Jolly for the groundwork that had been laid for those programs."

"I get it," Bill Jones continued. "This is politics. You gotta be tough. You gotta take credit. But the thing that was painful to watch was how Oleson destroyed Jolly's legacy. Doug had no conscience. A lot of us loved Jim Jolly. He didn't deserve the treatment he got. Nor did those of us who'd worked for the city for years. How fair was it for Oleson to take credit for everything we'd ever accomplished on the one hand and then to announce that we were incompetent a moment later? Daniels wasn't the greatest CFO, I'll grant you. Jolly knew it. Sure, it was time for Daniels to retire. But to blame Jim Jolly for that, well—that just wasn't fair."

At that point, Mary Anne took the baton. "Douglas Oleson took a lot of credit for the diversity in his administration. But many of the women and people of color he put in positions of power were originally hired by Jim.

Jolly coached them and taught them the skills that led to their success. If you compared us to Minneapolis' city government during Jolly's tenure, we employed a much higher percentage of women managers and people of color. We should probably have done a much better job communicating all we accomplished during Jim's administration. But we were focused on getting things done rather than taking credit. And we did things legally. Oleson's regime ignored legal restrictions. The developers who funded Oleson's election benefited more than anyone from his administration."

Mary Anne took a piece of paper out of her purse, handed it to me and said, "This is a list of zoning suits initiated against the city after Oleson came into power. A slew of their zoning decisions were questionable at best and just plain corrupt at worst."

She took a sip from her wine, then added, "One of the problems with Oleson quitting and leaving town the way he did was that he was never held accountable for many of the improper zoning decisions made by his administration."

I won't continue to recite all of the arguments Mary Anne and Bill Jones put forward to prove that Oleson had accomplished nothing. But the general accusation was that Douglas Oleson was ambitious, skirted the law and took credit for whatever Jim Jolly had accomplished.

*****

What I decided after the meeting with Bill Jones and Mary Anne Swenson was that Jim Jolly was like a boxer who had fought the fight but lost the bout as well as all the accolades that go with winning. I'm sure Jolly's regime probably did accomplish some things of value for which Oleson claimed credit. If Jolly had defeated Douglas Oleson, he and his supporters would've been able to take credit for their successes and could have ignored their failures.

But Jim Jolly and his team didn't win. Jolly's entourage had to watch as Oleson took office, pointing out all of Jolly's supposed failures and claiming credit for accomplishments—whether Oleson deserved credit for them or not.

And that, I decided, is our political process—like it or not.

Chapter 10 – Junior Year

It was early September. Webster took me out to lunch. Over a bacon, lettuce and tomato sandwich, he told me he'd enjoyed having me at the *Weekly Dispatch* and added that if I was interested, I was welcome to work there again during the following summer.

I thanked him and said I'd probably take him up on his offer.

*****

A couple of days later, I was on an Amtrak Empire Builder heading for Chicago. I planned to spend a week visiting my folks before returning to Carleton for my junior year.

My dad picked me up at the train station. The plan was for me to spend the first half of the week with him and the remainder of the week with my mother.

My father congratulated me on my summer internship. "I'm certain," he said with some parental authority, "that your work for the *Weekly Dispatch* will be well regarded by any law school to which you apply."

"Dad," I responded, "I'm not going to law school. Done. Final. Accept it. I'm a journalist headed for a career in journalism. I wish you could absorb that fact and live with it."

My father's simple response was, "You're saying that now, Paul. We'll see."

My mother was not that supportive. "I'm glad you enjoyed your summer," she said. "The internship was a good idea—much cheaper than sending you to a summer camp in the Rockies. But Paul, my question for you is when do you intend to grow up?"

*****

A week later, I was back at school.

Dr. Harris congratulated me on every aspect of the summer internship. She asked a lot of questions about how Webster was doing and told me that the Douglas Oleson project was brilliant.

"That is exactly the feather in the cap of your special major that you needed."

The school year moved forward. I was confident that the courses I was taking provided the right context and preparation for my future career. I didn't spend much time working on the Douglas Oleson project. It was not on my radar. My coursework received attention.

And, there was a new distraction. I had my first girlfriend.

I had been on very few dates in my life. I am not sure why. Maybe it was because I was shy. Maybe I just was leery of relationships having seen my parents treat their marriage as a psychological battlefield. Whatever the cause, I had not dated in high school or college.

I was a junior and Kathy was a freshman. Kathy didn't appear to have any real insecurities, certainly not about men, anyway. She had told her high school boyfriend *goodbye* when she left for college.

"He was a nice boy," she explained. "But I was ready to move on in my life."

I took Kathy to a campus film for our first date. As we waited for the film to start, I was pretty nervous. Kathy leaned over and whispered, "Relax, Paul. I won't bite."

I heard her but was a little distracted by the scent of her perfume. It was nice. Anyway, I didn't relax.

Kathy's perspective on *the relationship thing* was different than mine. Later that evening, she told me having a steady boyfriend at Carleton would remove unnecessary distractions so she could focus on her studies. Kathy's goal was to become an attorney. With no equivocation, she told me, "I intend to study hard and play hard."

A week later, a few friends threw a small party for my twentieth birthday. I invited Kathy to join us. It was our second date.

At the party, I was given a bottle of Jack Daniels whiskey. As we walked away from the party, Kathy said, "Let's take that bottle of whiskey back to your dorm room and open it up."

That caught me off guard. I had been struggling with how I could find the courage to kiss her when I walked her up to her dormitory at the end of the date.

When we got to my dorm room, we sat down on the side of my bed (which of course in a dorm room also serves as the couch).

Kathy said, "Listen Paul. It's up to you. I don't have the time to date a bunch of guys. But I like having a boyfriend and I'd be happy if it were you. I will respect it if you would rather not get into a serious relationship right now. If that's the case—if you don't feel like you want a relationship—let me know. You can walk me back to my dorm."

Then she scooted closer to me on the bedside. I again noticed the perfume.

"However," she continued, "on the other hand, if you want to have a relationship with me, let's go ahead and celebrate your birthday. Open that bottle of whiskey. Pour each of us a glass. I'd love to spend the night with you."

I was dumbfounded. I had never spent the night with a girl and wasn't sure I was ready to have a serious relationship. Still, Kathy was awfully cute and it's not like my social calendar was so full I couldn't fit her in.

I quickly processed her statements, considered all of my alternatives and reached for the bottle of whiskey.

I guess the rest is history.

*****

Having a steady girlfriend changed my life. Kathy was a serious student. We would go to the library every evening after dinner. What else was I going to do at the library? I studied. But I knew that after we returned to my room from the library, we would make love. So, I ended up studying more than I'd ever studied in my whole life. It wasn't like I enjoyed studying. I just didn't want to miss the reward that might be bestowed upon me after we returned to my room. My grades improved. No. My grades shot up. During the winter term, I made the dean's list.

We rode on the train together when we went home for spring break. Kathy's parents lived in Winnetka, a wealthy suburb just outside of Chicago.

During the break, Kathy's parents invited me to have dinner with them. As I drove up to her home, I was stunned as I drove along the long private road that led to their large Georgian mansion. That driveway spoke to me. It said *Kathy's parents have money.*

That evening, after a wonderful dinner of Beef Wellington, Kathy's father asked me what my plans were for the future.

I told him.

I could see he was being courteous when he responded, "I'm happy for you that you are excited about journalism."

When my parents found out I had a girlfriend, they put two and two together—Kathy and my grades—and were thrilled. Once they found out that Kathy lived in Winnetka and that I had been invited to her home for dinner, they put their heads together (which is not something that had often occurred) and invited Kathy to join our family for dinner at Mastro's Steakhouse, one of the most expensive restaurants in Chicago.

My parents had never praised me so much at one time as they did that evening after dinner. My God! They went on and on about how much they liked Kathy!

My father's words summed it up for both of them. "It seems like you've found a winner, Paul."

He was thoughtful enough to add, "We totally underestimated you. But I'm not sure you'll be able to support such a classy woman on a journalist's salary."

*****

Upon my return to Carleton after spring break, there was a letter waiting for me from Webster asking if I planned on working for the *Weekly Dispatch* that summer. The letter informed me that he could pay me a thousand dollars a month during the summer.

The letter went on, "How's the Douglas Oleson project going? Have you interviewed anyone else? I ran into Miki Oleson the other day. She is working as a realtor in Saint Paul. I told her you might contact her for a piece you were writing about her ex-husband. She suggested that you contact her sooner rather than later. She is planning on taking an overseas family trip in mid-May."

Webster included Miki Oleson's cell phone number.

I immediately wrote back telling Webster I would work for him, thanking him for the offer of compensation and letting him know I intended to be in Bloomington by mid-June. I added that I would contact Miki Oleson and set up a meeting with her.

Kathy was not pleased when I informed her that I would be returning to the paper that summer.

"I had hoped you would be in Chicago this summer. We could have had a lot of fun. My parents liked you. Daddy told me that he was going to offer you a summer internship at his advertising agency. Daddy always hires a couple of summer interns and pays them a lot more than your paper is going to pay you."

I sighed and said, "Tell your father I appreciate his interest, but I am committed to a career in journalism."

She pouted that evening. I ended up studying by myself.

*****

When I called Doug Oleson's ex-wife Miki, I led off with my standard *I'm a summer intern on a project* introduction.

Miki interrupted, "Webster told me about your project. It sounds fascinating. I'd love to go out to dinner with you and talk. I've got two weeks before I head off to Japan with Douglas Jr. and my folks. When would you like to get together?"

"Uhm, yeah," I gulped. "That would be great. Uh, I'd love to take you—uhm—out to dinner but—uh—well, my only problem is, you see I don't own a car—you know—here at school—no car—here. Maybe—maybe, we could meet at the Saint Paul bus station and just—uh—go from there."

I heard Miki giggle on the other end of the line. Then she said, "Don't worry. I remember what it's like being a student. It wasn't that many years ago that I was at St. Cloud State without a car. My home's not that far from the Saint Paul's bus depot. Why don't we get together this Friday evening? I can pick you up at about six. I know a good place where we can have a fun meal."

"Uhm, yeah. Sure. That would be great. I will be at the depot around six on Friday. I'll be the tall thin guy wearing a Chicago Cubs baseball hat."

*****

I was a little taken aback after the call by how quickly Miki had arranged the interview. I walked over to the Northfield bus station to get a bus schedule. I needed to figure out what time I should leave Northfield on Friday to meet her. My bigger issue, however, was that I was going to have to explain to Kathy why I was going to have dinner with the ex-wife of the ex-mayor of Saint Paul.

When I told Kathy, I could see she was trying to appear understanding. But in the end, she had more questions than I had answers.

I studied alone at the library for a second night in a row.

Chapter 11 – Meeting Miki Oleson

Friday afternoon, I caught a 2:15 bus out of Northfield arriving at the Saint Paul bus terminal at five. I walked around for forty-five minutes; then waited in front of the station for Miki. I waited and waited some more. When I checked my watch, it was 6:30. I was about to go to a pay phone to give her a call when a shiny, white, late-model Thunderbird pulled up in front of the station. The driver was a strikingly attractive Asian woman wearing a silky, blue Minnesota Twins baseball jacket.

Miki Oleson reached across the T-Bird's front seat to open the passenger door. "Hey, Mr. Chicago Cubs. I figured if baseball was going to be the theme, I'd better represent my hometown team. I have been looking forward to this evening all week. Webster told me you were cute—and he didn't exaggerate at all."

Miki Oleson's dark hair was pulled up into a ponytail. Her rose-colored lipstick was a match for the similar shade of eye shadow complimenting her large brown eyes. Miki Oleson was stunning and I was speechless. I got into the front seat of her car and strapped on my seatbelt.

Miki smiled and said, "I'm sorry I'm late. My son had a tough day. I just didn't want to take off until he felt better. Obāsan and Ojīsan, my parents, live with us and the three of them are now eating a ham and pineapple pizza. Now, I can go out on the town without any guilt. I haven't been out on a date in months. It's tough being a divorced mom and even tougher when your ex-husband is somebody everybody in town knows—and despises."

She smiled, gave me a sly look and said, "I hope you don't mind going out with an older woman."

I still had no clue what to say. I just checked to make sure my safety belt was buckled and uttered, "Hi Miki. I'm Paul."

As the T-Bird zoomed into heavy rush hour traffic, I noticed her perfume. It was delicate—almost like a whisp of flowers.

Miki continued to be the only one speaking. "I figured we could head off to one of my favorite dinner spots," she said. "It's a nice little steak house in Cottage Grove. It'll only take half an hour to get there."

It started raining and the traffic slowed down. I was trying to figure out how to start a conversation about her ex-husband when Miki Oleson grabbed a CD from the dashboard and slid it into the car stereo. For the rest of the drive, we listened to *Best Hits of the Rolling Stones*.

A short while later, we were sitting at a table in a corner of the Cottage Grove Outback Steakhouse. Our waiter asked what we wanted to drink. Miki said she'd have a strawberry daiquiri. The evening was quickly moving in a direction I hadn't anticipated. I didn't know what to do. I was underage and had never ordered a drink. But I decided I should try to look cool and ordered a margarita.

When the waiter asked me if I wanted my drink on the rocks, I tried to look at ease. I didn't know what he meant by the rocks but I said, "Why not."

Miki laughed as the waiter walked away, saying, "Well done, Paul. No one would ever guess you are underage."

I felt my cheeks turn bright red. She just laughed harder.

Our drinks came. She ordered shrimp scampi and I ordered a rib steak. I knew the bill was going to be more than I expected. However, I decided this just goes with the territory (though I was uncertain as to what that territory was).

While we sipped on our drinks, Miki told me about her upcoming trip. She would travel with her mother, father and son to a village located near Kyoto. Miki's grandparents had spent most of their lives in that village before coming to San Francisco in the early 1930's. Miki wanted to show her son his heritage.

"It's important that Douglas Jr. understand his family's history. We are so fortunate my folks were willing to go there with us."

Our waiter brought our dinner. He asked if we wanted another drink. Miki did. I passed. The Margarita was still doing its work on my ability to think straight.

We ate in silence. While I worked on my steak, I was trying to figure out how to turn the conversation into a discussion of Miki's ex-husband. Miki had been so warm. I felt like I was being manipulative by bringing up a subject that might make her feel uncomfortable.

After she finished her dinner, Miki asked, "What is it you want to know about Douglas?"

I had just put a big piece of steak in my mouth and was pretty high from the margarita. As I slowly chewed the bite, I opened my notebook to a list of questions I had assembled the previous evening.

1. *What was Douglas Oleson like in college?*
2. *How and why did he change over the years?*
3. *What sort of husband was he?*
4. *Why did Oleson and Miki break up?*

    5.   *What's he doing now?*

    6.   *Is there anything else I should know, anyone else I should speak with?"*

I wasn't feeling too sharp—the margarita was still buzzing in my brain. Miki watched me, waiting for a response. As I looked at the questions, I became concerned that she might think they were offensive. Maybe I should eliminate some of them? What should I have asked instead?

While I focused on how to ask Miki about her life with her ex-husband, I looked up and saw how closely she was watching me. She laughed and said, "Why don't you just break down and hand me your list of questions?"

Not knowing what else to do, I tore the page out of my notebook and handed it to her.

Now it was Miki's turn to study the questions.

"Good questions, Paul—not nasty nor too intrusive. They give me the room to tell you as much as I want to—or more, I guess, especially if that second Strawberry Daiquiri does the trick. Fortunately for you, I like you and am going to be open. In exchange, I ask that you not describe me as a ditzy ex-wife or include anything that you think will cause me too much—how can I best put it—too much new shame."

I felt like my teacher had just reviewed my homework and told me I had done a good job. I was pleased with the praise but felt that somehow the coolness I had been striving to achieve all evening had just vaporized.

As the waiter cleared Miki's plate, she ordered a third strawberry daiquiri. She gave me a coy smile and said, "It will lessen the pain."

Over the next forty-five minutes, Miki's candor earned my respect. She hardly stopped speaking except to take small sips from the pink liquid in the tall stemmed glass sitting in front of her.

*****

"I met Douglas during my first week at St Cloud State. I was so excited to be on a college campus, away from my folks, beginning the adventure of my lifetime. I was seated alone in the dining hall, eating dinner, when a handsome stranger sat down across from me. *Hi,* he said. *I'm Douglas. I think we need to get to know one another.*"

Miki's elbows were on the table, her softly closed and her hands held together, under her chin. As she spoke, her eyes had a glossy look as she gazed off into the distance.

"Douglas was a junior—a confident junior. I was a gaga freshman—one who was on the verge of falling in love. At that moment, my college experience became preordained. I was a virgin before I met Douglas—and proud of it. But I slept with Douglas that first night. He was so handsome, so wonderful, so full of ideas. Douglas had so many dreams—so much ambition. He could have had any girl he wanted. But he chose me, a mousy Japanese girl from Saint Paul Minnesota. Wow!"

As she spoke to me, Miki looked across the restaurant. She seemed to be seeing the events she was describing. She was glossy-eyed, as if still in love—at least with the person she had imagined when she met him.

She sighed. "Douglas taught me about the world—the world as he saw it. He explained politics and told me the thing wrong with the Democrats was that they were letting the Republicans shove them around too much. He intended to change that. Douglas wasn't as good a student as I was. But he was a lot smarter. Or at least that was what I thought. In retrospect, he was just a whole lot more confident."

Miki was quiet for a minute—all the while gazing into a vague distance. I am not sure what she was thinking— maybe she was wondering if she should be sharing all of this with some ignorant college student.

Miki looked down for a moment and sadly shook her head. When she looked up, she said, "My sophomore year, Douglas decided to run for student body president. I was so proud after he won. But what happened shortly afterwards should have given me ample warning that Douglas had huge honesty issues. Apparently, a bunch of counterfeit ballots had been stuffed into the ballot box. Everybody accused Douglas of being the culprit. But one of his buddies took the blame. Douglas was a big shot in saying he couldn't accept a victory under those conditions and resigned from an office he hadn't legitimately won in the first place."

She laughed quietly after saying this.

"He graduated after my sophomore year. We eloped—and got married in Sioux Falls, South Dakota. We spent our wedding night there at the Harrington Hotel. My parents were devastated that they were not included in our wedding. It took years for them to forgive me. But back then, I didn't care. I was so happy—so in love—with stars in my eyes—stars that distracted me from almost everything that should have mattered."

Miki told me about the second floor of the old gabled house they rented in Saint Paul and how much she enjoyed cooking special meals for Douglas, especially when he brought colleagues home for dinner. She loved the praise she received after those meals. Soon, Miki got a job in a real estate office as a receptionist. Before long, she was working as a realtor, making more money than her husband. But there never was a question of who was the star of the family show.

"Douglas treated politics the way other people treat a chess game—he was coldly analytical. He often would explain to me what he was doing and why he was doing it. The only thing he exaggerated was his justification for doing some of the things he did. He always claimed to be altruistic. What he didn't disclose were the lies he told and the compromises he made—and the ones he had other people make on his behalf."

She laughed softly and added, "He also didn't do a real good job of informing me about the women he slept with. He told me the newspapers were printing lies created by his enemies. Douglas denied he'd ever cheated on me."

She chuckled as she said, "His apologies were quite elegant."

She paused, took a deep breath and continued. "Then there was the sadness he shared, his stories about how his bad behavior was a result of his unhappy childhood. Douglas could have been an actor. And boy, Paul, was I ever the sucker audience. I believed it all—or talked myself into believing it all."

For a moment she was just silent—probably reliving some memory that she hadn't put into words.

"After the news articles more or less proved he'd been having an affair with his deputy mayor, after she resigned and split from her husband, we were done. I didn't publicly announce it. We still lived in the same house. We spent time with our son in public. But we didn't share a bed. And we both knew the marriage was over."

Miki spoke briefly about the last few months they lived together. "At first, I put on a show to help him. But after I read about the bimbo he was sleeping with at the end, well, that morning I lost it. I threw our set of fine China—one dish at a time—against our dining room wall. I told Douglas to get out of the house. I never wanted to see him again. I asked again and again; *How could you do this to me, Douglas? How could you?*"

The pain was so evident on Miki's face as she described that last morning with her husband. She stopped speaking and quietly sat there, taking one deep breath after another. After a while, tranquility returned to her face.

She took another deep breath, then said, "A couple of weeks later, he signed the divorce papers. He questioned nothing and gave no apology—nothing—not a one."

She turned toward me, gave a weak smile and said, "My ex-husband didn't tell me he was going to resign. He gave me no indication he was going to leave town. He didn't tell me where he was going. He disappeared for me just like he had for the whole damn city. Can you imagine how humiliating that was? I was a young woman. I had a little child. We had been the toast of the city—then became the butt of everyone's jokes. I saw the political cartoons. I heard the comments. I was humiliated in front of my parents, my friends, my work colleagues—in front of the whole city."

She took a deep breath and let it out slowly.

"I had to sell my home. My husband had extended our mortgage to lend the money to his campaigns. But he hadn't gotten around to paying those loans back. There was no equity left and I had no income to make the payments. I was left with nothing except my beautiful son. However, I did have real estate sales experience and had already completed two years of college. I moved to Moorhead, Minnesota, finished up my degree at Moorhead State

University and worked part-time for a real estate office there. After I got my degree, Douglas Jr. and I moved back to Saint Paul. I began working for my old real estate company. Soon, I was able to purchase a home. My parents sold their condominium and moved in with Douglas Jr. and me. My life is back on track."

Miki had a somber look as she said, "I think I've answered all of your questions, Paul. I've been through some tough times. Surviving my marriage with Douglas Oleson was the greatest accomplishment of my life. Douglas is—or was—how shall I put it—quite the character. He could charm your socks off. But then he would steal them. I am a stronger person for having known him. But I never again will submit myself to that sort of ordeal. Never."

It occurred to me that Miki might be able to give me some insight into the new mayor, Dave Dickens. I told her about my interview with him and how much he seemed to dislike her ex.

I asked her, "Do you have any idea what motivated Dickens's bitterness."

She looked down at the table, shook her head and laughed. "That little son of a bitch, that measly, short, son of a bitch. I never would have said anything too nice about him. But a couple of months after Douglas left town, Dickens calls me up and asks me out. Can you imagine that, Paul? Now I never would have dated him under any circumstances— never. But asking me out—at that point? That was way beyond the pale, even for a total creep!"

*****

I had finished my steak and the waiter had cleared my plate. Wanting to be a good host I asked Miki if she wanted a dessert.

81

She just laughed. "Maybe we ought to get going. There's a 10:30 bus out of Saint Paul going back to Northfield. I think we can catch it."

The waiter delivered the check. I looked at it and gulped while pulling out my checkbook. The bill was more than I had imagined. But I had asked Miki to join me and she had shared a lot with me.

However, Miki handed the waiter her credit card and said to me, "You are an absolute sweetheart, Paul. It was a pleasure going out with you. But you're a student and I am certain you can't afford this. I'll pick this up tonight. After you graduate, you can take me out on a real date. This evening, it's on me."

*****

We were soon in her car heading back to the bus station. We rode in silence, each of us lost in our thoughts. I imagine Miki was thinking about her life, her broken marriage and all the pain she had described.

But my thoughts drifted to the fact that I would be returning to Northfield after midnight. I was wondering, *How is Kathy going to take this?*

As we pulled in front of the bus station, Miki placed the tips of her right hand's pointer and middle fingers upon her lips. Then she placed those fingertips on my lips.

"Finish up your project, Paul. Do it justice. You have the charm I ascribed to Douglas. But you have an innocence and an honesty of which he never will be capable. Write a good paper. Become a wonderful journalist and stay sweet. Maybe we will meet again."

Chapter 12 – A Second Summer Internship

Spring term flew by. I continued to excel in my classes. But I ended up doing a lot more studying by myself. I had disappointed Kathy once too often. Chief among those disappointments was my decision to spend the coming summer working as an intern for Webster's newspaper.

I remember Kathy telling me one Friday evening near the end of the term, "I appreciate that you enjoy pretending to be a newspaper reporter. But what about your future, Paul? What about our future? I looked up what newspaper reporters earn. Unless you're the anchor for NBC or a columnist for the Washington Post, you won't earn squat. Is that what you want out of life? I can assure you that I want more than that."

I didn't give any ground.

That was one of those evenings I spent by myself. It had become evident to both of us that my dreams for the future conflicted with hers.

*****

We (read this as Kathy) decided we should take a break in our relationship for the summer. The term *break* may be an understatement of what she decided. Kathy told me that maybe I should be thinking about whether I wanted any sort of relationship with her. She intended to date other guys during the summer and made it clear to me that I should feel free to date anyone I wanted.

When Kathy's parents picked her up to take her home for the summer, they didn't ask to see me nor had I asked to see them. And Kathy didn't bother to say goodbye.

*****

That summer, I rented the same small room near the *Dispatch* that I'd had the prior year. I didn't require additional summer funding from my parents due to the thousand dollars per month I received from Webster. That income turned out to be a good thing because my parents had made it very clear that they weren't about to fund my summer plan.

In a phone conversation with my mother, I made the mistake of telling her that Kathy's father had offered me a job for the summer, an offer I'd turned down. I followed that by informing her that Kathy and I were taking a break in our relationship for the summer.

My mother was distraught. "What were you thinking, Paul? Are you planning on staying a child your whole life? Kathy is enchanting. You're not going to do better than her. Her father offered you the opportunity to start a real career! When will you start thinking about your future—when will you start acting like an adult?"

My parents rarely communicated with one another. Unfortunately, on this issue, they did communicate.

After my mother had relayed the news, my father was less ambiguous.

"Son," he said, "I recognize you need to live your own life. I will accept that. You can choose not to go to grad school. But once you graduate, you're on your own. Should you change your mind and choose to go to graduate school— well, I'll continue to underwrite your living and education expenditures. Someday, your mother and I will be gone and since you are the sole beneficiary for each of our estates, you'll have financial security. But until they toss that dirt onto our caskets, you'd better plan on making your way in the world. And hear me clearly, I speak for both your mother and myself when I say this."

*****

On the bus ride to Bloomington, I thought about how Kathy and my parents wanted me to follow their preferred path rather than listen to my heart. I decided I was not regretful about the outcome. I didn't need my folks' money and was better off without Kathy's vision of married suburban bliss. True, I would miss the sex. But I enjoyed the peace of mind that came in its place.

My attention turned to the summer internship. I planned to continue developing my craft as a reporter. In particular, I intended to write articles about Bloomington's government. (Webster had shared with me that the city manager was out on maternity leave and her replacement was the veritable bull in a China shop). I would also take another shot at writing about the city's high school football teams. (During the prior season, despite good intentions, each school's team had won only two games and lost eight). But what drove my enthusiasm was the challenge of my senior thesis. The paper now had a title: *What Happened to Douglas Oleson?*

*****

I reported to work the following Monday at 9 AM. Dolly gave me a warm welcome and Webster hollered from his office, "Grab a cup of coffee and c'mon in here and get to work."

After completing his ritual of lighting a Benson and Hedges cigarette, inhaling it deeply and propelling the smoke toward the ceiling, Webster said, "Based on what I heard from Sharon, it sounds like the powers in your life are intensely pressing you to become a successful American businessman. Do you regret your decision to work for me this summer?"

I laughed. "Dr. Harris did bring you up to speed, didn't she? The answer is no, I don't regret working here at all. I'm excited—hoping you can teach me how to cause some trouble."

Webster had just taken a long draw from his cigarette and coughed it out while laughing. Once he stopped coughing, he said, "I don't think you need a teacher for that Paul. I think you'll soon be ready to teach your own post-graduate course in causing trouble. In that light, are you planning on writing any interesting stories for the *Weekly* this summer?"

I told Webster about my intention to write about the city government and football teams. He chuckled at my description of how I would approach the stories.

"Well," he said, "I have a few new areas for you to contribute around here. You need to learn how to write an obituary. I'm sure that Bloomington will cooperate by producing enough voluntary subjects for you to develop your skills in that area. You should be proficient by September. I also want you to sell a few advertisements. I'm not trying to turn you into a salesman. That's my job. But if you want to know how to run a local paper, you'll need to be able to generate revenue. I also have a couple of people in mind for you to interview—you know, for your Oleson paper."

I listened to Webster's proposed assignments. The last item, the Oleson interviews, piqued my attention.

I quickly asked, "Like who?"

Webster gave a sly smile, reached for his cup of coffee and took a sip followed by a long drag from his cigarette.

After intently watching the cigarette smoke float into a halo and then disappear, Webster responded. "I thought you might enjoy meeting Douglas' vice-mayor. She's just returned to the Twin Cities. I had lunch with her the other day. After some cajoling, she agreed to meet with you. I had to promise that your final report will not include any intimate details about her relationship with the ex-mayor. However, I am directing you to secretly inform me of anything titillating that you learn from her. You just can't put it into print or communicate it to anyone else.

Webster roared with laughter after saying this and again, his laugh turned into a deep chest cough.

A moment later, composure regained, he said, "Yeah, and the other interview—the guy from the development community—you know the one who got all the attention for siphoning contributions into Douglas' campaign—that's your second opportunity to become this summer's Walter Winchell."

Just then, Webster's phone rang. He looked at the phone set and said, "I gotta take this. Dolly will help you log onto the system. We updated a few things on our computers. After you get that crap set up, why don't you schedule interviews for your football story?"

*****

A moment later as Dolly rummaged through her desk looking for the appropriate network login information, I whispered, "Webster's cough is awful. How's his health?"

Dolly looked over her shoulder. Then, in a quiet voice, she said, "Louise is worried sick. She says not only is the cough getting worse, but he sometimes ends up spitting out bloody phlegm. But Webster absolutely refuses to see a doctor. Louise says he tells her, *Wives worry too much.*"

Pausing while checking over her shoulder again, Dolly added, "I brought it up with him last fall—told him he was gonna kill himself if he didn't stop smoking. He told me he appreciated what a fine person I am. But he said he would appreciate me even more if I would mind my own damn business. I haven't dared to mention it since."

Dolly found the network instructions she had been looking for and we went over to my cubicle. After she turned on my PC and signed onto the new network, I was on my own.

During the summer, I produced more stories faster than I had the previous summer. But those stories remained absent of any real redeeming value.

Chapter 13 – The Former Deputy

Debbie Perth had served as Douglas Oleson's legislative assistant and later as his deputy mayor. She was also rumored to be his mistress. Miss Perth had recently been hired by a Minneapolis political consultant, returning to Minnesota from her position working with the New Democrats in the nation's capital.

At the end at the end of my first week back at the paper, I contacted Perth. After I introduced myself, she laughed and said Webster had twisted her arm to get her to give me an interview and almost broke it. She suggested we meet the following Friday evening at a hotel bar in downtown Minneapolis.

*****

I went into The Leamington Hotel's bar the following Friday. I knew what Perth looked like from news article photographs and quickly spotted her, sitting at the bar, drinking some sort of high ball.

Webster had said Perth was in her mid-thirties. But the petite woman with medium-length straight black hair dressed in a black silk shirt and tailored black slacks looked more like a teenager. Her fire-engine-red lipstick jumped out against her black hair and outfit.

I walked up to the bar stool on which she was sitting and introduced myself. Perth stood up and suggested we go to a table in the back corner of the room. "It'll be a bit quieter," she said as she led me across the room. "Some privacy is always nice."

We sat down and a waiter approached the table asking us if we were ready to order. Debbie suggested we split a bottle of wine with dinner. I gulped a little because there wasn't a lot of money in my checking account. Perth must have read my thoughts because she laughed and said, "Relax, Paul. I'm paying. My company gives me an expense account and, you know, if I don't use it, I lose it."

Along with a bottle of 1995 Chateau Neuf du Pape, Perth ordered rack of lamb, medium rare.

"I've had the rack here before," she said. "It's first-rate."

Relieved and now anticipating a good meal, I told the waiter I'd have the same.

"Webster told me you're going to be a senior at Carleton," she said. "Carleton is an excellent school. Are you a good student?"

I was a little taken aback. I responded, "I'm working at it, but being a good student has been a work in progress."

"Well good for you—Peter, isn't it?"

"No, it's Paul. But if you If you want to call me Peter, go for it. You won't be the first."

"Peter, Paul, John—I get I get all those old Christian Saints mixed up. But I'll try hard to remember to call you Paul. I should start by telling you a little about myself. I graduated from Vassar but was born and raised in good old Saint Paul. It was a big deal for me heading off east to college—you know, hitting the big time and all. While I've never regretted it, I never wanted to stay back there. Loved the culture, stimulated by the politics, but couldn't wait to return to the Midwest—don't have a clue why I felt that way for the life of me."

It seemed like I'd heard Debbie speak before. It took me a while to place the fast pace of her language and her accent. Then it hit me. She sounded exactly like Catherine Hepburn in *Bringing Up Baby*—light-hearted, affected and haughty—just like a New England aristocrat.

The waiter brought us the bottle of Chateau Neuf du Pape and poured a small amount into Debbie's glass. She tasted it. "It's excellent, Herbert."

"Thank you, Miss Perth," he responded. Debbie was a familiar patron at the bar.

We sat silently for a couple of minutes, sipping the wine and looking around at other guests in the restaurant. The wine had loosened me up and I decided I'd go for it. "You know Debbie, you sound a lot like Catherine Hepburn."

She leaned back, her head at an angle, and gave me an interesting smile. "I can't tell you how often I've heard that since I returned to Minnesota. Someone told me that all of us girls from Vassar sound like Hepburn. I don't know what it is. We arrived in Poughkeepsie as freshmen sounding like natives of whatever yokel village we came from and then, the next thing you know, we were all trying to talk like we were cast in a movie selling a classy piece of property in upper Vermont to Fred Astaire."

I laughed and said, "I couldn't afford even a cheap piece of property in Vermont."

"Neither could I—back then. But I'm seriously working on it. Someday, Peter; someday, I hope to be able to pull it off."

She paused, took a sip of wine and said, "Webster told me you had some questions. What are they?"

I had been a little tense when I arrived at the bar. But after my first glass of wine, I was relaxed enough to blurt out, "How did you meet Douglas Oleson? Can you tell me a little about your relationship with him, I mean how did it start and maybe even how did it end?"

"My Peter, don't we get to the point. Let me see. I came back from college—that was twelve years ago. I went into the Democratic-Farmer-Labor offices and told them I needed a job. The young guy I met with told me he was about to run for the state house seat that represented Saint Paul. He seemed smart and was pretty decent-looking. We went out for a drink and he asked me if I'd work on his campaign. I told him I'd think about it. I checked around and was told he was an up-and-comer worth hitching my wagon to. I was also told he was very married. I guess the rest is history."

The waiter brought us our salads and Debbie stopped speaking. Her single focus (and mine) was our food—first the salad, then the rack of lamb. The rack was as succulent as she had promised. After that, she ordered another bottle of wine. We didn't get back to my questions until after we had finished our dinners.

Once the waiter had cleared our plates and our glasses were filled, Debbie continued with the description of her career as if she had not been interrupted for forty minutes.

"Douglas won. He offered me a position as his legislative assistant. I liked working for the guy. He was ambitious, fully capable of listening—to a woman. Working for Douglas was fun and exciting. He often had me meet with constituents and let me draft several interesting pieces of legislation. We worked together on some pretty impressive bills that we guided through the legislature; ones that landed on the governor's desk."

I was not that used to alcohol and stopped drinking. Debbie, however, did not appear affected by the wine at all. She seemed to be energized. When the waiter offered us dessert, I ordered a piece of pecan pie ala mode. Debbie ordered a glass of twenty-year-old port.

"When Douglas ran for mayor, I ran the campaign. We worked well together. I knew who to talk to get the endorsements required to win the election. Once he was elected, it seemed only natural that I should be part of his administration. He offered me the deputy-mayor position and I didn't hesitate to accept."

She paused as the port was delivered. When the waiter left, she continued. "Saint Paul had been run forever by a gang of stooges who had no clue what they were doing. Douglas pulled together a bright and innovative cabinet. We put together a four-year plan like that city had never seen and accomplished some pretty innovative outcomes in the area of jobs, social programs, parks and public safety. Yup, Peter. We did it all."

She had finished her glass of port and ordered another.

She paused for a moment, looked off across the dining room, then shook her head sadly and sighed. "In politics, Peter, nothing creates enemies like success. Douglas' second term started out great. We were beginning where we left off at the end of his first. But people started working to ensure we would not be successful. Despite that, we accomplished a lot in that second term."

The waiter brought Debbie her port. She didn't sip from her glass this time. She tossed it down in one bottoms-up swallow; then continued her story. "When the third term began, there were huge targets painted on each of our backs.

Other local, city and state politicians who had been jealous of our successes from the outset worked with *The Minneapolis News Chronicle* and *The Saint Paul Daily Journal* to take us down. Each time we did something well, they identified a set of community members who had benefited most from our efforts and accused us of buying their support."

Debbie looked around the room with a wild touch in her eyes—I think it was a combination of intensity and intelligence.

"Numbers don't lie, Peter. Look at the trends. See what happened to the financial position of the city. See how businesses grew, how new businesses were locating in neighborhoods that had always been overlooked—ignored—how can I say it more clearly—redlined. Look at the crime statistics during our tenure; at the acres of parks that were added—all over the city. Study the cooperation that was going on between the schools, the police and the neighborhoods of color. These things really happened, Peter. We documented them. But it seems like that just pissed people off."

She paused for a moment, gave me a fiery look and added, "I know that government has a bad name. The old saying *it's good enough for government* has a real basis. Unfortunately, there is a lot of mediocrity in public service. When Douglas was elected, he went into a city government in which no one gave a damn about quality. The city's managers had been there for years—they just didn't want to be bothered and weren't going to be changed. It was a government run by the employees for the employees—not for the citizens. Those old managers who'd been there forever hated Douglas because he insisted on change. Go ahead. Talk to a few of them. Hear their criticisms. Then you'll begin to understand what we took on."

I interrupted her. "Can you give me a name of some of those managers?"

"Sure," she responded. "Go talk to Warren Daniels, the prior regime's director of finance and information technology. He liked working for the city. He was one of the good old boys. And let me tell you, they were all boys. Before Douglas' administration—during those good old days—there were almost no women in senior positions—and if your skin wasn't white, well, there wasn't any reason to even apply for work at the city. Yes, go talk to Warren. Get a sense of his perspectives. You'll understand better what we took on—what we changed."

Of course, I had talked to Warren. And that conversation confirmed a lot of what Debbie was saying. But I had also met Mary Anne Swenson. She had run Human Resources for Mayor Jolly.

Somehow, Debbie read my look and said, "Yes—Webster told me you met with their director of human resources. She was the only woman on Jolly's cabinet and did nothing to elevate any other women at the city. And talk about a snake? You've got one there. On anything of importance, she was run like a puppet—by the white men with whom she worked."

Debbie was looking down at the table, shaking her head as she said, "They accused us of trying to buy favor within the community—of corruption! But when a program was slow getting off the ground, we were incompetent and our managers were labeled as political hacks. Every personal shot in the world was taken at Douglas and anyone around him who was defamed, well, we were just collateral damage. It was awful. Of course, you've read the papers. You've heard all the accusations. I just didn't need it. I submitted my resignation and took a job working for the party in DC."

Debbie Perth took a deep breath, exhaled, then looked me straight in the eye and said, "There you have it, bud."

The waiter came over to the table. Debbie looked up at him and smiled. "Dinner was great, Herbert, as always. Please tell the chef he hit it out of the park one more time. Would you bring me the check, please?"

I took a drink of water and said, "Could I ask you a couple more questions?"

She gave me a defiant look. "You've heard the whole story. Now, I am willing to bet that what is going on in your little mind is what happened between Douglas and me. Right? You want to know if we were sleeping together."

She had me there. I don't know if it was my curiosity or the wine's bravery but I didn't back down.

"Yes," I said, "it's an important part of the story. Is there anything you want to comment on about those accusations?"

"Well," she said, looking at me with a fierce glare, "I'll be straight with you. The truth is it's no one else's Goddamned business. You should be asking me what major projects were completed during the nine years that Douglas ran the city. You should be asking for specifics about what happened to the parks. How much did we improve the city's financial position? How many more people of color were included in the city's social programs? How did we work with the city's underserved communities? Nobody gives a shit about those questions. They just want to know if

Douglas and I slept together—did we screw? Was there hot and dirty sex? What do I have to say to them? What do I have to say, Peter? I say, screw 'em...just screw 'em."

She stood up and leaned over to sign the credit card receipt.

I had to ask my last question. "Do you know what happened to Oleson since he left the city? Do you know where he is now? What he's doing?"

She scowled as she said, "I'll be honest, Peter, I don't know. But if I did, I sure as hell wouldn't tell you. The guy has been crucified enough. Sure, he was ambitious. But ambitious people sometimes accomplish a lot. I need to ask you a question, though. What the hell did he do to this city to be treated so poorly other than to try to be very successful as its leader? Do you want to look at the numbers? Do you want to find out how effective he was? No, you don't. And you won't. So, no, I don't know where he is or what he is doing. But if I did, Peter, if I did, I sure as hell wouldn't tell you...or anyone."

And as Debbie Perth looked at me, her face transformed. It gained a tranquility. She gave me a polite smile and Debbie Perth became, once again, the self-possessed woman who had been sitting at the bar when I arrived.

"It's been an absolute pleasure meeting you, Peter. Please give Webster my best regards...and enjoy your summer internship."

With that, Saint Paul's former deputy mayor gave me one more confident smile before looking away from me and walking out of the bar.

Chapter 14 –Dinner with Jeff

I spent the weekend pondering the nuances of my remarkable meeting with Debbie Perth.

As I walked into the office Monday morning, Webster called out for me to join him in his office. Wearing a wry smile, he looked at me—up and down, head to toe—then said, "I needed to take a quick inventory. Hmmm, two legs, two arms, a head still squarely on your shoulders. Yup, all the pieces are attached. Other than that, my boy, how was the play?"

Webster took a long drag from his cigarette and gave a deep laugh that was immediately followed by a deeper cough. Ashes fell from his cigarette onto his desk. Webster frowned, brushed the ashes onto the carpet and forcibly extinguished his cigarette in his crowded ashtray.

I gave Webster a brief rundown of the interview. His comment when I finished was, "That girl has some serious fire, doesn't she?"

He added, "I ran into Jeff Washington, the reporter who wrote many of *The Daily Journal* stories in the folder I gave you. After I told him about your project, he said he was surprised you hadn't contacted him already. Jeff Washington is a straight shooter. He has a keen ability to peer into other people's souls. Meet with him and you'll get new insights into Oleson."

*****

I called Washington that afternoon. We agreed to have lunch on Friday. Based on Webster's comment, I decided I should focus the interview on better understanding all of the major players in the drama.

I jotted down the following questions:

o   Was Oleson an effective mayor?
o   Tell me about the developer who contributed so much to Oleson. (Webster has already contacted the developer and I will meet him).
o   Who was the public information officer linked to Oleson?
o   What is Dave Dickens' backstory on Oleson?
o   What's your read on Debbie Perth?
o   On Miki Oleson?
o   Do you have any idea where Douglas Oleson is living now or what he is doing?
o   Are there aspects of this story I might be missing?

*****

It was a humid ninety-five degrees when I got into Washington's blue 1968 Ford Mustang. Jeff was a large, athletic-looking man with a grey beard and an afro. Webster had told me Jeff was about seventy—but he didn't look it. He was warm, engaging and had a sharp sense of humor.

We headed out to a diner Washington described as a *classy greasy spoon.*

Jeff suggested holding off on our discussion about Douglas Oleson until after we ate. Instead, as we drove, we chatted about how well the Minnesota Vikings football team might do that coming fall. Riding in that convertible with the top down on that hot day was refreshing.

Once in the diner, Washington didn't look at the menu. "This greasy spoon grills the best burger you'll ever taste. Their fries are hand-sliced and their coffee milkshakes, oh man, their coffee milkshakes are to die for. You'll thank me afterward for taking you here."

Jeff had not exaggerated about the quality of the food. We ate in silence. When our empty plates had been cleared, Jeff ordered a couple of cups of coffee and said, "OK rookie, let's go for it."

I figured the most straightforward approach would be to just hand Jeff my list of questions. He took the page, glanced over the list and said, "A pretty fine set of asks."

With that, he moved into speaking about Douglas Oleson. I turned on the pocket-size Sony voice recorder I had purchased earlier in the week and Jeff proceeded to speak almost nonstop for an hour.

*****

Jeff Washington met Douglas Oleson shortly after Oleson graduated from Saint Cloud State. Oleson was working for Minnesota's Democratic-Farmer-Labor Party. Early on, the two of them went out for occasional beers and once, Oleson had invited Jeff over to his home for dinner. Miki cooked spaghetti and meatballs. Jeff told me how much he enjoyed that evening. He told me it was clear from the outset that Miki was much nicer than her husband.

"In the beginning, Doug was the nicest guy in the world—my best buddy. A day or two before he announced he was running for state representative, he called me up and gave me a heads-up. I ended up writing a background story on him that was printed the day he announced. Once he was elected to the Legislature, he became a little bit more distant."

Jeff paused and took a sip of coffee and then chuckled while he shook his head. "When he became a candidate for mayor, he was once again my best buddy—

gave me some scoops and we'd go out for beers. Oleson and I stayed in pretty close touch until a few months after he was elected when I committed the terrible crime of stating in an article that Oleson had taken credit for accomplishments of former mayor Jim Jolly."

Washington laughed. "After that, forget about it. Oleson and his team gave me the total freeze. They stopped talking to me. They liked to control what was said about their administration and I had committed the sin of being beyond their control."

Jeff looked at my list of questions and said, "Was he an effective mayor? If you listened to Oleson and his cronies, you couldn't help but believe his whole administration was effective. But if you listened to his critics, you'd hear that Oleson's team focused too much on public relations rather than production. I tried to always parse through their rhetoric, to report an accurate account of how well they were doing. But was he an effective mayor? I'll answer that if you define *effective*."

He laughed, took a sip of coffee and looked at the list of questions.

Then he glanced across the room gave an odd grin and said, "What do I think of Debbie Perth? She was quite the talker—a great connector. She gets credit for pulling together a bunch of different groups in the city and got them to work in support of what were often innovative programs. She used me to connect with some of my brothers in the 'hood. They ended up working with Oleson's team on some pretty good stuff."

He paused, looking off for a moment. Then he leaned forward and said, "But Debbie Perth was one smart cookie. She could manipulate any circumstance; making a sow's ear look like a purse. She seemed to always describe her own efforts as being perfect and everybody else's as being mediocre. But don't get me wrong. This woman was an excellent administrator. When she asked her staff to jump, they asked her, *How high?* The bottom line in was if anyone was going to benefit from anything, it always began and ended with the mayor and herself."

Washington gave a sly smile and said, "One time, I wrote this story about a human services program that the mayor had bragged about. But I had found that the city had actually added staff and renamed an old program—one that had been around for years. They had doubled overall program costs and given it a new name. My article documented that for all that expense, the program's outcomes hadn't increased or improved. Perth called me up and chewed me out. *What was I trying to do? What was my problem? Was I afraid of change?* She let me have it. Then, she sent me a written analysis full of statistics that at first glance might have seemed impressive. But it was misleading. If Debbie were a scorekeeper, the Minnesota Twins would seem like the best baseball team in history. But there is a difference between *hits* and *at-bats*. Well, the next time I saw Debbie, I let her know what I thought of her analysis. That was five or six years ago. She hasn't spoken to me since."

Jeff Washington looked down at my list of questions and gave a pensive look.

"What's my read on Oleson's wife? Miki's a total sweetheart. At times I thought of her as being like a wounded deer. But sweet as she was, she was also complicit in his manipulative politics and went along with a lot of his bullshit. In the end, however, Miki was the one who got hurt.

She didn't deserve it—not at all. I think she thought of their marriage as a partnership. She learned that that was a fantasy. Yeah, Miki got hurt more in this whole charade than anyone else."

I interrupted, "I don't understand what you mean by *a wounded deer.*"

Jeff sighed and gave a kind smile. "There was this gentleness about her—I don't know if it was her culture? But there was something about the way she interacted—maybe a Zen quality in the way she lived. I guess she had a general lack of greediness. She wasn't on the make in any regard. I could see why Douglas had chosen her for his wife. Her characteristics were the antithesis of his. Her qualities might lead someone who met both of them to trust him more than they otherwise would have."

I interrupted Jeff. "I spoke with Chris Thompson of the labor federation. He spoke highly about how well Olesen managed the city. Now I understand that Chris was a buddy of Oleson's, but I listened closely to the things he said about the city's finances. Then I did some research to confirm them. His facts bore out. Oleson made big improvements— at least as measured by information from the city's financial reports. And I confirmed my conclusion by speaking to an employee who is still with the city's accounting department. She agreed that Oleson had made a huge difference. She said other departments also became more effective. Doesn't that sort of support Debbie Perth's contention?"

Jeff chuckled. "You're pretty a thorough man, Paul. Checking out the back story, eh? I guess you're going to become an ace reporter. Oh, by the way, the woman who backed up Thompson's story—she wasn't by any chance named Barbara Robbins, was she?"

I wasn't sure how he could have known that, but I said, "Yes. That was her."

"Yeah, Barb's a pretty good accounts payable supervisor. Her live-in boyfriend, Chris Thompson, really respects her opinion a lot."

I felt deflated.

Jeff was kind enough not to rub it in. He just looked down, rubbed his large hands together and continued to speak. "Now, the developer you asked about who contributed so much to Oleson is an entirely different story. Chuck Persons is from an old Saint Paul family. His great-grandfather started one of the city's first banks around the turn of the century. Chuck lives in one of those grand prairie homes on Summit Avenue. By the way, if you've never driven down that street, you should. The architecture is old, rich and beautiful. Anyway, Chuck comes from old money in this city."

Jeff explained that Persons' company owned property near downtown that was zoned for low-income multifamily homes.

"Persons had tried to rezone that property to commercial for years. The city wasn't having it—at least not until Douglas Oleson got elected. Oleson brought in a new planning director who upgraded zoning for a variety of projects owned by Persons and his administration did the same thing for projects belonging to several other members of the development community—all of this was done, of course, in the name of economic development. Coincidentally most of those who benefited from zoning changes had been contributors to Oleson's campaign. If you follow the money, Paul, you'll see that many of those campaign contributions flowed through Chuck Persons. He ended up getting fined after twisting campaign finance rules all over hell. But I'll bet you anything, he thinks the fine was a worthwhile expenditure to obtain those zoning changes."

Jeff frowned. "What's the point of having campaign finance laws when anybody who ignores the laws by making a $200 thousand contribution is able to get off with a ten grand fine? That's a five-percent entrance fee! It allows rich people to ignore the rules. And Persons' company was also the organizer of that seminar Oleson and his wife attended in Mexico. I checked out its agenda. There were a few tours of Mexican multi-family dwellings. But other than that, it was a series of cocktail parties for developers and elected officials. While Oleson was not the only elected official there, he was the only one who didn't pay for any of the junket's expenses until after the trip. And he didn't sign that check until the whole thing ended up in *The Daily Journal*."

Jeff looked back at my list of questions. He paused for a couple of minutes before continuing. "The story that outed the public information officer's relationship to Oleson? That was a *News Chronicle* article."

He took a deep breath, let it out slowly and said, "However, I do know Sandy Benoit—the girl that got hired. Before going to work at the city, she was a junior reporter at *The Daily Journal*. She's awfully cute and knows how to get what she wants. I wouldn't describe her as overly bright. She is, how shall I say it, uhm—socially skilled."

I interrupted him. "Do you think Oleson was involved with her before she got hired by the city?"

Jeff appeared to mull over his response before speaking. "Several reporters in the area applied for that city public information officer position when it opened. In addition to Sandy, two reporters from *The News Chronicle* applied. There were also two or three reporters from *The Daily Journal* who applied. I was one of them. And there were several other highly qualified candidates. It was a good-paying gig and, if you work for a newspaper, job security and good pay look awfully damn sweet. I don't think Sandy slept with the mayor before she got the position. I don't know that she slept with him after she got the position. But she was definitely not the most highly qualified candidate. Of that, I am certain. In any case, the two of them took multiple trips together after she was hired—apparently to accomplish the city's critical business needs. Anyway, after the story came out about those busy business trips, Sandy resigned. Coincidentally, she ended up getting hired by Chuck Persons' company. Small world, ain't it?"

He chuckled again.

I was going to ask several follow-up questions about Benoit, but Jeff looked at his watch and said, "Hey man, I'm sorry but we got to get going. I have a dental appointment this afternoon. You have one more question on your list—the relationship between Dickens and Oleson. I'll talk about that as I chauffeur you back to the *Dispatch*."

I pulled out my wallet but Jeff insisted on paying for lunch.

A few minutes later we were in his car heading toward Bloomington. Once again, I enjoyed the fresh air blowing past me as Jeff wove through traffic in his Mustang convertible.

"So, you wanna know how Dave Dickens and Oleson got along?" He continued. "I would describe the two of them as being a lot like Italian dressing. Italian dressing is vinegar, oil and spices. You have to shake the hell out of the bottle before you pour any dressing onto the lettuce because oil and vinegar don't mix. One basic fact: Dave Dickens and Doug Oleson were not allies."

For most of the rest of the ride, Jeff spoke about the two Saint Paul mayors. "Before Oleson was elected, Dickens was council chair, well on his way toward his goal of becoming emperor of the city. But once Oleson announced his run for the office—with enthusiastic endorsement from party leaders—Dickens had no choice but to be the good soldier. He endorsed Oleson."

We were only a couple of minutes from my office. Jeff checked his watch and finished up the interview. "Sometime, probably in high school, Dickens must have decided his lifetime goal was to become mayor of Saint Paul. My read is that he resented Douglas Oleson for delaying his achievement of that goal. Meanwhile, the moment Oleson was elected, he started treating Dickens like he was a leper. Those two bureaucrats were like a couple of nasty old ladies sniping at one another whenever they could, undercutting the other person whenever possible—and always refusing to admit it."

As he made that last statement, Jeff pulled up in front of the *Weekly Dispatch*. I thanked him for the lunch. We said goodbye and promised to get together again in the future.

Chapter 15 – A Magnificent Dinner

One Thursday afternoon, Webster approached me while I was waiting at the printer. Webster had a serious look when he said, "Louise asked me why I'd never brought you home for dinner. I told her it was her fault—she'd never suggested it. Well, she says, *In that case, wise guy, I'm suggesting it now. Get your intern over here for dinner tomorrow evening. In exchange, I promise to fix your favorite—chicken fricassee.*"

Webster gave me a *don't give me any crap* look and said, "So, unless you're meeting with President Clinton or the Pope tomorrow evening, you're coming home with me for dinner. Got a problem with that?"

I laughed and said, "No."

Webster gave a pleased smile, pivoted on his heels and headed back into his office.

*****

Friday at 4 PM, Webster came to my cubicle. After an exaggerated inspection of how I was dressed, he said, "I'm not too impressed with the shoes. But other than that, you'll pass muster. Let's get out of here."

I had often seen but never ridden in Webster's classic, 1975 Mercedes Benz 240D. The light blue car looked new. It turned out that the comfort of its leather seats and solid ride were as impressive as the name *Mercedes Benz*.

As Webster drove us out of his parking space behind the *Weekly's* office, he popped a CD into the car's disc player and with Billy Holiday singing "Am I Blue" in the background, Webster spoke about his car. "I know the

240D's gas mileage isn't outstanding. But every other aspect of this vehicle is beyond reproach. Louise and I find absolute tranquility traveling the back roads of this country in this artisan-crafted chariot. Each day, as I drive into work, this little blue baby gives me the unique satisfaction of driving a classic machine at a time in this country's history when quality is not a prominent aspect of how we live. This automobile is functional, rational and exquisitely engineered. I know it's a bit hedonistic for me to say all that—but Paul, if the shoe fits, I guess I will happily stick it on my foot."

Webster had a smile of satisfaction on his face and didn't speak again for the rest of the drive to his home. During the drive, I enjoyed the Mercedes' luxury ride and relaxed while listening to the buttery voice of Billy Holiday.

After a half hour of fairly heavy commuter traffic, Webster turned off of the state highway onto a quiet gravel county road and we headed into farm country. Ten minutes later, he pulled into the yard of a two-story white farmhouse. The beautifully maintained, green-roofed and shuttered, home had to be from the turn of the century.

Webster's wife Louise was standing inside the home's wooden screen door. Louise was of medium height and wore wire-rim glasses. Her white hair was pinned up in a bun.

As she opened the screen door and walked toward us, Louise had a big smile. "Paul, I had begun to worry if you really existed. I was concerned you might be just another figment of Webster's over-active imagination—you know, like his six-foot rabbit. Come on in. Our feast is in the oven and you look like you could use a drink. Webster, can you tear yourself away from your magical Mercedes and make us gin and tonics?"

The Pedersen's living room looked like it had been furnished in the nineteen-forties. Its seating was provided by an antique oak rocker, an overstuffed deep blue mohair couch and a matching chair. The room's worn oak floors were covered with a dark red oriental carpet. Against the wall, facing the couch, was a black and chrome wood-burning stove.

Louise suggested I sit on the wooden rocker. From there, I watched Webster carefully measure jiggers of Tanqueray Gin into three tall cut-crystal glasses. Meanwhile, Louise brought two wooden bowls of honey-roasted peanuts into the room. She placed one on a small wooden table next to my rocker and the other on the coffee table in front of the couch. A moment later, Webster set a gin and tonic down next to me. After eating a small handful of the delectable nuts, my first long sip of the gin and tonic seemed like a match made in heaven. I'd never had a gin and tonic before. Its tart, bubbly pine taste was completely refreshing—perfect for that hot humid afternoon.

"Do you enjoy jazz?" Webster inquired.

I said, "Yes."

Webster walked over to a beautifully carved wooden bookcase that was loaded with LP record albums. He selected one, removed its vinyl record from the cover and placed it on a turntable located on top of the bookcase. A moment later we were listening to the elegant shoo-be-doo of Ella Fitzgerald. That was the first of many swing-era albums we listened to during the evening. We heard duets by Ella and Satchmo, orchestral compositions by Duke Ellington and clarinet improvisations by Benny Goodman.

Before each album played, Webster shared a few biographic comments about the album and its performers.

Several albums and a couple of gin and tonics later, Louise hollered from the kitchen, "If you guys don't get to the table soon, I'm going to eat dinner by myself."

*****

The dining room's Duncan Phyfe table was covered with a lace tablecloth and a China setting. The room's elegance was from another age.

Webster said, "Louise grew all the salad fixings and we managed to raise and butcher this chicken as a team. Tonight, you're eating homegrown, boy."

Not much was said during the dinner of chicken stew with dumplings accompanied by a fresh green salad with radishes and tomatoes. The meal was served with a Chardonnay from Washington State. I made the mistake of having seconds on everything before I learned that there was a wonderful dessert which, because I wanted to be a good guest, I could not pass up.

Louise handed me a plate with a large piece of fresh apple pie and a huge scoop of vanilla ice cream.

"Last fall," Webster said "Louise traded a couple of bushels of our apples to a neighbor in exchange for future deliveries of cream from their small organic dairy. The ice cream melting in your mouth is literally the fruits of our labor."

After the meal, Louise suggested we go back into the living room. Webster put on an Errol Garner piano LP and our conversation continued. I remember noting that Webster did not smoke one cigarette all evening—and that their house did not have any of the foul smell of old cigarette smoke. While that seemed odd, I did not bring it up.

I did ask, "How did you acquire this home?"

It was Louise who responded. "I get the credit for that, Paul. I've lived in this house my whole life. My parents owned and farmed the two hundred acres surrounding the home. We haven't changed the place much since Dad passed away. I was still in college then and Mom was so ill, so I stayed on. Mom died a few months after Webster and I were married."

"It's a wonderful house," I said.

Webster added, "I was raised on a farm about fifteen miles east of here. Louise and I went to high school together."

"We like rural America," said Louise. "On most of our vacations, we just relax in Webster's Mercedes and tour blue highways across the Midwest. We're going to be taking a trip the week after next. We'll be visiting some of Webster's relatives in Nebraska. On the way, we'll pass through some of my favorite farm country."

Webster jumped in. "I'll be out of the office for two weeks, Paul. Dolly knows that if there are any emergencies while I'm out, you're in charge."

The rest of the evening was small talk. Louise asked me a few questions about my family and what it was like growing up in Chicago. She wanted to know if I liked college and whether I intended to continue in the newspaper business.

To that last question, I responded, "Yes, I'm enjoying working for a paper. Webster is teaching me a lot and I have a project that's been really interesting."

Louise smiled. "Webster told me about your project. Beware. It's a tangled ball of yarn. Best of luck on it."

A little while later, I made the mistake of yawning. Webster commented that if he didn't drive me home soon, they would have to put me to bed in the guest room.

*****

On the way home, we listened to Bessie Smith singing songs of troubled love. As we got near my place, I thanked Webster for the wonderful evening.

Then, I asked my question. "You didn't smoke one cigarette all evening. Why?"

"Well," Webster responded, "my lovely wife keeps telling me that my cancer sticks are going to be my death. The best deal I could negotiate was that I would never smoke a cigarette in front of her. Sure, she knows I smoke at work. She harps on me about it all the time. But what are you gonna do?"

I was going to follow up on that—maybe tell him what I thought he should do—when Webster changed the subject, taking away my opportunity to preach against the tobacco industry.

"The other day," he said, "I thought of someone else for you to interview for the Oleson story. We can probably get to her this summer. Edith Hanson is a teacher at Horace Mann Elementary School. She taught Doug Oleson when he was in the fourth grade. The old lady is close to retiring now. But she and I have talked about Doug in the past. I think she would enjoy speaking with you and could certainly give you some interesting insights into the former mayor of Saint Paul.

*****

The following week, I worked in earnest on the articles about the two Bloomington High School football teams. I met with the schools' coaches. Each must have

113

forgotten he had met with me the prior year because their stories were the same as they had been in our first interviews. Each was enthusiastic about the upcoming season, confident that this year they would be able to turn things around and maybe get a championship.

I considered writing about how bad those high school teams had been over the years. Then I remembered the advice that Webster had given me: *Let discretion be the better part of valor*. He didn't want me making enemies for the paper.

In deference to Webster's concerns, I didn't discuss how strong the two football teams would be in the upcoming season. Instead, I chose to focus on each coach's back story— that they had grown up on Minnesota farms, gone to school in small towns and how they had played college football for Minnesota State Universities. And, probably most importantly, I emphasized that they were nice guys— and that was the truth. I described their families, their philosophies of life and their hopes for their players' future lives.

At the end of the week, Webster looked at the completed stories and said, "My, how diplomatic you've become. Go ahead and publish them. I'm out for the next two weeks. You can work on finishing up the story about the Bloomington City Council. And oh yeah, while I'm out of the office, try not to publish anything that will have the citizens of Bloomington hanging me in effigy before I return."

Then, almost as an afterthought, he added, "Oh, by the way, the superintendent of schools has promised to get us the home phone number for Edith Hanson."

Chapter 16 – Miss Edith Hanson

During the next two weeks, it was just Dolly and me in the office. I enjoyed the opportunity to get to know her.

Dolly's husband had been drafted before their son and daughter had begun school. He was killed in Vietnam less than a year later. Dolly ended up raising the two kids and supporting herself as an administrative assistant at a state agency. She retired from the State about the time Webster bought the *Bloomington Weekly Dispatch*. Her kids had grown up and moved from the area. So, Dolly went to work for Webster out of boredom rather than because of financial need.

*****

Tuesday morning, Dolly stopped me as I passed her desk. "I got a call," she said, "from the school district. They gave me the home phone number for Oleson's former teacher, Edith Hanson."

Later that day, when I called Miss Hanson, the woman who answered the phone sounded like the fairy godmother from Cinderella. "Hello? Why yes, this is Miss Edith Hanson. Why do you ask?"

After I explained to her how I had gotten her phone number and told her about the project I was working on, she responded brightly, "How very nice. Webster Pedersen is such a kind newspaperman. And Carleton College is an excellent college. I would love to help you. And yes, I remember Douglas very well. I would enjoy telling you all about him. Why don't you come over to my home tomorrow morning? I can make us each a cup of tea and we will talk."

*****

There weren't good bus connections to get to Edith Hanson's home in South Saint Paul. Dolly offered me the use of her ten-year-old Ford Escort to get there. I parked the Escort in front of Miss Hanson's small white rambler, rang the doorbell and Edith Hanson invited me in. She looked every bit the grade school teacher during her summer vacation. Her white hair was cut in a bob and she was wearing an embroidered Mexican-style blouse with worn blue jeans.

Miss Hanson invited me into her brightly colored living room. Surrounding a red and yellow needlepoint rug were a pair of yellow upholstered chairs and a matching settee. In between the chairs and the settee was an elegant mahogany coffee table. On top of it were a coral-colored teapot, two matching tea cups with saucers and a plate of homemade chocolate chip cookies.

I sat down on the settee across from Miss Hanson who was in one of the chairs. After pouring us each a cup of tea, we made small talk about the weather and how much she liked living in Saint Paul. Then, I asked her if we could speak about Douglas Oleson.

"I remember Dougie so well," she said. "He tried so hard and was always so helpful. He joined my class a month after the start of the school year—his mother had just moved into our district. Dougie always worked so hard, always listened to instructions and never spoke when he was supposed to be silent. I don't remember him ever challenging me. Years later, I was so proud of Dougie when I read in *The Daily Journal* that he had been elected to the legislature. And then, after he was elected mayor, he invited me to his office. His wife was there too. She was such a gentle and beautiful woman. They both treated me like I was someone special."

I listened to her babble on about what a sweet boy Douglas Oleson had been. Everything she said made it sound like he had been the perfect fourth grader. I began to wonder why Webster had suggested I interview her. Finally, I decided I needed to find out if she had any more nuanced perspectives to share.

I asked, "Was there anyone in the school who didn't like Douglas?"

"Oh, you misunderstand me, Paul. I thought Dougie was a sweet child. But the kids in his class? Well, I don't recall any of the kids in his class liking him very much. They were mean to Dougie. I always felt so sorry for him. Sometimes, to make him feel a little bit special, I'd ask Dougie to stay in from recess and help me in the classroom. Well, the kids didn't like that either. Kids can be so mean. And the meanest kids, well, they often become the leaders. Initially, they just teased him—his clothing wasn't very nice. His shoes were worn and his shirts and pants were often dirty."

She was quiet for a moment. Then she sighed and said, "Later, after he had had it with the teasing, he got into a few fights in the playground—you know, with the kids who teased him the most. Well, they stopped teasing him after that. But after that, they liked Dougie even less. You've heard the old saying, *darned if you do and darned if you don't.* The other kids enjoyed pushing his buttons. But they didn't think it was so nice when he pushed theirs."

We sipped tea in silence for a little while. Miss Hanson offered me more tea. I thanked her and held out my cup. After she refilled it, she began to speak again.

"There was one boy in our class, Jimmy Childs. His dad was an executive with General Mills. Jimmy was one confident little boy. And oh, he had such a mean streak in him. He was the leader of the kids who were mean to Dougie. One day that spring, Jimmy decided he was going to teach Dougie a lesson. As I learned later, he caught up with Dougie after school about a block from the schoolyard. Jimmy beat Dougie up pretty badly."

Miss Hanson looked out the picture window in her living room. She sighed as if she was visualizing what had happened.

"The next day, Jimmy did not come to school. When Dougie arrived, he looked upset. I asked him what was wrong. He told me what had happened the previous day. When he got home after Jimmy had beaten him up, he had a nosebleed, his shirt was ripped and he had a pretty good shiner. Dougie's mother asked her son what happened. He told her. She asked him if he knew where Jimmy lived. He nodded yes, he did. Dougie's mother told him to go over to Jimmy's house and not to return home until he had given Jimmy a licking—one just as bad as Jimmy had given him. It sounded like Dougie followed his mother's instructions to a T."

Miss Hanson looked down and shook her head sadly. "As you might imagine, I was horrified. Later that day I was asked to go to the principal's office and meet with Jimmy's parents. Mr. Turner—he was our principal then—had me listen to their rendition of Dougie being the bully. I tried to explain to them that Dougie had been treated horribly by Jimmy and the other boys; that Jimmy had beaten him up earlier that day after school. But Mr. Turner interrupted me and said, *Let's talk about this later, Edith. Now please return to your class.*"

Miss Hanson gave a long sigh. "At the end of the school day, Mr. Turner asked me to come to his office. He told me he had called Mrs. Oleson and informed her that Dougie was suspended for the rest of the school year—about four weeks. I tried once again to explain what had happened. But Mr. Turner interrupted me and said, *Edith, it's over now. It has been taken care of.*"

Miss Hanson stood up slowly and walked to her living room's picture window. She stood there, her back to me, and silently looked out.

"I wanted to challenge Mr. Turner," she said in a voice full of sadness. "I wanted to explain to him that he was wrong. But Mr. Turner often got angry when people disagreed with him. And I was awfully young. Anyway, Mr. Turner frightened me and I chose not to take him on. I returned to my classroom."

Miss Hanson continued to stand with her back toward me. A quiet tension filled her living room. I knew better than to interrupt the silence. Maybe she was done with her story?

But after a few minutes, Miss Hanson, still looking out the window, continued to speak. "The following fall, I looked for Dougie in the fifth-grade classrooms. It seemed he had not returned to our school. I asked Mr. Turner if he knew what had happened to the Oleson boy. He told me he didn't know but that Dougie and his mother had probably moved away."

Miss Hanson turned back towards me and returned to her seat.

"You know, Paul. Every grade school teacher wants every one of their students to be successful. But some of our—I don't know how I should say it—some of our more special students—we want them to overcome the obstacles they face even more. I felt so badly for Dougie. I wasn't able to get him out of my mind. And then, years later, when I saw he had become so successful, it made me happy. I thought to myself, sometimes God takes care of his children—takes care of the ones who have been given the tougher path."

Miss Hanson took a handkerchief out of her jeans pocket and wiped her eyes. There was sadness in her voice as she said, "When he was driven out of political office by the mean things people said in the paper, it made me sad all over again. That boy, he tried so hard, Paul. It just wasn't fair."

Miss Edith Hanson looked down at the table, shook her head slowly from side to side, took a deep breath, then exhaled and repeated, "It just wasn't fair."

She was silent for a couple of minutes before saying, "If you ever see Dougie, be sure to tell him that I often thought of him—that I think of him. He was one of the sweetest kids I have ever known. Tell him I hope he is doing well."

*****

As I drove back to the office, I thought back to when I was a little kid. I thought about how mean some other kids sometimes had been.

And, I must admit, I felt sad for Douglas Oleson.

Chapter 17 – Development

Monday morning, I called Chuck Persons, the developer who had been a major contributor to Douglas Oleson's campaigns. Persons suggested we get together for lunch at his home on Wednesday.

When Dolly heard we would be meeting at Persons' Summit Avenue home, she said, "Ooh-la-la! You lucky bum. Those mansions are big and beautiful. Why don't you borrow my car again? It will take forever to get there by bus."

I felt guilty borrowing her car. But after looking at the city bus connections, I was relieved she'd offered her car.

*****

As I drove down the four-and-a-half-mile-long ash tree-lined boulevard, I understood why Dolly had been so enthusiastic. The street was a parade of classic nineteenth-century architecture—a castle followed by a mansion next to a large classic home and on and on along the entire route. As I drove past the mansions, I thought about the books of F. Scott Fitzgerald. I could see part of where that Saint Paul native had found inspiration for *The Great Gatsby*. That was the first time it occurred to me that Gatsby's curious qualities were eerily similar to Douglas Oleson's.

I spotted Persons' three-story brick mansion early on my drive, but drove past it, wanting to complete my tour of the rest of the Summit manor houses before my meeting. A short while later, I was back at to the Persons mansion, driving up its curved brick driveway and parking Dolly's Ford Escort right next to a fire-engine-red Porsche Carrera convertible.

Chuck Persons, a big man—probably six feet four inches and built like a wrestler, came out of the stately home's entrance to welcome me. Persons was dressed casually in white Bermuda shorts and a red polo shirt as if he were on vacation in the tropics.

"Hey there," he welcomed me. "Thanks for coming to my home. My wife is out of town and I didn't want to go into work today. So, you gave me an excuse to stay home. If it's okay with you, we'll have lunch before we go over your questions."

We walked into the home's walnut-paneled grand entry, passed a couple of carved mahogany doors and entered a magnificent dining room that was dominated by a gold-trimmed, wood-inlay dining table with a dozen matching chairs. The room's cherry floors gleamed and a crystal chandelier that hung over the dining room table seemed to say, *This is what prosperity looks like.*

A white paper bag sat at the head of the table and Persons sat down in front of it. He invited me to take a seat next to him.

While he opened the bag, Persons said, "Sorry, I didn't ask if you were a vegetarian. I took the liberty of ordering us each a hot corned beef and rye sandwich from Cecil's Delicatessen. If you've never eaten there, you're in for a treat. Since my wife was out of town and I can't cook worth a damn, Cecil's seemed like the best option."

He asked, "Can I offer you something to drink? A beer? Maybe some sparkling water?"

"Sparkling water sounds nice," I responded.

Webster had mentioned Cecil's Delicatessen once or twice but I'd never eaten there. The sandwich was extraordinary. The fresh rye bread and the delicate corned beef melted in my mouth. The sparkling water Persons gave served me in a crystal glass was the perfect complement.

After we finished our sandwiches, Persons excused himself for a moment, exited through the swinging white door into the kitchen and came back with two mugs of coffee.

"You take cream?"

I told him the coffee would be fine, black.

Chuck needed no prompting to begin the interview. "My great-granddaddy built this house—or more accurately he had it built. He was one of the founding fathers of this city. He started a bank here as a young man; then sold the bank and started a construction company. After that, he met my great-grandma, became a city council member and initiated one civic innovation after another."

Persons let that soak in, then continued, "His son, my grandfather followed in his footsteps constructing several of the classic downtown buildings that people around here cherish. Grandpa established a reputation for helping out families who struggled during the Depression. Then he was off to Europe to fight Hitler with distinction. My daddy—he kept the ball rolling; built a couple of downtown commercial buildings; served in the state legislature and was head of the Minnesota GOP. I guess I sort of picked up where Daddy left off."

Persons took a drink from his coffee mug and said, "My family has always loved this city. We've tried to do whatever we could to keep it moving forward. That means we have worked for almost a century to keep Saint Paul's economic engine running smoothly. Part of the reason that we were successful is that we worked with politicians who understood that economic development helps everyone."

He looked at me as if he was trying to see if what he had said had registered with me. "Now," he said. "Go ahead and shoot. Ask me your questions."

I started with my standard *I'm a senior at Carleton* introduction moving into, "I've interviewed a variety of people from your community already. Some like Oleson—some don't. I was told that you contributed to his campaigns and were a strong supporter of his efforts after he got into office. I've also been told that he was your good friend. I'd like to hear your perspectives on Oleson and what he meant to this community."

"Like I said," he responded, "I'm the fourth generation of Persons who has built commercial buildings in Saint Paul. Do you want to guess what my great-granddad, my grandad and my father ran into when they had new ideas? Do you think everybody was in favor of building the hotels, the clinics, the hospitals, the schools and the office buildings? Of course, they weren't. But the Persons clan finds people they can work with. So, did I support Douglas Oleson? You bet your sweet ass I did. Oleson understood that to stimulate governmental revenues, he had to stimulate the economy. I didn't have to twist his arm into zoning flexibility. He understood it had to happen to achieve economic growth."

Persons paused, drained his cup of coffee and went back into the kitchen, returning with the pot.

After he'd poured each of us a full cup, he picked up where he had left off. "Did Oleson bring in a planning director who understood development and its community impacts? Of course, he did. Without that planning director, you wouldn't have the new parks or the low-income housing we built in conjunction with new condominiums—all of which the NIMBYs fought tooth and nail. These are the same parks and low-income housing for which Mayor Dickens is now taking credit. How did Oleson get those parks and low-income housing? It was part of deals he negotiated with developers. The commercial buildings? They benefit the whole community—check them out—they are full of offices and small manufacturers—full of new employers who give jobs to Saint Paul residents. Wasn't that what Oleson and his planning director should have been doing? The fact that we could communicate with the guy, that he understood what we were about and spoke directly with us—wasn't that a success rather than a failure?"

He waited. I am not sure if he wanted me to answer, but the pause in his speech increased the effect of his words.

"Did Oleson or his planning director approve everything I submitted to the city? No. Did they agree with me on all policy issues? Certainly not. There were times when neither Oleson nor his planning director gave an inch. And I'll tell you today, they were wrong! Those were good ideas that they turned down. But those decisions never got reported in *The Daily Journal*. You wonder why?"

Again, he waited. If this was an eight-ball game, Persons wasn't hesitating as he ran the table.

"I am sure as hell that you got a lot of input from Jeff Washington about all this. Jeff is a bright guy. He became successful as a reporter because he always found controversy. And when Jeff couldn't find that controversy, he created it. Newspapers depend upon their ability to stir the pot. That doesn't make a community stronger. The controversy creates fear of innovation."

Persons had his speech down and was enjoying delivering it. He changed gears and, with a sly smile, said,

"Did I finesse the campaign finance laws? The American economic system was built by people who finessed campaign finance laws. I sure as hell hope that you spend some time meeting with labor leaders who sent out their members to work door-to-door for Oleson, labor leaders whose unions were rewarded with contracts and richer healthcare benefits. Most successful political candidates have groups that push for them. Those groups push the edges. Why do I say most political candidates? Because there are a few candidates who go by the book. Do you want to know which city council members go by the book? None of them—not a single one! Most of the candidates who go by the book run one unsuccessful campaign and are done."

Our coffee cups were empty. Persons reached for the pot and asked if I wanted another cup of coffee. I declined. I could see he was wrapping up his one-man rally.

"Do I feel justified in having swung the development community in support of Douglas? Have you seen the analysis of what happened to Saint Paul's economy when Oleson was mayor? It was remarkable. Oleson was a partner. He benefited from our support and the community benefited from the fact that Oleson and the developers worked together."

Persons' cell phone rang. He looked to see who was calling, then answered it. For two or three minutes, I listened to him telling whoever was on the other end that they were full of crap and he wasn't gonna take any of it. Persons kept scowling as he shook his head and said more than once, *that's a bunch of crap.*

After he was done speaking on the phone, he looked back at me and gave a pleasant smile, paused and I could see he was trying to remember what he was about to say.

Then his face lit up and he continued. "The other red herring is that so-called *junket* to Mexico that Oleson and his wife took. Sure, they met with developers. Jeff Washington complained in his articles that we had unfair access to the mayor. He also accused Oleson of partying throughout the junket. Those statements are contradictions as well as outright lies. There were more discussions on Twin Cities economic development on that trip than there had been with the city in years. You don't get things done unless you talk to one another."

Persons laughed and said, "I'm sorry if I got carried away a little bit. I care about these things a lot. It's almost like the way I feel about the Minnesota Vikings. I'm passionate!"

He paused and added, "Now, is there anything else you wanted to ask?"

Persons had taken most of the wind out of my sails and I was taken aback by his bluster. It's not that I felt that what he had said was correct. It's just that he had moved so quickly without any prompting that I had fallen behind in matching what he said to the questions I had intended to ask.

I look down at my preparation notes. There were a couple of areas that he had not addressed. "What did you think of Oleson's deputy mayor?"

Persons gave me a sly look. Then he said, "By now you have figured out that I will tell you what I think. So, you probably won't be surprised. Debbie Perth is one smart cookie. She picked things up quickly; analyzed them thoroughly; and could always come up with a plan. Then she managed that plan as well as any private-sector project manager. If she disagreed with you, she told you to your face. Your big question—the one you haven't asked—is if, on those business trips, the two of them fucked? And my answer is, Paul, I just don't give a damn."

He paused, letting that sink in.

"What does that have to do with running the city? Can you tell me?"

He looked me in the eye and said, "And I'll save you your other related question. You're about to ask me, *didn't I hire Sandy Benoit? What's the story with her?* Sandy is a smart and independent woman, Paul. She can answer those questions herself. I think it would make a whole hell of a lot more sense for you to ask those questions of her rather than of me. You can reach her at our office."

Chuck Persons picked up his cellular phone again and stood up.

"I'm sorry, Paul," he said, "but I've got to call a couple of subcontractors who are screwing up royally. You had questions today. I gave you some pretty straight answers. I've enjoyed meeting you. If you have of more questions, give me a ring. Otherwise, good luck on your term paper. And yes, please give Webster my best regards. He's one good man. I miss having him on *The News Chronicle.* The man has integrity and is as smart as a fox."

I had no idea if I would have other questions for Persons. It seemed like he had touched upon everything I was going to ask. He led me out of the dining room, down the hall and back to the front door which he opened for me. As I climbed back into Dolly's Ford Escort (while glancing at Person's shiny Porsche), Persons wished me a good day and headed back into his house—already on another phone call.

*****

I was learning. My experience with Chris Thompson of the Labor Federation had taught me not to ask Persons for input as to who I might check with regarding how well Oleson's administration had managed zoning and the planning permit process. As I drove back to the office, I decided I would ask Webster for advice about who could give me some insight into those areas.

Chapter 18 – Lunch with Dolly

To thank her for the use of her car, I invited Dolly out to lunch at Cecil's Delicatessen. She gave me a warm smile and said, "You've got yourself a date. I love Cecil's!"

About 40 minutes later, we were seated at the delicatessen. I'd ordered a bowl of matzo ball soup and a hot pastrami sandwich. Dolly ordered blintzes and we each had a cup of coffee. We chatted about my projects at the newspaper. When the conversation turned toward Webster, I told Dolly about my dinner with Webster and Louise.

"Oh, yes," she said. "They've had me out there a few times. Louise is an incredible cook and Webster's jazz and blues record collection—wow! He was always interested in jazz, but do you know who got him into the blues?"

"I have no idea," I responded.

"Webster was taught to love the blues by his daughter, Ingrid. Ingrid had a beautiful voice. She would accompany herself on her guitar while she sang old blues classics. In high school, she got into singing Billy Holiday. That was when Webster started buying blues albums."

I was surprised to hear that the Pedersens had a daughter. Webster had never mentioned her to me. I'd assumed that he and Louise had just decided they didn't want kids or had been unable to have them.

"Webster didn't tell me anything about Ingrid," I said. "Where is she now?"

Just then, the waiter brought us our lunches. I attacked my soup first, then moved on to the hot pastrami. The soup was as good as any matzo ball soup I'd ever had and the sandwich seemed even better than the sandwich I ate with Chuck Persons. I put a lot of French's mustard on my plate and dipped each bite of that hot pastrami and rye into the mustard before devouring it. I lost myself in the rich flavor. Dolly was similarly focused on her blitzes. They had been served with a large dollop of sour cream and a fresh glob of strawberry jam.

After the waiter had cleared our plates and I'd paid the check, I asked again, "So, where is Webster's daughter living now?"

Speaking in a hushed voice, Dolly said, "I should have known Webster wouldn't have mentioned Ingrid. It's so painful for him. He was so proud of her. I've known the Pedersens for years. Both our families attended Saint James Lutheran Church in Saint Paul. Even after Ingrid graduated from the university and started working as a social worker in Minneapolis, she generally attended services with her folks."

Dolly's look took on some pain. "For her birthday about five years ago, Webster gave Ingrid his 1950s Triumph sports car. It was the classic he used to drive around town before he purchased the blue Mercedes. Ingrid fell in love with that roadster."

Dolly shook her head and looked down. "A few months after they gave her that little red car, she visited them after church. It was early October—a couple of years after Webster had retired and purchased *The Dispatch*. The day had been warm and rainy. In the evening, the temperature plunged. After dinner, on her way home to her apartment, the Triumph spun out and flipped into a ditch. Ingrid died instantly."

We sat there for a couple of minutes in silence. Then, we got up from our table, left the delicatessen and returned to the Ford Escort for our drive back to Bloomington.

We had driven for several minutes before Dolly continued. "Both Webster and Louise were devastated. They seemed to age ten years within a matter of months. Since Ingrid's funeral, I have not seen Webster or Louise at Saint James Church. Nor has he not brought up Ingrid's name once. But when Webster is at home and plays those classic blues records, I see the emotion on his face—his thoughts— I am certain they are with her. That man loved his daughter so much."

*****

Before leaving on vacation, Webster had written down a list of tasks he wanted me to address while he was on his two-week road odyssey. It included writing brief obituaries for a series of recently departed locals (he included their names and some background notes and attending the weekly Rotary luncheon meetings on his behalf.

I wrote the obituaries (and found the process fascinating); but skipped the Rotary meetings. Webster also asked Dolly to have me do a prepublication review of the *Weekly Dispatche*s. In doing the review, I discovered how much Dolly produced for the newspaper. Between the syndicated columns she compiled, the advertisements she laid out, the brief articles she wrote and the obituaries I authored, the newspapers seemed complete.

Chapter 19 – Wrapping up the Summer

Shortly after his return from the road trip, Webster invited Dolly and me to join him in his office for a cup of coffee. While we filled our cups, he took out a cigarette which he lit.

"I have to tell you guys about an unexpected highlight of our trip," he said. "It was a sun-scorched day in farm country. We were rambling along on a desolate state highway—we'd just gotten into Nebraska—when Louise declared, *Let's do some exploring Webster. Let's find a special out-of-the-way spot.*"

Webster sucked in some smoke from his cigarette and repeated his ritual of expelling it. Dolly and I watched while harboring our concern that this habit was killing him.

After blowing the smoke toward the center of his office's ceiling, he went on with his story. "Exploring sounded good to me. So, I turned onto the next no-name county byway we came across. It led to a gravel access road which I also followed. We raised a trail of dust on that gravel road for about fifteen minutes. Suddenly, Louise pointed out the window and said, *Park the Mercedes on the side of the road—now.* I followed her instructions. Then I saw it. About a quarter of a mile into a plowed field were some structures. It looked like they might be an abandoned farmstead."

He took a deep inhale of smoke, blew it out, and managed to retain the burnt ash intact on his cigarette. He looked at us and raised his eyebrows with an amused pleasure at that achievement.

Then he returned to his narrative. "We walked and walked into that field—maybe half an hour—and ended up in an old barnyard. I took a few photographs of the farmstead's old weathered buildings. The grey, dilapidated barn was leaning so far over that even though its large doors were open, I didn't dare explore it. The chicken coop was just a worn-down wooden skeleton from days past."

Webster stopped speaking for a moment. He had a quizzical look on his face as he said, "The fact that the farmstead was surrounded by so much plowed acreage might be the reason it had been so well preserved. Those fields had served as a metaphorical moat protecting that little kingdom of the past from the ravages of passing motorists. The farmstead's only enemy had been time and the weather."

He paused for a moment, looking off as if he was visualizing the farmstead.

"We walked up to the farmhouse. Its siding was dark gray weathered boards speckled with decades-old flecks of white paint. Louise approached the back door. When she turned its rusted doorknob, she was taken aback—the door opened. She pushed it open the rest of the way and we walked into a small empty mud room and then on into the kitchen. The kitchen counter was well-worn blackened wood with a beaten-up white kitchen sink in its center. The sink held a couple of old rusted-through pans. Across from the counter, was a heavily corroded iron cookstove."

Webster paused and shook his head. "We moved on through a doorway into the house's main room. We were stunned. The furniture was all still there—covered in dust, it's true—but still in fairly good condition. There was a small dining table and a couple of chairs drawn up to it. In front of an old leather couch (that had been seriously chewed on by rats and was covered with almost an inch of dust) was a small wooden coffee table. On that coffee table, again covered with a layer of dust, were a few old magazines. I picked one of them up and shook off the dust."

Webster stopped for a moment and repeated his cigarette ritual.

Then he smiled. "That magazine, Dolly and Paul, that magazine was the November 1937 issue of *National Geographic!* Its cover listed the month's stories—several articles focusing on Native Americans. One article was entitled *America's First Settlers, the Indians.* Another was entitled *When Redmen Ruled our Forests.* We opened the magazine to those stories. You can probably visualize the photographs."

Webster gave a disgusted look, shook his head sideways, and said, "Those of us with European ancestry have so little respect for the people who were here before us. Even when we try to be respectful, we end up patronizing. How shameful."

He stopped speaking for about a minute, taking a deep breath, then blowing it out as he gazed across the room. I could tell he was seeing that old farmhouse living room.

"On the table there, right next to the magazines were two empty coffee cups. Someone—two people, I guess—had left that home in 1937—probably in a hurry. Where were they going? Had the farm failed? Were they headed toward California? Perhaps someone had died? We'll never know. I guess that's the way of history. Stuff happens—relics are left...."

Webster sighed, then completed the thought, "and then it's all forgotten."

An intense silence followed Webster's monologue. How can one respond to a story like that? Dolly and I just sat there, stunned by his description of a scene that had been set six decades before.

Finally, Webster broke the silence. "Hey, why are you two sitting there like statues? Don't we have a newspaper to get out? Dolly, can you get me copies of the issues that were published while I was out and about with Louise? And Paul, come back in about an hour. I want you to go over your progress on the article about Bloomington's city leaders. You need to get hustling. There are only a few weeks before you go back to school. I expect that article to be done before you vanish—and to be done well. And also, I want an update on what's happening on the Oleson story. You're going to go back to school and Sharon's going to ask you what you've gotten done on it. I don't want to have to be embarrassed because you sat on your ass all summer."

As I walked out of Webster's office toward my cubicle, I heard him cough—a heavy cough that seemed like it came from the depth of his chest. I looked at Dolly. She was looking at me. She shrugged, raised her eyebrows and gave a look of resignation. I responded in kind and headed back to my cubicle.

*****

Later in the day, I updated Webster on my meeting with Chuck Persons. I told him I wanted to do some checking at the city on the accuracy of Persons' comments about permitting. I had already told Webster about my mistake of trying to get confirmation of everything Chris Thompson had said from his live-in girlfriend Barbara Robbins.

"I'm glad you're learning," Webster responded. "There's nothing wrong with making a mistake. But there's something sinful about repeating it. Sure. I'll help you find someone who can give you some perspective on Oleson's impact on permitting and zoning—someone who wasn't the beneficiary of a permit—or a cousin of Chuck Persons."

Webster opened his rolodex and started going through business cards. He selected a card, wrote a name and phone number on a scratch pad and handed me the page saying, "Call him. Dennis Cameron has been with Saint Paul's Planning Department for years. He was its assistant director before Oleson was elected. Oleson sort of moved him aside. But Dennis still works there. Give him a call. I'm sure he'll be able to share some useful insights."

*****

I called Cameron that afternoon. I gave him my well-rehearsed spiel about being a Carleton student and newspaper intern and told him that Webster had suggested he might give me some context on how well Oleson's regime had managed planning and development services.

"Sure," he replied. "That'd be fine. I have a lot of respect for Webster. He's a class act." Dennis Cameron paused for a moment before adding, "I've got the time right now—if you want to just do this on the phone."

"My main request," I said, "is for you to compare the planning department before Douglas Oleson was elected to what it was like during Oleson's regime and then, maybe also to what it's been like since he left office."

"Certainly. I've worked for the department for a couple of decades. I was its assistant director before Oleson was elected. I heard Oleson's campaign spiel and voted for him. Oleson spoke about innovation, integrity and making the city a model of good service. That sounded great. We weren't a bad department before he got here. Sometimes, a customer wanted approval on a complicated project that was full of problems. When we hold a project up, the customer gets angry. That is particularly true with the commercial development community. They always have the most complicated projects and often stretch their interpretation of building codes."

He was interrupted by somebody in his office. I heard his muffled response—he probably had his hand over the transmitter on his phone. "Yes," he said, "Tell them to submit it. I'll go over it in the next day or two and get back to them. Thank you."

A moment later he was back to our conversation. "Sorry. This place can get a little crazy. Where was I? Oh yeah. Before Oleson was elected we weren't perfect, but we worked with integrity and always tried to listen when permit applicants were frustrated. Our office probably was pretty bureaucratic. I knew we could have done our job better. But I think we always tried to be fair."

Dennis Cameron paused for a moment. "When Oleson came in, he fired the old director. The rank and file in our department were excited. We had heard Oleson's verbiage and wondered what sort of person he would bring in to turn us into an agency providing the standard of excellence he had promised. A few days later, we found out he had appointed a guy who had been fired by the City of Minneapolis for cutting corners and catering to developers. The guy used every quality improvement phrase and promised big changes to the development community. His mantra was, *We promise efficiency, courtesy and excellence.*"

Cameron stopped speaking. For a moment I thought we might have been cut off but I realized he was just considering what he would say next. "What a bunch of crap that was. Our new director told us to speed up work and approve projects even when the analysis wasn't complete. He told us economic development was an engine that would make Saint Paul a great place. Whenever a developer complained about a permitting decision, our new director chastised the staff person who had performed the analysis and almost always overrode the decision. Developers were thrilled. But my perspective was that the department had stopped enforcing our code. When I objected to what was going on, I was reassigned. Our new director put me on the special project from hell."

"How are things going today?" I asked.

I heard Cameron chuckle. "Mediocre—at best. They fired that hack from Minneapolis and brought back the guy who had been in charge before Oleson was elected. We're back to being bureaucratic. I had always hoped our department would someday become innovative. It wasn't innovative before Oleson. It didn't become innovative during his tenure and we're back to mediocrity now. I'm going to retire in a couple of months so I'm just keeping my yapper shut."

He stopped speaking for a second. I waited, not sure what would come next.

"Look," he continued. "I spoke with you because I trust Webster. Please don't quote me—at least not until I'm fully retired. I'm pleased to have had the chance to say these things. They needed to be said. But it won't make people happy. Anyway, I need to get back to work. I hope what I've shared with you is useful. Good luck with your project."

I thanked him and wished him the best in the future.

*****

As I sat in my cubicle considering what I had just heard, I realized that Chuck Persons hadn't lied. He'd just told me about the world as he saw it—or maybe as he wanted it to be. Persons was a developer. Oleson had made things easier for him. But Dennis Cameron saw things differently—he was trying to enforce Saint Paul's development code.

I was learning a lot about the city. But there was a whole lot I just didn't have the expertise to evaluate. If I wasn't going to become an expert on planning permits, economic development or measurement of effectiveness in government, how could I evaluate the quality of work, the efficiency of work or the economic impacts of planning department decisions that came out of Oleson's administration?

*****

During that summer, I spoke on the phone with other local special interest representatives. I chatted with a credible representative of the NAACP who argued that Douglas Oleson was all talk and no action. "Oleson had plenty of opportunities to initiate changes. Instead of exploring them, he took credit for federal grants that benefitted lower-income areas even when his administration had not supported the acquisition of those grants. Oleson was your typical carpetbagging liberal. He claimed to be all about minorities. But his senior level cabinet included no people of color."

On the other side of the coin, I spoke with a respected church leader who led the board of a local boys' club. "Douglas Oleson did more to help disadvantaged young people in our community than anyone in the history of this city. His people facilitated funding to our organization and to other community groups that reach out to young people in need. His human services staff worked with us in building partnerships that have made a lasting difference. Sure, I saw him make mistakes. I saw him initiate efforts that reflected no understanding of the culture or of the diversity in our community. But he tried. He wanted to do the right thing."

This church leader paused for a moment. Then his voice expressed some disappointment when he said, "However, Oleson still was a white dude who didn't know how to communicate with a community that had learned not to trust government. But when he was driven from power, I was disappointed. The man and his administration had tried—they had tried. And yes, they had made a difference."

Again and again, during conversations with members of the community, I ran into divergent, polarized judgments about Olesen and his administration. I commented to Webster once how much easier pulling together my senior thesis would have been if there had been a consistent perspective on Oleson and his administration's effectiveness.

Webster just smiled, raised his cigarette to his lips, inhaled the smoke, blew it toward the ceiling, and said, "You know Paul, the lessons of life—they are sometimes awfully elusive."

*****

I wanted to have at least one more interview before the end of the summer. The following day, I called Chuck Persons' development office and asked to speak to Sandy Benoit.

The woman who answered the phone simply responded, "You're speaking with her already."

I went through my dismal introduction—who I was and why I was contacting her. Then I asked if she would meet with me to answer a few questions.

When I was done with my monologue, Benoit said, "I've been expecting your call. Chuck told me about you. He said I'd need to drive—you don't have a car—but that I should expect you to take me out for a nice dinner. Chuck told me I might find you to be cute."

Then she laughed. By this point, I was flummoxed. What was I supposed to say? I had planned on going to her office and being super-professional. But that was proving difficult. She suggested we go to a restaurant near the Mall of America. She added it wouldn't be too expensive. We agreed she would pick me up at 5:30 that Friday evening.

She closed out the conversation with, "Have some really good questions for me and I'll try to have some really interesting answers for you."

*****

That wasn't the only interview I set up that week. Tuesday afternoon, Webster stopped by my desk and handed me a piece of paper with a phone number elegantly written in a woman's handwriting.

Webster placed both of his open hands on my desk, leaned over and said softly, "Millie Oleson—that's Douglas' mother, is in town for some sort of medical procedure. I ran into Miki Oleson at a Democratic Farmer Labor meeting last night. She told me she figured you'd want to meet with Millie. She gave me Millie's phone number. She will tell her former mother-in-law to expect a call from you. If I were you, I'd set up an interview as soon as possible."

I listened to the urgency with which Webster had imparted scheduling the interview. As soon as he left my desk, I dialed the number Miki had given him. I was a little taken aback when my call was answered by a woman who said, "Hennepin County Medical Center."

A few minutes later, I was on the phone with Millie Oleson. We set up a Wednesday morning time to meet in her hospital room. She told me she was pleased somebody would be visiting her.

Millie Oleson wasn't the only change I made to my schedule. Later that day, I got a call from my mother.

My mom's voice sounded stressed. "Paul, I know you're going to start school in a few weeks, but we haven't seen each other in six months. I was hoping you could come back to Chicago for a few days before you return to school. There are a few things I need to discuss with you. Your dad is out of town. So, this will be a time just for you and me."

I told my mom I'd finish off the internship early so I could visit her. Ordinarily, I stayed with my dad when I returned home. But in this instance, she told me I'd be staying with her.

I asked, "What's up?" She just told me she'd rather speak with me about it in person.

The call from my mom caused me a fair amount of angst. What was up with my mom? She generally seemed like she wanted to avoid me. At least that's how I felt. After considering every option, I decided she was probably going to try to pressure me to go to grad school after I graduated. Kathy had probably gotten to her and it wouldn't surprise me at all if it turned out that Kathy showed up for dinner the evening my mom was planning on putting on the pressure.

I went into Webster's office and told him I'd like to finish up my internship a week early. When he asked why, I explained.

Webster laughed as he snuffed out his cigarette saying, "You gotta do what your mom says, old man."

Then he laughed.

Webster was so great.

Chapter 20 – Douglas' Mother

Dolly lent me her car to me to travel to the Hennepin Hospital. After finding the correct elevator and then the right nurse's station, I asked for Millie Oleson's room.

The charge nurse said, "It's nice you're here. Facing a serious procedure when hardly anyone visits is tough."

That was my first notice that Douglas' mother's hospital visit wasn't routine.

A moment later I was in Millie Oleson's hospital room. A couple of medical machines were beeping as she slept. I sat on a chair next to her bed and studied her. She was overweight, had short curly gray hair and the multitude of wrinkles on her face spoke of a hard life. The yellowish color of her skin confirmed she might be pretty ill.

Millie opened her eyes. She smiled as she said, "Oh, you must be my visitor. Why are you here? What is your name? Were you a friend of Dougie?"

Her face and voice expressed an innocence I hadn't anticipated.

"Hi, Mrs. Oleson. My name is Paul. I've never met your son but I have heard a lot about him. I've got a homework assignment to write a paper about someone in politics. I am writing about Douglas. I was hoping you could tell me a little about him."

"Yes, Dougie is a very sweet boy."

"I am sorry you have to be in the hospital. Can you tell me what you are being treated for?"

"I was going to ask you if you could ask the doctors why they brought me here. Nobody will tell me. Everybody is nice and they treat me well. But no one will explain why I am here."

"I will ask the nurse when I leave and return to your room to tell you what I learn."

"Thank you. You are a nice man, Peter."

"How long has it been since you've seen your son, Mrs. Oleson?"

"Oh, it's been a while."

"Could you tell me a little about Douglas?"

"I would love to. Dougie has always been a hard worker. In high school, he worked at the doughnut shop. He made the doughnuts, sold the doughnuts and always sneaked some extra doughnuts home to me. He worked summers there and saved enough money to go to college. I encouraged him to go to a college near home. But he wanted to live in a dormitory. I don't know why. He found a job near the college and paid his room and board by working on weekends and summer breaks."

She closed her eyes and I was afraid she was going to fall asleep.

But suddenly Millie's eyes popped open and she continued to speak. "So, he didn't come home a whole lot. I moved back to Fergus Falls after my ma passed away. I inherited the house I grew up in. So, Dougie was pretty far away. Then, after he graduated from college, he was just always so busy. There wasn't a lot of time for him to visit, not in Fergus Falls. After Miki had Douglas Jr., she sometimes would visit me. I was so proud to be a grandma."

"But when did you last see your son?" I asked. "Was it at all recent?"

She gave a pensive look. "No. No, I don't think it was recent. After Dougie became a legislator, he was so—uh—so busy. Then he became mayor and he was even more busy."

She gave a quizzical look and said, "In fact, I don't remember the last time I saw him."

She paused. "He didn't visit me in the hospital. Miki has been here a few times. She brought Douglas Jr. He is such a sweetheart. Junior reminds me of his father. But no. Dougie wasn't here."

A nurse came into the room with a small plastic cup that contained several pills. "Time for your morning pills, Miss Millie."

I could see how weak Douglas' mother was as she struggled to raise her head. The nurse pushed a button on the bed to raise Millie's head and shoulders. Then she tipped the container so the pills fell into Millie's mouth and held a cup of water with a straw. Millie sucked on the straw to wash the pills down.

After the nurse left the room, I asked, "What was Douglas like as a child, Mrs. Oleson?"

"Oh, you know. Boys are rascals. They don't want to clean their rooms; don't want to do their homework; and, well, they get into trouble at school. Dougie was like that. I needed to give him an occasional whipping—you know, just to get him to pay attention to me. But he was a sweet boy."

Mrs. Oleson struggled to lean forward and took another sip of water, then said, "It was just Dougie and me, Peter. We depended on one another a lot. We would go for walks in the neighborhood. I would tell him stories about when his grandma and grandpa had the farm back in Williston, North Dakota. Dougie loved those stories so much. He would ask me to repeat them when he went to bed.

After a few minutes, I would look down, and there he was, asleep."

She took a deep breath and sighed. "I didn't earn a lot of money. So, we had to move a lot and, well, Dougie had to change schools often. He always wanted a dog. But you can't have a dog when you're renting a house—or an apartment—or a room—or living with other folks. You just can't do it."

She closed her eyes, smiled and said very quietly, "I'm sorry I never got him that dog, though. I know boys like dogs. But then, what are you gonna do?"

"I met with Douglas' fourth-grade teacher, Miss Hanson," I said. "She agreed that he was a sweet boy. Miss Hanson told me about a time when Douglas was beaten up by a boy after school. She said that when he got home, you told him to go to that kid's house and do to him what he had done to Doug. Is that true?"

Millie Oleson gave a childish giggle and said, "Miss Hanson ratted me out."

But then her face changed and she took on a somber tone. "The principal just didn't understand. The kids were so mean to Dougie. They showed him no mercy. Some mornings," she sighed, "some mornings, he just didn't want to go to school because he knew they were gonna be that mean. They would make fun of the way he dressed. They teased him whenever he did poorly on a test and they teased him when he did better than them on a test. They told him he had big ears; that he smelled; that he had bad breath. Those kids were so mean."

She sighed, shook her head and said. "What's a mother to do? I told the principal. He said, *Kids will be kids.* That's just a pile of hooie. When Dougie came home that day, his shirt was ripped and his nose was bleeding. I had it. It just wasn't right. Yes, I sent him back there. And yes, I told him to do to that kid what the kid had done to him. If Dougie was going to be hurt so often, he needed to learn to fight back. I told Dougie I expected him to always fight back. And the sons of bitches—they threw my sweet son out of the school. Can you imagine that? The rich kid beat up my poor little boy—after being mean to him again and again and again. So, Dougie finally fights back and what did they do? They threw him out of the school. Welcome to America."

*****

A nurse entered the room and said, "Mrs. Oleson mustn't get too excited. She will need as much rest as possible today. I'm afraid you're going to have to leave."

I promised to leave in a couple of minutes.

When the nurse had left the room, I said, "I have one more question, Millie. I don't know anything about Douglas' father. Is there anything you'd be willing to share with me about his father?"

Millie Erickson turned her head away from me and looked out a window. She was silent. My father once told me as he was describing a successful court case that after you ask someone a tough question; when that person you're asking doesn't immediately respond; you need to be patient. Be prepared to let the tension of the silence build. He told me that silence is uncomfortable for most people and eventually, the discomfort will take over. The person will give you a response. I remembered that conversation and waited for Millie Oleson to respond.

Finally, she did what my father had predicted. Millie Oleson turned to me and said, "You ask tough questions, Peter—personal questions. I was a young woman. I met a

149

guy. He was good-looking. We went out on a date. We had a nice dinner and a whole lot of fun. We ended up in the sack."

She was silent for a moment, then said, "And I ended up giving birth to a son."

Millie took a deep breath and slowly let it escape. She looked away at nothing in particular as she said, "The guy ended up having a nice life. He married somebody—somebody who he must have felt was his equal—not some trailer trash like me. He's still around—respected by the community. He and I—well, we never spoke again. So, what the hell difference does it make if he was a butcher, a baker, or a candlestick maker? What the hell difference does it make?"

Millie Oleson turned on her side with some effort. Her back was now facing me.

I stood up and said, "Thank you, Mrs. Oleson. I appreciate your time and willingness to share so much. I wish you the best."

Without turning to face me, Millie Oleson said in a quiet voice, "You're a nice young man, Paul. I wish you a good life. And if you find my son, if you find him, if you speak to him, tell him..."

She stopped speaking for a moment before finishing her thought. "Tell him his mother does love him. Tell him I'm sorry about the things I did wrong, I'm sorry for anything bad that I said. Tell him I wished I'd gotten him that dog. Tell him."

She took a deep breath and said, "Tell him I'm sorry."

I sat there watching her. Soon, her breaths were coming at regular intervals. She was asleep.

*****

I retraced my steps to the nurse's station. I approached the nurse who had been in the room minutes before. "Mrs. Oleson was confused about her illness. She asked me to inquire on her behalf. Why is she in here?"

The nurse bit her bottom lip before speaking. "You know," she said, "by law, we're not supposed to say anything about a patient's medical condition—not unless the patient has authorized us to do so. I could get fired for saying anything."

I waited. I could see the nurse wasn't sure what to do. Once again, I employed my father's stratagem and was patient.

Finally, the nurse continued. "Millie is a lonely soul. I am certain she appreciated someone caring enough to visit her. I can tell you this much. She's in here for something serious, very serious. Tomorrow," she paused and looked over her shoulder in both directions, "well tomorrow there is a scheduled procedure, and...and we'll have to see what happens. I shouldn't have said that much. But thank you for coming in to say goodbye to her."

*****

I drove back to the *Bloomington Weekly Dispatch* Office in silence. Millie exuded sadness. She had centered her life on a son who she hadn't seen in years. Decades ago, she had had a fun and exciting evening. It had changed her life. Now, she lay in the hospital—alone. I didn't know. Maybe her life was slipping away? Life is sometimes so tenuous.

At the office, I went to my cubicle to begin writing up my notes from my time with Millie.

Webster shouted out from his office, "Hey intern. Time to brief the grand poohbah. Get yourself a cup of coffee and sit down."

A few minutes later, I was sitting in Webster's office. He had just lit a cigarette and was performing his cigarette trick. I sipped my coffee and waited.

When the smoke had disappeared and the ash had fallen onto his sleeve only to be brushed to the floor, Webster asked, "What did you find?"

I took him through the entire visit. I shared Millie's comments about her son's childhood and about how long it had been since she had seen him. I went over her responses to my questions about Douglas' father. I described how ill she looked and repeated the comments the nurse made as I left the hospital ward. Webster didn't interrupt me once. He listened attentively, occasionally sipping his coffee and drawing smoke from his cigarette. It took about ten minutes to describe the entire meeting. Webster showed no reaction after I finished my narrative. I waited a moment, then returned to my cubicle.

I spent the rest of that day writing up my notes from my morning with Millie.

*****

As I summarized the hour's conversation, I couldn't put Millie's sadness out of my mind. I wondered what Douglas Oleson was really like. Rather than becoming easier to stereotype the former mayor of Saint Paul, it seemed like it was all becoming more and more elusive.

Chapter 21 – A Night Out

Friday evening, as I stood in front of the *Dispatch* wondering whether Sandy Benoit had forgotten about our interview, a bright yellow VW Bug convertible pulled up to the curb.

"Heh, Slim," The driver said as she looked me up and down. "Chuck described you pretty darn well. Why don't you hop on in and we'll head on out. We're going to Kincaid's. Their menu covers just about everything including some pretty awesome drinks."

I got in and we sped off toward the Mall of America. Sandy Benoit's shoulder-length light brown hair whipped around in the open air of the VW convertible. She was wearing white jeans, a blue Minnesota Twins T-shirt and pink flip-flops. With the VW's top down, the traffic noise didn't allow any conversation. Nothing was said until the bug was parked and we were entering the restaurant.

Sandy told me she'd eaten at Kincaid's often. When we sat down, she didn't even look at the menu before ordering their blue cheese salad, barbecue shrimp and a mojito. I told the waiter I'd have the same.

As soon as the waiter had walked away, Sandy took over, almost as if she was the one doing the interview. "So, you're a student at Carleton, eh? Where are you from and how did you end up there?"

During that first fifteen minutes, Sandy learned my life story and I didn't ask a single question. When our drinks arrived, she raised her stemmed cocktail glass and said, "To freedom of the press."

How could I not toast that?

When our salads were served, Sandy stopped asking questions and I jumped into my spiel. "I'm doing a research article on Douglas Oleson. Your name came up as one of Oleson's, uhm, colleagues so that's why I—uh—asked to interview you. Can you tell me a little about your career—and how you ended up going to work for the city?"

Sandy looked up from her salad, gave me an engaging smile, and said, "I was paying my way through the University of Minnesota. I ran out of money after my sophomore year and got a full-time job at *The Saint Paul Daily Journal.* I worked there for a year and a half before the city communications job came up. The job with the city paid a whole hell of a lot more than I had been earning."

She leaned her head to the side and gave me a clever smile that said, *There, I've answered your question.*

I kept going. "Did you know Douglas Oleson before you applied for the job?"

She gave me that same look and said very simply, "No."

I was trying to figure out what question to pose next when Sandy put down her fork and once again gave me that smile. Then she said, "Look, we both know what you're angling at—what it is you want to know. I've read the articles. You want to know when there were such highly qualified and experienced journalists around, why did they give the job to me? You want to know if it was because I am an attractive woman? But you don't know how to ask that question without sounding like a sexist pig. My guess is you've already talked to Jeff Washington and he told you I'm a bimbo. Am I right?"

Sandy had quickly retaken control of the interview and I had no idea how I was going to get it back.

I was about to try to respond to her question when she said, "Don't worry, Paul. I won't make you answer that question. But am I right about the general drift of what you want to know?"

I shrugged my shoulders and gave a meager nod.

She chuckled before saying, "I don't blame you for wanting me to answer those questions. They are the obvious things to ask. But let me start by telling you, I'm no bimbo. I'm one pretty smart woman. I pick things up quickly and I don't play by the book. I use my imagination. I was selected for that position because I can think on my feet—far better than any other candidate who applied. The city was looking for somebody who could think outside the box. That's me. I do it—always. I may not be the best person for writing a news story about a local charity, but I was able to create backstories that resulted in others writing articles that the city wanted printed."

I had to give her this. She was smart—and awfully direct.

"Next, you want to know what was going on between me and Douglas. Douglas also happens to be a pretty smart guy. When he told me about an issue, it was because the city needed a strategy for communication of that issue. I was immediately able to frame the problem in a manner that was useful for him—and then come up with a strategy for communicating it to the public—a strategy that accomplished whatever was needed. Sometimes we just had to explain things. Other times, we wanted to distract people from a stupid error that some idiot bureaucrat had made. But we never lied. We just helped people turn their attention to what we wanted them to be looking at—in the way that we wanted them to look at it. It's the same principle that a magician uses when he or she pulls a rabbit out of a hat or a coin out of a child's ear."

The waiter brought us our dinners and Sandy ordered another mojito. I followed suit.

Sandy was able to eat and, between bites, speak quickly and coherently.

"Douglas had a nimble mind. I enjoyed working with him from the outset because I didn't have to spoon-feed him. And Douglas appreciated how quick I was—how smart I am. A lot of men feel threatened by smart women. Most women go through their whole damn careers trying to make ignorant men feel comfortable and secure—and trying to get things done despite that distraction. I know how to do that too. But Douglas didn't need that crap. He wanted me to be straight with him, to tell him what I thought. I did that and the two of us hit it off."

She stopped speaking and focused entirely on her dinner. Nothing more was said until our plates were clean and our second mojitos had disappeared. At that point, we each ordered a third.

"You know Slim, the person who had the biggest problem with me being hired and becoming successful in that job? It was Jeff Washington. Jeff was a damn good reporter. But the pay for a good newspaper reporter is pitiful. He had his eye on a job that I took and after I got the position, he was angry. I have no doubt he told you that you needed to speak with me because I was an example of what was wrong with Douglas' administration."

I had no idea how to respond. Fortunately, Sandy chose that moment to excuse herself to go to the women's restroom.

When Sandy returned, she continued what had become a questionless interview. "I'm certain Jeff wasn't the only person who told you that you needed to interview me. I'm sure that spineless little prick who now sits in the mayor's office took a shot at me as well. Dickens was always such a creep. He was a snake when he was a councilman and he is a snake now that he's mayor. Dickens never had the balls to say anything negative to anyone's face. He just shoots people in the back. What a slimeball!"

Sandy took a sip from her mojito, then continued. "It was Dickens who spread the rumor that I lost custody of my son because of problems I'd run into at the city. Let me be super-clear about that one. I was married—true. But a new fact—my husband had a son from a previous marriage. A second new fact—it was my husband who cheated on me— not me on him."

Sandy took another sip from her mojito. There was fire in her eyes.

"When my husband and I were divorced, he kept custody of his son. But that slimeball Dickens has been undercutting me all over town with the accusation that I lost my kid because I had an affair. What a shit!"

Sandy finished her mojito. "So, I'm about to get to the next question you felt awkward asking. Did I have an affair with Douglas Oleson? As far as sex goes, most people think it's OK for men to have affairs. That's a part of our culture. However, it's not OK for women to do the same thing. If a man and a woman get along well and if that man has sex with the woman, well good for him. But the woman—well, she's a scheming slut."

Sandy glared at me for a moment then finished the thought. "So, you want to know if I had an affair with Douglas. The answer is yes—yes, I did. But that affair followed my separation from my husband. It did not precede it. And I liked Douglas. He attracted me. And goddamn Dickens anyway for even insinuating that I did anything inappropriate."

Sandy was becoming more intense and I guess I didn't blame her. "Next, Mr. Cub reporter, you want to ask about my breaking up the marriage between Douglas and Miki? Right?"

She was making me feel uncomfortable and the whole interview (if you could call it that) was becoming so much more personal than I ever would have anticipated. But Sandy had nailed it and I meekly nodded ascent.

"Miki is a sweet woman, Slim. I'm not proud of sleeping with her husband. But I was not the first person—other than Miki—to sleep with him during their marriage. That's the truth."

Sandy paused, looked me straight in the eye again, and said, "I hope in your little story about Douglas Oleson, that you do not treat me unkindly for being honest with you. It is my style to be direct. And in that regard, I'm a little bit different than most of the other people you've interviewed."

I could think of nothing to say. Fortunately, I didn't try.

Sandy continued. "I can tell what you would ask next, Slim. That is if I hadn't thrown you back on your heels already. You'd be asking if I didn't do anything wrong, why did I resign from the city?"

She looked at me—this time out of the corner of her eye—probably just to catch my reaction. Again, I said nothing and she continued. "Try to put yourself in my shoes. I felt uncomfortable with all of the public attention that had generously been thrown my way. It was awful. And why did Chuck hire me? Well, Chuck knew I was smart. He hired me because I had the skills his business needed. Does that sound so strange? Chuck has never made a pass at me—not once—and that's not something I can say for Dickens."

Sandy's face relaxed.

She laughed and concluded, "Other than that, how was the play? Heh? I think I caught you off guard. You didn't anticipate that I would be so tough. Attractive women aren't supposed to be tough cookies. However Slim, this one who is sitting in front of you; she sure as hell is. And she's honest to boot—something that, over the years, has occasionally gotten her into a whole hell of a lot of trouble."

Sandy grinned. The conversation moved on. She asked me a few questions about what it was like working for Webster. We talked about newspaper reporters and discussed both the thoughtful and the two-faced folks who work in government.

She looked at her watch. It was 9 o'clock. "My, how time flies when you're having fun," she said. "I appreciate your seeking me out and giving me a chance to tell my side of the story. You seem like a sympathetic soul. But I need to get going. I better pay up and we'll be on our way."

I said, "But wait, this was supposed to be on me. I was taking you out to dinner."

"Listen," she gave a thoughtful look as she responded. "Chuck told me you probably don't have a whole lot of money. He said I should put the meal on the company credit card and I'm sure as hell going to do that. I enjoyed having dinner with you, Slim. And I'll have a ball telling Chuck about my mild-mannered skills as an interviewee. He will know his money—paying for dinner, that is—was well spent. You excelled at your job this evening, Slim. The woman you interviewed appreciated your ability to listen. You, my friend, are one wonderful listener."

It had been one heck of an interview. I was the one wearing a smile on my face as we headed back to her car.

*****

As Sandy drove me back to my rooming house, we listened to Nirvana on her CD player. About halfway back to my place, she gave me a funny look and said, "Hey Slim, ever do much weed?"

I was a little taken aback, but answered, "Yeah. A few times in my dorm."

"Look, it's just that it's still early—9:30," she said. "I mean it's Friday night. I don't want to just go home and call it a night. Would you like to come on over to my place and smoke some hash with me?"

I was taken aback, but pleased to receive the invitation.

"Sure, that'd be neat."

Sandy started laughing as she made a U-turn in the middle of the block and headed north.

I asked, "Why are you laughing?"

"Oh, it's just that it's been a long time since anybody told me that something was *neat*. I like it, Slim. You're a character—a character from off the beaten path."

With that, she popped another CD into her car stereo and we listened to The Foo Fighters as Sandy drove us to her apartment.

*****

Sandy lived near downtown Saint Paul in a fairly new medium-sized apartment building. She parked her car and we walked up to her apartment.

I was nervous. I didn't know where this was going—although I was quite pleased with the general direction. It seemed cool to be smoking some dope late in the evening with a beautiful woman. But Sandy was older than me and I had no idea what she had in mind. And I felt a little guilty about being with her. Kathy was the only woman I'd ever slept with. But Kathy had said she was seeing some guy in Chicago and well—yeah—what's good for the gander is good for the goose.

The living room in Sandy's one-bedroom apartment had brightly colored modern furniture and a series of framed art deco German travel posters.

I asked, "Are those posters originals?"

She laughed and said, "I'm glad you noticed. Yes, they are, Slim. They're collector's items. I bought 'em off of eBay. Aren't they neat?"

She laughed after saying *neat* and I couldn't help but join her.

"Would you like a beer," she asked.

"That'd be neat," I responded and again we both laughed.

A couple of minutes later, we were sitting on the floor with our backs against her couch. I was sipping from a bottle of Heinekens, listening to a *Grateful Dead* CD while Sandy packed a small pipe with hashish.

"This is really good hash," she said. "I don't smoke it a lot. But it is a hell of a nice way to start a weekend. Don't you agree?

I smiled and nodded.

A moment later, I was sucking in acrid smoke and holding it in my lungs as long as I could. After I coughed the harsh smoke out, Sandy handed me back the pipe and I repeated the process."

I felt great. This was the life.

Sandy turned to me and said, "I'm probably ten years older than you. Is that a problem?"

I smiled and said, "Not for me."

Then I kissed her.

*****

The next morning, I woke up in Sandy's bed. She was still sleeping. While I couldn't remember too much too clearly from the previous night, I knew it had been nice. I felt relaxed.

I looked around her bedroom. There were three framed Salvador Dali prints hanging on the walls. I like Salvador Dali. I had taken a survey of art course when I was a sophomore. Dali was one of my favorite twentieth-century artists.

I must have studied those prints for more than five minutes when I looked at Sandy. She was lying on her side, her head on an elbow, intently watching me.

"Dali's pretty neat. Isn't he Slim? I oftentimes wake up in the morning and just look at those prints and lose myself in his imagination. He's...he's...so surreal."

We both laughed.

"Listen Slim," she said, "I could go make us some coffee or we could do another round. What d'you think?"

I grinned.

*****

About forty-five minutes later, Sandy brought a tray to bed. It held two steaming mugs of coffee. I hadn't known that a cup of coffee could taste so good.

One hour later, we were sitting in her VW in front of my rooming house. We chatted for a few minutes, talking about the weather and about me going back to school—totally small talk.

Before driving off, Sandy Benoit gave me a warm smile and a peck on the lips saying, "Thank you, Slim. Thank you for being such a sweetheart."

Chapter 22 – A Funeral

Monday morning, while I was working on a story about the city manager's new baby, Webster approached me with a grave look on his face.

"I just received a call from Miki Oleson," he said. "Her mother-in-law passed away Friday. Millie's procedure was a heart valve replacement. She just wasn't strong enough." Webster sighed. "She just didn't make it."

He shook his head sadly and added, "You were probably one of the last people she had a conversation with."

Webster stood there for a moment, took a slow drag from his lit cigarette, blew out the smoke while for once ignoring its trajectory, and returned to his office.

*****

Wednesday afternoon, I rode to Millie's funeral with Webster and Louise. "Millie didn't worship at Saint James," Louise said. "But Miki did. That's why the service is being held there. We used to belong to Saint James. That was how we became friends with Miki."

Nothing else was said during the half-hour drive to the church.

*****

As we entered the large sanctuary, I saw Miki Oleson, wearing a simple black dress, standing in front of the closed coffin. Next to her stood a boy in a dark navy sports coat, white shirt and dark tie. I assumed he was her son.

Webster, Louise and I sat near the front of the sanctuary. An organ began to play *Amazing Grace*. After the music stopped, the large, almost empty church was filled with an eerie silence. I heard footsteps. It was a priest in a black floor-length gown approaching the front of the sanctuary. The priest said several prayers. I don't remember what those prayers were. I'm not sure anyone there listened. Then the organ player played a hymn and the priest spoke about all of us experiencing earthly lives before moving on to the next world where God would embrace us as he was now embracing Millie.

For me, it seemed empty. Was the priest saying that the pain that dominated Millie's life had somehow disappeared—or maybe no longer mattered? I began to reflect on the conversation I had had with Millie several days before—how disappointing and painful her life had been. People get lost. Their lives quietly become sad and lonely. Millie would have appreciated receiving in this world some of the love the priest was promising she would get in the next.

And then, *Amazing Grace* was being played again. And the service was over.

I looked around. The only people in the sanctuary were Miki, Douglas Jr., the Pedersens, the priest, the organ player and myself.

Miki stood up and slowly walked with stooped shoulders toward the exit of the sanctuary. She had such a sad look on her face. She approached Louise and the two women embraced. Then Miki's body shook as she wept. Soon, Louise joined her in shedding tears.

Webster wore a stoic look as he watched the two women embrace. Then the five of us silently walked out of Saint James Lutheran Church into a bright day's sunlight.

Chapter 23 – Back to Chicago

Webster drove me to Saint Paul's Union Depot to catch an Amtrak Empire Builder back to Chicago.

"You're entering your final year of college," Webster said. "In nine months, you'll be the new version of Don Quixote, riding out into the real world, pursuing a personal Rocinante. What's your plan?"

I laughed softly. "Boy, isn't that the sixty-four-thousand-dollar question? I have no clue, Webster. I'd like to continue in journalism. But how do I pull that one off? Newspapers have been laying off skilled reporters left and right."

Webster cleared his throat and said, "The reason I'm bringing this up, Paul, is because Louise tells me that before too long, I need to hang up my spurs. If I do, there might be an opportunity to run the *Dispatch*. Let's talk during the school year. Who knows? Maybe we can continue working together."

I responded, "I'd like that."

*****

The last few weeks of the summer had been intense. As soon as I'd taken my seat in the dome car, I realized I was exhausted. I spent the nine-hour train trip staring out the window, gazing at farms, forests, towns and cities as they passed me by. My only break from that stupor was when I went to the dining car where I enjoyed a delicious bacon-lettuce-and-tomato sandwich.

The Empire Builder arrived in Chicago around five that evening. My mother and I had agreed to meet at a steakhouse located next to her condominium. The restaurant was a refreshing ten-minute walk from the train station.

As I sat down at her table at the steakhouse, I could see my mother looked tired. I asked her how she was doing.

"Oh, I'm fine, Paul," she responded. "Let's talk after we eat. I'm famished."

We each ordered Steaks. I ordered a New York cut. She had a small filet mignon. I devoured my steak, baked potato and trimmings. My mother picked at hers. I was pleased to finish her filet and afterwards, I even had room for a large piece of lemon meringue pie.

Once our plates had been cleared, my mom asked about my summer internship. I gave a complete report.

"...and so," I finished up, "it was a great summer. How are you doing, mom?"

"Well, Paul, that was why I wanted you to come home before school started."

A chill ran down my spine. This was serious. My mother was a trained psychologist. She tended to understate everything and would never make a comment like that without a lot of forethought. She had just told me to prepare for what she was about to say. At her suggestion, we walked back to her nearby condominium before continuing the conversation. The walk was tense. Nothing was said. We took the elevator up to her apartment and went inside.

My mom had lived and worked in downtown Chicago ever since she left my father. She had an almost non-existent commute to work—her clinical office was on the third floor of the same building in which her apartment was on the twenty-third floor.

When we got to her place, my mom fixed each of us a cup of ginger tea. Then we sat down in her living room. She started by thanking me for coming home so quickly. She was silent for a minute as she looked out across her living room, through her apartment's picture window in the direction of Centennial Park and Lake Michigan.

Then she broke it. She took a deep breath and said, "A couple of weeks ago, I had my regular visit with Dr. Lee, my primary care physician. I told her I had had some back pain, and that I felt listless. Dr. Lee told me it was probably just overwork. She ordered a battery of blood tests and referred me to a back specialist. However, a couple of days later, Lee called and let me know there were concerns regarding some of the blood test results. She told me to call the office of a colleague of hers, an oncologist."

My mother's face showed strain—something I wasn't used to seeing in her.

She took another deep breath, slowly exhaled, then continued to speak. "I spoke with the oncologist later a couple of hours later. I will save you any detailed build-up, Paul. I have pancreatic cancer."

She stopped speaking, giving me a chance to absorb what she'd said.

A moment later, speaking in a slow, dispassionate cadence, she said. "I have quickly learned that pancreatic cancer is one of the disease's deadliest forms. The outlook for stage-four patients is bleak—and that is what I am, Paul, stage-four. It means the cancer has metastasized. The outlook for my life is measured in months, not years."

There was an ominous silence throughout the apartment. We each sipped our cups of ginger tea.

Finally, she continued, "I've always tried to be upfront with you. Chemotherapy can slow down pancreatic tumors. It won't stop them."

She stood up, took a deep breath and walked to the window looking out toward the lake.

Her back was to me as she said, "I wish there was something positive I could say. I love you so much, Paul. No one means more to me than you."

She sighed before saying, "I've been evaluating my life. I am sorry about so many things. But above all, I wish I had been a better mother to you. I wish your father and I had each been more supportive. But things are as they are and I am not able to turn the clock back."

Still, with her back to me, I watched her raise both hands to her face, bend her head forward and weep. Her whole body shook.

I was stunned. I had never seen my mom cry. Inside me, emotions of guilt, surprise, anger, compassion and panic collided with one another. Could my mom really be about to die?

I walked up to her and put my arms around her. She continued to weep. I felt helpless. I didn't know what to say.

Finally, I said, "Is there any way they could be wrong—wrong about the diagnosis—about the...about the hopelessness of it all?"

"Paul. Part of my job as a psychologist is to assist people going through things like this. It's different being on this side of—well—of the bad news. But what's true for my patients is also true for me. Bad stuff happens. I intend to fight it as hard as I can. But it is what it is."

"I will take a leave of absence from Carleton. You need support here. I can..."

"No Paul. My sister lives in Chicago. She will be staying with me for part of the time. You need to continue with your education. However, I do want to spend more time with you—more time together until…"

And she turned to me. Her face was twisted in a pained look. Then, she leaned into me, her head against my chest and she wept. I put my arms around her. Again, her entire body shook.

Once she collected herself, she took on a more dispassionate approach. "I would appreciate it if you could visit on weekends—when you are able. We need to talk. There are so many things that need to be said—so many things we probably should have spoken about in the past— but now," she took a deep breath and slowly let the air out, "we will speak about them now."

I got each of us another cup of ginger tea and we sat down.

"I can't drive anymore—the chemotherapy—the weakness. I just can't drive. Take my car—when you return to school. Spend weekends with me whenever you can. We can watch some old movies on television. We can talk. It would be, it would be a big comfort."

She smiled for a moment before adding, "My only request—which comes as no surprise to you—is that you take good care of that car. Drive it carefully, Paul. Service it. And find a garage at school to park it in."

It all seemed so strange. After my mom left my dad, she purchased a dark navy blue 1984 Mercedes-Benz 280SL convertible/hardtop. The two-seater was her prized possession. When she purchased it in 1988, the car looked like new. It had only ten thousand miles on it. She babied that Mercedes in every way during the decade she'd owned it, only driving it another ten thousand miles over those years. Her willingness to let me borrow it made sense. But it was jarring.

"Sure, mom. Of course, I'll take care of it."

I paused, then added, "This coming term, I don't have any classes after noon on Thursdays. So, I will be here for dinners on Thursdays and can stay till Sundays."

*****

That week became something truly special. My mom and I had conversations that were far more open and intimate than any we had had before.

For example, Monday evening, we were looking out the window at Lake Michigan. I was enjoying a small glass of crème de menthe while my mom nursed a cup of ginger tea. She said to me, "I've never been religious, Paul—never will be. Still, I'm finding a sort of peacefulness in all that is transpiring. It's not like I'm tired of living. That's the furthest thing from the truth. I've enjoyed my life. And I'm not giving up and I don't want you to feel sorry for me. But it's just that I'm finding a weird kind of serenity that has been missing from my life."

Later that evening, she asked, "What are your thoughts on Kathy? She's obviously a beautiful and bright girl who knows what she wants. What do you think of her?"

I gave a nervous laugh. It wasn't that I thought her question was funny. It was just such an uncomfortable question—something I hadn't fully resolved. I was honest and told her I just didn't know.

My mom gave me a direct look and said, "You know Paul, this is your life. It's not your father's life. It's not mine. As I look back, I'm not sure your dad and I made such smart decisions when we were your age. It seems like you're trying to do better than we did, to do what's right for you. I don't want you to repeat the mistakes we made."

She paused, looked down, took a full breath and gave a hard sigh, "No, Paul. You need to listen to your instincts." She paused and then repeated, "You need to trust your heart."

A little while later I asked her, "How did dad take it when you told him about the cancer?"

"I haven't told that son-of-a-bitch yet. He's off with his thirty-year-old girlfriend in Indianapolis. I'll let him know when he gets back. He'll act sympathetically. But he won't give a damn. Your father has always been primarily about himself."

That was more honest than my mom had ever been about my dad. The two of them had always tried to keep up the good front for their only kid. But back when I was small, before they separated, I remember hearing them fight. Those arguments were brutal.

I was glad my mom felt like she could be honest with me. This was not a time for holding back. I stayed with my mom for almost a week. My departure for school was full of sadness. But I had never felt so close to her.

*****

Before that week, I had ridden in my mom's 280 SL, but she had never let me drive it. I drove the roadster back to school on a sunny early autumn day. Maple trees along the way had turned red and yellow, their leaves beginning to drop. As I drove, I experienced a weird combination of sadness, exhilaration and dread.

Upon arriving in Northfield, I was able to meet the single specific concern my mother had expressed regarding the use of her beautiful little roadster; that it should have secure covered parking. Dr. Harris resolved my dilemma with one call to a visiting professor who had no car but whose rented house had an empty garage.

Chapter 24 – Fall Term, Senior Year

Three years earlier as a freshman, I had watched in awe as upper-class students confidently paraded around the campus. Their careless laughter, serious, knowledgeable way of speaking to one another, and the authority with which they addressed us freshmen had humbled and impressed me.

Upon returning to campus, I saw new freshmen looking around with the same Alice in Wonderland sense of awe that I had once had. Now, I was the one with the confidence I had once ascribed to upperclassmen. While I was full of concerns about my mother and had no clue what I would do after I graduated, I felt fully prepared to deal with the great challenges of life that were less than a year away.

As I look back, I realize how young and innocent I was. Maybe the process of aging is a continual discovery of one's previous naivete.

*****

A day after I returned to campus, I ran into Kathy in a dining hall. Or, I should say, she ran into me. She brought her tray up to my table, gave me a bright smile and said, "Can I join you?"

She sat down and we ate quietly. When our plates were empty, she asked if I wanted to go for a walk.

We walked into the arboretum; the park-like area adjacent to the Carleton campus. It was a pleasant September day—leaves were falling from a big old oak that stood in the middle of the meadow through which we walked. Around the tree, squirrels were busily gathering their bounty.

We moved on, walking for half an hour without exchanging a word.

Kathy broke the silence. "You didn't write this summer. I wondered what that meant. I thought maybe you had a girlfriend in the Twin Cities or perhaps you were just working so hard for your newspaper. During the summer, I thought a lot about the fun we had last year. I began to wonder if maybe it was just me who had the fun—and if you, well, if you didn't like me so much?"

We walked quietly for a while before I responded.

"Yeah," I said. "We sure did have a lot of fun last year. The snowball fights, the movies, the walks in the middle of the night and the meals we cooked together. We had more fun than I'd ever had with anyone—in my life. And no, Kathy. No, I don't have a girlfriend in the Twin Cities. It's true I was working hard at the paper. But that didn't take that much time. I went for a lot of long walks by myself. I thought about a lot about things—things like what I want from life. Part of the reason I didn't write to you is because I wasn't able to answer that particular question. You know who you are so well, Kathy. But I don't know who I am or what I want to become."

Kathy looked up at me. The intent expression on her face told me she was listening closely and understood what I was saying. I recognized that she had grown over the summer as well.

As we entered a dense area of oak and maple, I was looking down at the path as I said, "You want to achieve a lot, Kathy—I mean professionally. I watched my folks do that."

I sighed and said, "It didn't work out that well for them. Working for a newspaper—it doesn't pay a whole hell of a lot. It certainly won't provide the level of affluence that you and I enjoyed while growing up. But it was so fascinating. And for that reason, the summer was satisfying."

We walked for a while before I spoke again. "Last spring, you were upset that I wasn't interested in working for your dad. Then, if you recall, you told me you wanted to have a bit of a break—in our relationship. I took that to heart."

We came upon a clearing. I sat down on a log and she sat next to me. A woodpecker was tap-tap-tapping on an old dead tree. The sound of his beak on the dead wood was like an odd sort of drumbeat. We sat there, totally absorbed by the sounds created by that bird.

After a while, I said, "One thing you don't know...."

I took a deep breath and slowly blew it out, "One thing you don't know is that my mom is ill—really ill."

Kathy turned toward me. I could tell she was studying my face. I looked up at the woodpecker and was quiet. Kathy allowed me that space.

I continued in a soft voice. "Yeah. My mom has stage four pancreatic cancer. Pretty awful shit."

Kathy was the first person I had spoken to about the illness. I found it difficult to say much more than that. I couldn't force the words out—couldn't say that my mother was about to die—to die maybe soon. I just sighed. It seemed like Kathy understood and was gracious by not pressing me.

"I borrowed my mom's car. For the next few months, I'll be heading back to Chicago, going there each week on

Thursdays and returning to school on Sundays. You know, so I can be with her. That sort of has become my priority."

I paused, trying to figure out what I should say next.

"I would be outright lying to you if I said my mom's illness had anything to do with why I didn't write this summer. Kathy, I like you a lot. The time I spent with you is the best I've had at Carleton. But the bottom line is you know what you want—and I don't know what I want—and it would be dishonest for me to pretend otherwise."

We remained there, sitting, watching and listening to the woodpecker do his thing for another five minutes. Then Kathy stood up. I followed suit and we headed back to the campus.

When we reached the campus, Kathy said, "I'm sorry to hear about your mother. That's tough. I guess I'm not too surprised about the rest of it. You're right. We'll just have to see. And you're also correct, I do know what I want. I had a blast this summer. I dated a guy from the tennis club. He fell in love with me. I just haven't decided how interested I am in him."

We walked for a few minutes before she continued. "We'll just have to see about the future, won't we?"

There was an uncomfortable silence. She stopped walking and we faced one another. Then she shrugged and said, "I have to go to the bookstore and pick up a bunch of books. I'm sorry to hear about your mother. She seemed like such a nice person. What you're going through, Paul—it's tough. I'm sorry."

Then she stood on her tip-toes and kissed me on the cheek. Then she turned away, heading in the direction of the bookstore.

*****

The fall term was challenging. In addition to a heavy courseload, I drove to Chicago each Thursday afternoon and returned to Northfield on Sundays. My mother's health continued to deteriorate. She had never been a large woman, but her size—along with her energy and spirits—was now diminishing. She had always been a stylish woman and proud of her appearance. It was a terrible blow for her when her hair fell out. And while she acquired a couple of stylish wigs, the loss of her confidence was overwhelming. We only left her apartment for medical appointments.

Throughout my childhood, the tension related to my parents' arguments had impeded my getting to know my mother. But now, we were making up for lost time. We spent those long weekends speaking about the important things. Mom told me about her parents and how kind they were, about her sister who lived nearby and about her brother who had died years before. She told me about her childhood; growing up on a small farm in Illinois. I hadn't known her family raised pigs. She said that when she was a kid, she worked every day after school doing farm chores. She laughed when she recounted how she once had forgotten to latch the gate on the pigpen. My mom had to spend an entire weekend—along with the rest of her family—chasing pigs all over the county.

She spoke about the satisfaction she had found in her career. She shared how much she had admired my father before they married—and about the pain each of them had endured as their marriage fell apart.

My mom may not have been healthy, but her mind was sharp as a tack. She shared perspectives on life with an alert sense of humor that I'd never known. She asked me about my life, about my internship, about the news stories I had written and about my plans for the future. I will never forget the thoughtful looks she gave as I responded to each question.

I shared the conversation I had had with Kathy during our recent walk in the arboretum. Afterward, my mom took a deep breath and looked away, gazing out the window into a grey stormy sky. After a couple of minutes, she said, "You're a good person Paul. You'll make the right decisions. Trust your gut. That's something I didn't always do."

She shrugged, then added, "Wish I had."

Months after my mom passed away, I thought about how closely she had listened when I repeated that conversation with Kathy and how thoughtful her response had been. I realized—maybe for the first time—what a wonderful and effective psychologist my mom must have been.

*****

I saw my father a few times when I was in Chicago. He always asked how my mom was doing and tried to be consoling. But I could see that mom was not the most important thing on his mind. One time, he took me out to dinner with his new girlfriend Peggy. Peggy was a confident, well-dressed Indianapolis attorney. Even though she probably was twenty years younger than my father, they appeared to get along well.

My dad continued to seize every opportunity to remind me that I should be applying to law school. And lo and behold, Peggy agreed with him. Who would have guessed?

I let them talk. But at that point in my life, I'd heard it all too often. It occurred to me that my father had never taken the time to listen to me when I spoke about journalism.

*****

I came home for Thanksgiving. Mom's disease had progressed. The day after a small Thanksgiving dinner in her apartment, she allowed me to initiate hospice services. A few days later she stopped eating.

My mom had shared her thoughts on a funeral. "I never liked funerals, Paul. I hope that the people who told me good things while I was alive meant them. That will have to do."

I was sitting with her, holding her hand, when she passed away.

*****

My father was the executor of her will. I was her sole beneficiary.

My dad asked me if I wanted to take a term off from school. I told him *no*. We agreed that he would leave the apartment as it was and we would defer to the future the conversation about how to deal with the apartment's contents and the rest of the estate.

Chapter 25 – Winter Term, Senior Year

I spent a quiet winter break alone in the apartment which I now owned. I focused on editing my notes from meetings with Douglas Oleson's colleagues, critics and family. As I reviewed those meetings, I realized I had learned a lot—and nothing. Douglas Oleson was proving to be an enigma.

It was 1999. I was close to completing my college education. As I packed my clothes into my mother's roadster preparing to head back to school for winter term, my focus moved to a single challenge: What would be next in my life?

I felt like an empty vessel. I had begun my education with hopes and dreams—maybe they were vague hopes and dreams—but they were good enough to give me confidence in the future. I had expected that I would leave Carleton with a sense of purpose and would have a plan for the future. But things hadn't evolved in that manner. As I drove back to school along winter Wisconsin's icy roads that were lined with frozen ponds, empty fields and barren trees, I kept thinking to myself, *I have no plan. There is no plan.*

*****

The day after returning to campus, I approached the same person I had asked for advice each time I had been confused about how to proceed.

Dr. Harris smiled when she saw who had knocked on her door. "How are you, Paul? How's your mom doing? How's the progress on your paper?"

It was hard to reciprocate her positive response. I felt like life had been beating me up.

"It's good to see you, Dr. Harris. I'm not sure how I'm doing. I've been working on the paper. But I'm not sure I'm reaching any conclusions that would give anybody a halfway decent reason to want to read it."

She watched me. "You look like a broken sparrow, Paul. What's wrong?"

I wasn't sure how to respond. I fought the tears. When they came to my eyes, I brushed them away. But then they returned and soon they were streaming. I couldn't bring myself to say anything. Dr. Harris was kind enough not to question my response.

Finally, I got control of myself. I took the Kleenex she offered and wiped my eyes, then blew my nose.

"It's been tough, Dr. Harris. And it has nothing to do with Carleton—nothing to do with my education."

She waited. I composed myself further. "I'm sorry to come to your office sniveling. These have just been a few tough months. Unfortunately...."

And I couldn't finish the damn sentence. She waited.

After about a minute, I tried again. "You knew about my mom's cancer. Well, she died a few weeks ago. I've felt so alone ever since. My father, well my father—he is doing his own thing. I don't blame him. It's his life. But I just don't know who to go to."

As soon as I finished that sentence, the dam burst and I wept. Dr. Harris stood up, calmly walked over to me and softly rubbed my back while my entire body shook.

Then she said, "Sometimes life can be so difficult, Paul. It can seem unforgiving. But you're wrong. You said this has nothing to do with Carleton and that it has nothing to do with your education. It has everything to do with Carleton and this is a part of your education. I have been so proud of you. You have been fearless in the face of bureaucratic challenges—things that would cause most people to give up. I am so sorry to hear about the loss of your mother. But I can tell you one thing. Your mother would be touched that you care so much. She must have been so proud of your courage and integrity."

I collected my emotions.

Dr. Harris returned to her seat and continued to speak. "I don't have any easy or simple solutions for you. The pain you are feeling isn't going to go away tonight—or in a week—or a year. I'm not sure there is anything anyone can say to you that will relieve that pain. But I will make one suggestion. It's dark outside now. Northfield is a beautiful little town. I have always found that when the snow is falling heavily, as it is tonight, it gives me a sense of peace to walk down this city's residential streets and enjoy the beauty of the falling snow; the silence of being alone while walking through it."

She stopped speaking for a moment and leaned forward while closely watching my face. "When you finish your walk, Paul, don't go to the dormitory dining hall for dinner. Walk downtown. Go to a restaurant. Have a nice dinner. Order a mug of beer or a glass of fine wine to go with your dinner. Propose a toast to your mother and enjoy the meal. I think your mom would approve of that. Then, I bet you'll be able to return to your room and sleep like a baby. You look very tired."

It was not the first nor the last time I took Dr. Harris's advice. Once again, I did not regret it.

*****

I once heard my mom describe the advice she gave to one of her patients who was grieving the loss of a family member. Mom told her young client to follow one simple rule, "Left foot, right foot, left foot, right foot. You have to move forward. I know you don't feel like it," she had told her patient. "But there is no substitute for this technique."

I took the advice my mother had offered that patient. During winter term, in addition to getting my coursework done, I did not leave my dormitory room often. I communicated with very few people. After attending classes and completing my classwork, I spent every spare minute alone in my room, working on my Douglas Oleson paper.

In one regard, the Oleson paper was coming together. I was able to describe each of the interviews and pull them together into one large document. But I was troubled because the document was simply a collection of episodes that led nowhere.

What could I conclude from all of those facts? Well, Dickens was a creep. Chris Thompson was a smooth operator. Miki Oleson was an innocent. Jeff Washington had perspectives as a reporter—but a different view of the world as a job applicant who had been ignored. Chuck Persons was a successful developer who knew how to use the political process and Douglas' mother—well, she was a special kind of tragedy.

I had wanted to reach some brilliant conclusion about who or what Douglas Oleson was and to enlarge it to make a profound comment about the nature of our political system—maybe even about life.

But I could see I had failed.

*****

Toward the end of the term, I approached Dr. Harris for advice about how to proceed. As I walked into her office, she said, "I'm glad you stopped by, Paul. I was going to contact you. I don't know if you've already heard, but Webster is very ill."

I was stunned. *What next*? I thought to myself as I sat down in silence, trying to absorb the shock of what had just been shared.

Dr. Harris had a gaunt look on her face as she spoke quietly. "Webster always loved his cigarettes. We all told him, *They're going to kill you, Webster. You gotta kick that habit.* But to no avail. The fool has been battling lung cancer for the last six months. He gave Louise strict instructions not to tell anyone. He continued working at the *Weekly Dispatch* until a month ago. Since then, an old friend, Jeff Washington, has relieved him at the paper. I got a call this morning from Louise. Webster is going fast. I'm going up there tomorrow. You're welcome to ride along."

*****

The next morning, Dr. Harris drove us to Hennepin Hospital, where I had visited Millie Oleson nine months before. As she drove, Dr. Harris shared stories about Webster. I had had no idea that Webster and Dr. Harris had known one another for so many years. I was even more stunned when I learned they'd lived together—as a couple—while attending the University of Minnesota.

"One weekend, we were camping near Lake Itasca up in Northern Minnesota. Webster insisted we needed to camp without a tent in order to appreciate nature. That night we just laid there in our sleeping bags under a million brilliant stars. Unfortunately, after we fell asleep on that enchanting summer evening, a large thunderstorm approached and dumped its load. We quickly moved to sit under a large pine tree, kept mostly dry by our ponchos, as we watched hundreds of lightning strikes light up the sky and the lake and listened to the horrid thunder that accompanied each furious lightning strike. That was one of the most frightening nights of my life."

Dr. Harris laughed softly. "One other time, we tried to sneak into a Minnesota Twins baseball game at the old Metropolitan Stadium."

She glanced at me and chuckled, "Paul—Have you ever been inside a county jail?"

I digested what she had shared with me and asked, "What happened? It seems like the two of you were quite the couple."

Dr. Harris was silent for a couple of minutes.

Then she took a deep breath and said, "You know what you're going through? It's not really that rare. Webster knew what he wanted. He started working for *The Minneapolis News Chronicle* before we graduated. He was happy living with me but I wasn't sure what I wanted from life. I ended up pursuing a PhD in Literature at Penn."

Her voice became wistful. "Time passes. Things change. And Webster was not one to sit on his hands. He dated around. Then he and Louise got together—again— they had known one another during high school. And the rest is history."

Dr. Harris was silent for the last ten minutes of our drive. The tension on her face increased as we pulled into the hospital parking lot.

Minutes later as we exited an elevator and approached a nurse's station, a voice called out to us, "Sharon, thank God you are here. Paul, thank you for coming."

I turned and saw Louise Pedersen walking toward us down a long hall of open hospital room doors.

"How is Webster?" Dr. Harris asked.

"I'm afraid not well," Louise responded. "Not well at all."

Louise led us back to Webster's room. He had aged a decade since I had seen him last. He did not appear to be conscious. Several small monitors next to his bed kept beeping and flashing. The smell of the hospital, the sounds and lights of the machines and the sound of oxygen being pumped into Webster brought back a flood of painful memories from my recent visits to the University of Chicago Cancer Center.

We stood by Webster's bedside for fifteen minutes. Then Louise said, "I need to get something to eat. How about going to the cafeteria with me? We can talk there."

The quality of hospital cafeteria food can only be measured by its blandness. Hospital menus always offer diverse options that somehow feature no flavor. At the cafeteria, Louise got a plate of tasteless spaghetti and Dr. Harris and I just had a cup of overheated coffee.

Louise told us how Webster's disease had progressed over the past few months. She lamented that her husband had refused to stop smoking cigarettes. She talked about how his coughing had gotten progressively worse and how he had refused to set up an appointment with his doctor.

"Finally, he started coughing up blood. The last two months have been hard. Webster refused to allow me to tell anyone. When Jeff Washington stopped by the house to see why Webster wasn't at the paper, I told him Webster couldn't go into the paper anymore. Jeff volunteered to pick up the slack. Since then, he and Dolly have run the weekly."

*****

I listened and learned. About a year after Louise and Webster married, Dr. Harris was hired by Carleton. The three of them got together often in those early years. I sat quietly as Louise and Dr. Harris talked about the past and how the three of them often cooked dinners together. I enjoyed hearing those stories, imagining what each of them had been like when they were closer to my age.

We returned to Webster's hospital room and stood next to his bed, each of us speaking to him as if he were just resting with his eyes closed. We told Webster the ways in which he was important to us—that we wanted him to know he would never be forgotten.

Afterward, out in the hospital floor's lobby. Dr. Harris told Louise, "I think Paul and I ought to be going now. We'll be seeing a lot of you over the next few days and be certain to know," Dr. Harris said softly, "I'll be saying my prayers for Webster."

The two women embraced.

Then Louise looked at me and said, "Thank you for coming Paul. You meant an awful lot to Webster—more than you can understand. The hardest thing in Webster's life was losing our daughter. In you, Webster seemed to find some of the freshness and joy Ingrid brought into our lives. Your presence lifted him. It would mean a lot for him to know that you were here. Please visit again."

Dr. Harris said very little on the drive home. I realized that I might be losing a mentor but Dr. Harris was losing someone who had an important role in defining her life.

*****

That night, I did not sleep well. I couldn't stop thinking about what it meant to lose Webster. The following day, I got up early and drove to Minneapolis to visit him again. I was hoping against hope that somehow the illness would not devour him.

Louise was not at the hospital when I arrived.

I sat down on the chair next to Webster's bed and spoke aloud. "Thank you for what you've done for me, Webster. You offered a level of kindness and affection that was otherwise absent in my life. You are my mentor, my friend and my role model."

I took a deep painful breath and blew out the air. I sat silently for several minutes.

Suddenly, I heard Webster's rasping voice. "Paul, what are you doing here?"

He looked around the hospital room slowly and said, "Oh. I see. You came to say goodbye, didn't you?"

I didn't know what to say. But it was now or never.

"You know Webster, there's a lot I don't understand. I don't know what I'm gonna do after I graduate. I don't know where the Douglas Oleson project is going. But between working for you and applying myself to that project, I feel I have found some bearings for my life. I will be eternally grateful for these gifts. You are a good man. You gave me a lot."

He listened to what I had said, then coughed heavily. "Thank you, Paul."

He coughed again and said, "We all struggle. We all try to do the right thing—even though we often screw it up. I'm no exception. But the thing I've learned is—the thing I learned—is that you just have to try."

He coughed again and the small machine next to him started to beep. Its lights flashed. Then, Webster coughed up blood.

A nurse rushed into the room saying, "You have to leave."

Webster raised his hand and said, "Wait Paul. Please tell Louise I love her."

He coughed again and another nurse came into the room. I stepped back as Webster closed his eyes and seemed to go back to sleep.

The first nurse said, "You must leave the room."

A short while after I had returned to the lobby, I saw Louise rush down the hall toward Webster's Room. As she passed, she glanced at me for a moment with a lost, almost wild look in her eyes. Then she headed toward Webster's room.

Half an hour later, Louise walked into the lobby.

Her face was gray. She spoke almost in a whisper, "He's gone," she said. "He's gone."

Chapter 26 – Another Funeral

A week later, I rode with Dr. Harris to Webster's funeral. The service was held at Saint James Lutheran Church. It had also been the location of Millie Oleson's funeral.

There were quite a few people in the sanctuary, most of whom I didn't recognize. Dolly was sitting next to Jeff Washington. She looked lost. Miki Oleson and Douglas Jr. were seated next to a man I didn't recognize. And of course, Louise was there, walking up and down the aisle, thanking folks for coming. When the ceremony was about to begin, she sat down next to Dolly and Jeff.

There wasn't a coffin. On the way up to the service, Dr. Harris had explained to me that Webster thought that the burial of a person's body was a primitive custom. She quoted Webster as having said, "When I die, I want to be cremated—before I get burnt to a crisp in hell."

As we waited for the service to start, we listened to a recording of Billie Holiday singing "God Bless the Child." It was followed by Ella Fitzgerald singing "Summertime."

The service was brief. Jeff Washington spoke about Webster's integrity and kindness. He told a couple of funny stories, one of which was about Webster challenging the Governor of the State of Minnesota. "So, Webster says to the governor, that's great sir—but what are you going to do about it?"

Everyone laughed.

Bud Harmon, a sports columnist with *The* Minneapolis *News Chronicle* spoke about Webster's work ethic. "I like to think of myself as one of the hardest working reporters around. But I would get into work and Webster Pedersen was already at it. At the end of the day, after I submitted my column, Pedersen was still working on his. His dedication, the quality of his work and his constant integrity earned him the unqualified admiration of his colleagues in the newspaper industry."

Afterward, Dr. Harris stood up. Without going to the front of the sanctuary, she spoke about her memories of Webster as a young man. Most of the brief incidents she recalled brought laughter. Her voice turned somber as she said, "Webster was as honest a man as any of us will ever know."

She paused and added, "I know if Webster could tell me what to say today, he would ask me to thank his loving wife, Louise. He would want me to tell her that she was the greatest pleasure in his life, that the time he spent with her and their beautiful daughter Ingrid gave his life fullness and meaning."

*****

At the conclusion of the ceremony, folks stood around and chatted. We were treated to more of the music that Webster had loved. We listened to Duke Ellington's "Moon Indigo" and "It Don't Mean a Thing If It Ain't Got That Swing." The service closed out with Billie Holiday singing "I'll Be Seeing You." Everybody in the sanctuary stopped chatting and listened to Holiday's haunting rendition:

> *I'll be seeing you in every lovely, summer's day*
> *and everything that's bright and gay;*
> *I'll always think of you that way.*
> *I'll find you in the morning sun*

and when the night is new.
I'll be looking at the moon but I'll be seeing you.

There was not a person who had a dry eye after the recording ended.

*****

Miki Oleson came up to me and introduced her son and boyfriend. The boyfriend probably was a few years older than her. He seemed like a nice guy and I was happy for her. Her son seemed to be sweet. I told her as much. She thanked me.

Dolly walked up and gave me a hug. You could see that she had cried.

She gave a brave smile and said, "In your fresh naivete, I think Webster saw himself as a young man. He found a lot of joy as you explored the newspaper business. And your sweetness brought back memories of his daughter. That was good for him. Recently, there hadn't been that much in his life that had been uplifting."

Jeff approached me. "Heh, youngster. How's the Douglas Oleson novel coming?"

I chuckled and said, "Seeing all of you here today was a strong reminder that I don't have a good answer to that question. I still have no real clue who Douglas Oleson was or what happened to him."

Jeff laughed. "Life is such a Goddamned elusive process, ain't it?"

Louise spent a lot of time speaking with Dr. Harris. Afterward, she came up to me and said, "Paul, Sharon filled me in on what has happened in your life in the past year. I'm so sorry. I know it's just about your spring break, but I would enjoy it if we could have dinner at my place sometime after you get back from it."

I told her, "It's a date."

As she drove us back to Northfield, Dr. Harris appeared lost in her thoughts. While I would have liked to have asked her for advice about my senior project, I realized that that was not the time. We hardly spoke.

*****

I had one more week of classes before the winter term's final exams. After returning from the funeral, I dug into my studies, refusing to think about all the uncertainties facing me. I would struggle with those questions about my future after my exams had been completed.

Chapter 27 – Spring Break, Senior Year

I left Northfield on a sunny Friday morning, bound for Chicago for spring break. My sunglasses were no match for the brilliance of the day's sunlight but it was a pleasure driving the 240 SL. Along the way, I saw the snow had melted and the river ice was breaking up. I decided to take that as an omen. Spring was coming and the long hard winter might be coming to an end.

*****

It felt strange being in my mother's condominium without her. It had been cleaned, its refrigerator emptied and my mother's clothing removed. Everything else was as it had been. It all seemed so quiet, so eerily empty.

I did not change bedrooms. My mother's room would remain my mother's room. I went into my bedroom and threw my backpack and suitcase on the bed. Fifteen minutes later, I was in the living room fixing myself a whiskey and soda, a drink my mother had often enjoyed.

I stood in front of the picture window overlooking Lake Michigan. Lifting my glass, I toasted her out loud, "Mom—here's to you. Thank you for the wonderful conversations we had last fall. I'm sorry for all of the pain you had to endure—but so appreciative I got to know you before you—before you went away."

I sat down on the wingback chair next to my mother's and sipped the whiskey and soda. I thought about the last few months of her life. After having been through a couple of funerals recently, I couldn't blame her for not wanting one. She wouldn't have enjoyed the idea of being eulogized by my father. She wouldn't have wanted professional associates who hadn't contacted her during her illness to come together and have a social hour over her dead body.

****

After I finished my drink, I called my father.

"Paul," he said, "I'm relieved you got to Chicago safely. I have reservations for seven at *Harry Carey's* Steakhouse—just the two of us. Does that work?"

I was pleased he hadn't invited Peggy to join us. She meant nothing to me and I had dreaded spending the evening watching the two of them flirt with one another.

I had an hour before I needed to leave for dinner. I found a family photo album. It had pictures of me from when I was a little kid—maybe four or five. There was one snapshot of me at the state fair in Springfield. I was wearing a cowboy hat while sitting on a pony. I remembered the day when that picture was taken. I had felt like the king of the world.

There were photographs of my parents from when they were younger and happier. One must have been taken at a Chicago Cubs baseball game. My parents had big smiles on their faces and were each holding a plastic glass of beer as if offering a toast to whoever snapped the photo.

"Life is so strange," I thought to myself as I turned the pages. "Every time you think you sort of understand it, it eludes you. It sort of slips out of your grasp. A couple of years ago, I was so confident about so many aspects of my life. All of that certainty has evaporated."

****

As I walked to meet my father, I tried to anticipate the things he would ask. Would I keep the roadster? How were things going between me and Kathy? He would begin to ask about the disposal of my mom's assets and what I wanted him to do with her apartment. But his big ask would be about my plan for next year. Had I applied to law school yet?

I was not looking forward to telling him I had no answers. The closer I got to the steakhouse, the more I wished I could avoid the conversation that was about to occur.

I thought about the one person I would not discuss with my father—Sandy. My night with her had been the most special time I had had since I arrived at college—maybe ever. OK, Sandy was ten years older than me. So be it. But it wasn't just the sex—I liked her freshness, her openness. I felt comfortable with her sense of humor and directness.

Over the last six months, I had thought about Sandy often. A few times, I considered driving up to the Twin Cities and asking her if she wanted to go out on a date. I would have shown her the roadster. Maybe she would have been impressed.

But I hadn't gone up there to see her or attempted to contact her in any other way. As I got close to *Harry Carey's*, I resolved to contact Sandy after I returned to school.

*****

My father was already seated at the restaurant when I arrived. He ordered a scotch and soda. I asked for a Guinness.

"I'm sure you're anticipating that I'm going to give you the third degree," was how my father started the conversation. "But I realize that you've got to be overwhelmed right now. So instead, I want to know how you're doing—not what decisions you've made about the future"

I was stunned.

"But first of all," he said, "I need to give you a personal update. Peggy and I are no longer seeing one another."

My father gave no details but I considered that information to be good news.

The waiter brought our drinks and took our orders.

My father continued. "So, how you are doing?"

"I'm missing mom," I said. "The time I had with her in the fall—it was really special. I wasn't ready to let go."

I told my father how empty winter term had felt; about Webster Pedersen passing away and how important Webster had been in my life. I told him it was disconcerting that I didn't know what I wanted to do in the future, but that I was appreciative he hadn't pushed that question.

We sipped on our drinks and the conversation turned to the upcoming Chicago Cubs season. I told my dad I had become a Minnesota Twins fan.

He laughed and said, "You've moved your allegiances from one really bad baseball team to another. The Cubs and the Twins are probably the two worst teams in baseball."

*****

After dinner, my dad turned briefly to business. "As your mom's executor, I could give you a large legal spiel on your mother's will. But my guess is you don't need or want that. Let me just run over it at a high level and answer any questions you have."

I responded, "That would be nice."

"The estate's primary assets were your mom's practice, her apartment and her retirement accounts. After your mom got ill, she sold her practice to the psychologist who covered for her when she was on vacation. What that means is for the next decade, you'll have a steady cash flow."

My dad took a deep breath and blew it out. "Your mom's apartment is worth somewhere around a million dollars. Monthly maintenance and taxes will be absorbed by the stream from the sale of her practice. She has a significant amount of retirement savings and other liquid assets as well as a half-million-dollar life insurance policy for which you are the only beneficiary."

The waiter came to our table. We each ordered a piece of pecan pie with a scoop of their homemade vanilla ice cream.

My dad finished up. "You've got the car. Her other valuables are in the apartment. Those things are yours to do with as you wish. If you need any help or advice, I'm here."

I was taken aback by the brevity of his summary and the breadth of what I had inherited. I gave a nervous laugh.

Finally, I was able to tell him, "That's an awful lot to process, Dad. Thank you."

It had been a long day. After dinner, my dad offered to give me a ride back to the condominium which I gladly accepted.

*****

After I got back to the apartment, I spent the evening thinking about my life. I had reached an important juncture. My mom was gone. My dad and I were communicating. And I would soon have the value of a college diploma. Now, what did I want to do with my life?

The next morning, I called my dad and thanked him for the previous evening. I told him I needed a few quiet days to just decompress. We agreed to get together a week later on a Saturday afternoon at Grant Park. The park was located along the waterfront of Lake Michigan, walking distance from my mom's condominium. After our phone conversation, I walked over to a local grocery store and got some basic supplies including coffee, eggs, bacon, bread and an early edition of the Sunday Chicago Tribune. I intended to have a good breakfast the following morning.

That evening, after a spaghetti and meatball dinner at *Acanto*, a nearby Italian restaurant, I took in the film *Pleasantville*. The light positive tenor of the film was a great distraction from the stressful issues upon which I had been dwelling.

I was back at the condominium by ten-thirty and went right to sleep.

*****

The week passed quickly. I spent a lot of time walking along the shores of Lake Michigan, thinking about my life, trying to figure out how to move forward. Saturday, I met my dad at Grand Park. The day was breezy, but the air felt good.

As we walked along the lake, I asked my dad what happened between him and Peggy.

He laughed, shook his head and said, "I was afraid you'd ask. I think Peggy decided she needed a younger guy. Let me put that more honestly. Peggy found a younger guy. In any case, the moral of the story is that Peggy turned out to be that special lesson about arrogance and humility that I guess I needed. What else can I say?"

We both laughed.

We stopped and watched a small blue sailboat battling the winds. I commented, "That boat is a good metaphor for how I've been feeling the past six months."

Nothing more was said for at least fifteen minutes.

*****

My dad broke the silence. "I've done a lot of thinking. I don't regret separating from your mother. She was a fine person who I often took for granted. But we fought a lot over the years."

We sat down on a park bench and gazed at the lake.

"But I've also been thinking about the type of parent I was for you. I often tried to control your life. I know that. Dads want their kids to do well—even if the life directions they push would not make their kids happy. Sure, becoming an attorney would have been a safe option if you had chosen it. It would have offered financial and social security. But would such a path have made you happy? Probably not. I was not wise enough to understand or accept that."

I thanked my dad for those words. We got up and walked for half an hour without conversation.

Then I said, "I've done some thinking, too. Here are my grand decisions. I'm gonna keep the car—at least for now. I'll take good care of it. It was important to mom. When I get to the point that I don't need a car, I'll talk to you before I sell it."

I looked at my dad. He was listening closely.

"As far as her condominium goes, I don't need such a nice place. I'll go through it and set aside things I want to keep. Later, if there are things you want, go ahead and take them. I would appreciate it if you could find a realtor to sell the property and someone to dispose of its other contents.

Finally, I'd like your advice on who I should use to invest and manage the proceeds from the estate."

My dad was watching me closely. He winked and laughed before saying, "But damn, you would have made some hell of a good attorney."

We walked for another hour only making small talk about the beauty of the day and the changing of the seasons. It had been a lovely afternoon. I felt like I was getting to know my father.

*****

The next morning, I packed up my beautiful little Mercedes roadster and headed back to school.

Chapter 28 – Spring Term, Senior Year

During my drive back to school, I thought about Sandy and resolved to call her as soon as I arrived in Northfield. I would ask her if she wanted to go out to dinner the following Saturday night. I could pick her up and we would go out for an expensive dinner. I hoped I would be able to rekindle some of the excitement we had enjoyed during our date in August.

After arriving at Carleton, I dialed Sandy's cell phone number and was greeted with a recording, "The number you have dialed is not in use." I tried the number again and got the same message.

Monday morning, I called her at Chuck Person's office. The receptionist who answered my call said, "Sandy no longer works here."

I told the receptionist, "I'm a friend of Sandy's. I haven't been in touch with her in a while. Do you have a number that she can be reached at?"

"No, sorry. Sandy left us in December. We were sorry to see her go. She told us she just needed to take some time off, maybe go on some sort of trip. We haven't heard from her since. If you do speak with her, give her our regards and tell her to stop by when she's in the area."

I was totally deflated. So much for that fantasy.

*****

Later that day, I went to meet with Dr. Harris in her office.

After some small talk about my spring break in Chicago, I said, "I'm embarrassed to say this because every

203

time I come to your office, I tell you I'm confused about stuff. Well, today, Dr. Harris, I'm super confused about stuff."

Dr. Harris laughed and responded, "Three years ago you told me you didn't have any idea what you what you wanted to study. Now, you are about to complete a special major with distinction. All that's left for you is to finish your senior thesis. What's the problem?"

I took a deep breath before explaining, "I followed through on my thesis project plan. I met with a slew of people who knew Douglas Oleson. Since then, I've gone over my notes from those meetings—multiple times. But I haven't even begun to respond to the questions the project was supposed to answer. Douglas Oleson remains a mystery to me—maybe even more than when I started the project. I don't know what caused him to run off the rails, where he has gone or what he is now doing. I can't decide whether he was a fraud, a genius or a victim. I don't have any sort of conclusion that would turn my paper into a complete story. What I have is a collection of seemingly unrelated tidbits about a person I never met rather than a meaningful distillation of who he was or what happened to him."

I paused for a moment, then tied it all together—for Dr Harris and myself. "Dr. Harris, this project means more to me than just a senior thesis. Completing this paper has turned into an attempt at personal validation. And, oh yeah—I have no clue what I'm gonna do next year." I laughed and said, "One more time I have to ask, what's your advice?"

She gave a big warm smile, looked down for a moment and began to speak. "First of all, you don't deserve criticism. You deserve congratulations. You have accomplished so much. You've created and executed a special major in journalism. You've excelled in it. Your internship was supposed to last three months. But you've expanded it into a two-year project. That's incredible. You've worked hard and have not only come to understand what journalism is, it appears you've become a journalist. Your pursuit of the ghost of Douglas Oleson has, in itself, been an exploration of the challenge of journalism."

Dr. Harris took a deep breath and let it out slowly. "Sometimes, Paul—sometimes in life—after you ask a question—you discover there is no simple answer."

She paused and looked directly at me.

"Don't let that truth defeat you, Paul. Wisdom is not about answers. Wisdom is knowing where to look for an answer. Sometimes it is simply the ability to understand a question; the diligence to explore it; and the bravery to admit when you haven't found the answer. Don't be afraid to admit that in your paper."

I was taken aback by her passion. But I recognized she was delivering an important lesson. I listened intently and have never forgotten her words.

"You're about to graduate, Paul. Graduate to what? An education is much more than technical skills. Education is about discovery. You'll find a way to finish that paper, a paper you intended to be a definitive analysis of a politician whose life fell apart. Your path will be different than you anticipated. Your final paper may not seem like a page out of the *New York Times*. But you can turn it into an interesting discussion of the difficulty of tying the pieces of a complex question together. It might turn into something different than what you had anticipated—but maybe it will be something even more special."

I was thrown back. Dr. Harris had not just given me a path, she had just given me clear and meaningful direction. I was ready to go back to my dorm room and get to work on finishing my project.

"But," she continued, "as you stated, your senior thesis isn't the only thing that is causing you angst. You haven't decided what you're going to do next year—or for the rest of your life. But Paul, you do not need to decide—and probably cannot decide—what you're gonna do for the rest of your life. All you need to do now is to decide what you're going to start doing after you graduate."

She paused.

Then looking intently at me, she said, "And you have options. You could apply to newspapers or you could take some time off on a trip to Europe. You certainly have the finances now to afford that. You could go to grad school or, if you wanted, you could just get some meaningless job somewhere and do it until another path becomes clear. Those are ideas off the top of my head. I'm sure it's not a complete list of your options. Ask your friends if they have ideas to be added to the list. Rather than brooding about not knowing what you are going to do, celebrate the uncertainty of the adventure of a lifetime that is in front of you. But one thing for certain, Paul—don't worry about it. Everything is going to work out."

I walked away from that conversation with a lightness and a focus. I was going to use Dr. Harris's strategy to complete my paper. And yes, she was right. I had options for the future.

*****

That evening, I ran into Kathy in the dining hall. We hadn't talked in months. We ate together and after dinner, we went for a walk in the arboretum. Kathy was silent which is not her normal pattern. I finally asked her how she was doing.

She gave me an odd look, but still said nothing.

"What's up," I repeated.

She stopped walking, sat down on a log, and started speaking in a hushed, quiet, tentative voice. "I found out just before I went home for spring break that my parents had split up. The whole thing turned out to be pretty ugly. My mother told me she had suspected my dad had been cheating on her. One evening, he came home and told her he had grown beyond her. They needed to get a divorce."

Kathy stopped speaking. I sat down on the log next to her and just waited.

After a couple of minutes of silence, she said, "His girlfriend is fifteen years younger than he. Mom is moving out of our home. And my dad, I didn't even hear from him once. So, spring break was just awful."

We stood up and walked on in silence. Then Kathy asked me how I was doing.

I told her how Dr. Harris had suggested I should finish my paper. Kathy told me she liked that approach. Then Kathy asked what I intended to do that summer and next year.

It was my turn to walk in silence. Finally, I said, "I don't know, Kathy. I've been trying to work through that one. I haven't given up on becoming a journalist. But somehow, Webster's death sort of put a spear through that whole profession. Don't ask me to explain that because I can't."

"That's tough," Kathy said. "After watching all of the crap with my father, I decided I don't want to go to law school. You know what I decided to do? Don't laugh, Paul. I think I'm going to become a high school teacher. Can you believe it?"

I told her I thought she'd be a fantastic high school teacher. "What do you want to teach?"

"Prepare yourself to be shocked again. I want to teach French."

This time I couldn't help but laugh. But I was a little bit envious. Kathy had spent a year in high school living in France and had always talked about her love for that language.

Good for Kathy. She had found something that had meaning for her.

*****

Over the next few weeks, I dug into my senior thesis. Dr. Harris had told me to push through it, not to worry about making everything perfect and that's just what I did.

"Damn the torpedoes," I kept saying to myself in a mocking voice. "Full speed ahead."

The first chapter of my thesis paper included the facts I had put together from Webster's newspaper clippings. Most interviews became a separate chapter. I described the interviews and the person I interviewed. For each interviewee, I tried to identify their interests, biases and insights. The second to last chapter would be entitled *What I Think I Know About Douglas Oleson*. I waited until I had written all of the preliminary chapters before I began to work on it. The final chapter would be titled, *What This Internship Taught Me about People, Journalism and Life*. I would not begin work on that until I felt satisfied with the rest of the paper.

Chapter 29 – My Dinner with Louise

I had promised to visit Louise during the term. I gave her a call.

Her voice bubbled. "Paul I am so glad to hear from you. I have been looking forward to having you over for dinner. Webster enjoyed you so much. Having you come over will bring me a touch of his humor, enthusiasm, creativity and joy. And there are a few things about Webster I want to share with you. When can you come?"

We agreed I would come over for dinner on the following Saturday evening.

*****

I was relieved that Louise had given me detailed instructions on how to get to her place and that I had been wise enough to write those directions down. Otherwise, I never would have found it.

The last time I had been to the Pedersen home, Webster had driven and Louise had been standing in the home's doorway when we pulled into the farmyard.

She was standing there again when I arrived. She came out to the car and gave me a hug. Then she walked around my mom's roadster, inspecting every detail. When her inspection was complete, she said, "Webster would have been thrilled to see you driving into our farmyard in this magical magnificent chariot."

*****

We went into her home. The aroma was extraordinary.

Louise asked, "Can I fix you a drink?"

"That would be lovely," I said.

After she went to the bar to pour the drinks, she reached into the stereo cabinet. A moment later, I was listening to the soft sounds of Erroll Garner playing *Misty* on the vibraphones. A few minutes later she carried in two gin and tonics.

"So much has changed," she said as she sat down, "Since the last time you were here. My world has been turned upside-down. But it sounds like your world has changed almost as much."

I agreed. Then I lifted my glass and said, "To Webster."

She lifted hers and, with a lump in her throat, she repeated the toast.

She asked me about my mother's passing and about my senior year. I filled her in on the past nine months. After I finished updating her on my senior thesis, we went to the table. A minute later, Louise had filled my plate with chicken fricassee.

"I know this was what I fixed last time you were here. But it was Webster's favorite meal. I haven't had the opportunity to cook it in some time and if our goal today is partly to honor Webster—well, he wouldn't have it any other way."

She poured us each a glass from a dusty bottle of Pouilly-Fusse'. I had never drunk that white Burgundy, but had heard it was really special and saw that the bottle from which Louise poured it was almost twenty years old.

The meal was fabulous and I told Louise as much. However, Louise looked pensive. I became worried that maybe I'd said something wrong.

She poured us each a second glass of wine.

After taking a sip from her glass, Louise said, "I'm going to share something with you, Paul. Something I'm not sure I should share. What I'm going to tell you about your senior project will—well, at a minimum, it will catch you off guard."

She took another sip of the wine and paused as she swished it around in her mouth, tasting it fully.

Then she gave a resolute look and said, "Webster would oftentimes talk to me about his work. In addition to being his wife, I happened to be his best friend and excelled as his major critic. He was so enthusiastic when you started your internship a couple of years ago. I could see that part of his pleasure in working with you was that your freshness reminded him of our daughter."

She took a deep breath, slowly blew it out and continued. "Webster was depressed before you started. He wasn't feeling that well physically and there wasn't much in his life that gave him joy. But you changed that. He enjoyed the naive sparkle you brought into the office each day. However, when Webster told me about the project, he was suggesting you take on, I told him he was wrong."

Louise stopped and took another sip of wine, then looked down for a moment.

When she looked up, she said, "Something Webster shared with no one but me is that before the two of us got together, he had had a short affair with a young woman. As he described her later, *the woman wasn't highly educated but she was very sexy.* A year after Webster and I were married, he learned that the woman had become pregnant during that brief relationship and had given birth to a child that she was raising by herself. Webster did the honorable thing. He contacted her and offered to provide child support. She swore at him and told him to get out of her life for good."

Louise poured the rest of the wine into her glass. "So, you are asking now, what does this have to do with you and your project?"

She paused, looked directly at me and said, "Douglas Oleson was Webster's son. Webster offered multiple times to provide financial support to Millie but the woman remained adamant that he should stay out of her life—and out of her son's. Eventually, he stopped making any comments to me that he was the parent of a boy he didn't know. However, once Douglas ran for the state legislature, Webster began to follow his career religiously. He scoured *The Minneapolis News Chronicle* and *The Saint Paul Daily Journal* for articles about Douglas and carefully clipped each one out, dated it and put it into his file."

Louise offered me a cup of coffee.

I needed it. After she served the coffee, she brought out a fresh blueberry pie with a container of her neighbor's vanilla ice cream. She cut each of us a piece of pie and added a big scoop of vanilla ice cream on top of each piece.

That blueberry pie was as good as the apple pie I remembered. We ate it in silence—a silence that was deafening.

Then Louise continued. "I could see how proud Webster was of Douglas' success. He never mentioned anything about his secret to any of his colleagues or acquaintances. But I could see his pride as he carefully read the articles and clipped them out of the morning papers.

When Webster told me he was going to give you this project, we argued intensely. I told him it was dishonest for him to assign this project to you and not to tell you about his ulterior motive. But Webster wanted to know what had happened to his son. His secret desire was that you would find Douglas."

We sat in silence. Our pie, ice cream and coffee were gone. But we continued to sit there for several minutes with nothing being said.

Finally, Louise said, "I think Webster's secret hope was that someday Douglas would return to the Twin Cities and resurrect his career. And Webster probably dreamed that he would be able to speak with Douglas, to explain to him what had happened. I think his fantasy was that Douglas would somehow understand."

After she had stated this, she stood up and quietly cleared the table. Once the table was cleared, Louise suggested we return to the living room for a second cup of coffee.

We sat down. No music played on the stereo. Instead, we just drank our coffee—each of us digesting what Louise had shared with me—each of us thinking about it in a unique context.

"This meal was probably more interesting than you had anticipated," she said as she gave a soft chuckle. "I've debated back and forth whether to tell you. Now, after having spit it all out, I am feeling disloyal to my husband— but maybe even more loyal to him on a much higher plane. What I ask of you is that you not share this with Dr. Harris— or with anyone—for now. After I die, you can tell the world. But until I pass, let it be our secret."

I gave her my word. And I have kept it.

*****

I sat with Louise for another half hour. We made small talk about a variety of things including the Minnesota

Twins, the weather and the future of humanity. Webster's name did not come up again.

I was lost in reverie during my drive back to Northfield.

Chapter 30 – Graduation and Onward

Once the term's coursework was complete, I spent a lot of time walking in the arboretum, trying to figure out how to commence the rest of my life. I considered applying for a position with one of the Twin Cities' larger newspapers (following the example set by Webster). I thought about going to law school (emulating my father). I even considered getting a master's in English literature with the intent of eventually getting a Ph.D. and teaching (embracing the path Dr. Harris had chosen for herself).

But none of those paths seemed right.

I asked for advice from my father (by phone), from Dr. Harris, and from Kathy. Each responded differently. But all of them backed off from suggesting what I should do.

My father who had seemed to have grown immensely since my mother's passing, said, "Paul, I think I would be doing you a favor by letting you figure this one out for yourself. But while I don't have the right answer to offer you, I am confident that if you work at it, you will find it."

Dr. Harris' response was, "You've had a tough year. I suggest you take some time off. After that, I have no doubt you'll find a path that works."

And Kathy laughed when I asked her. "You shouldn't be asking me. The last time I gave you any career advice, it was to work for my father. If you'd taken that advice, Paul, I'd probably hate you. I can tell you this, however. I'm confident that whatever you do, it will be done with integrity."

*****

For my senior thesis, I ended up following the approach Dr. Harris had suggested earlier in the spring.

I pushed the project through to completion. The simple focus of the project that Webster had suggested to me—find out what sort of person Douglas Oleson was and what happened to him—had turned into a multifaceted riddle, one which I in no way had solved. In the paper's conclusion, I spoke about the difference between answering a question and exploring a riddle. And I honored Louise's wishes. I did not refer in any way to Webster's relationship with his son.

A week before I walked across the stage and accepted my diploma, I made a few decisions. Maybe, more accurately, I committed to a plan to kick the ball down the road.

I guess I sort of followed Dr. Harris's advice and decided to take some time off. I would go to Europe for the summer and visit the major cities of France, Italy and Spain. During my trip, I would try not to think about Carleton or Douglas Oleson. And I would avoid dealing with the fact that I had no plans for what I would do once I returned to the States. That was not going to become a distraction from all I would see.

The only other decision I made was that upon returning from that vacation, I would rent an apartment in Minnesota's Twin Cities.

Once there, I would figure out what I would do next.

Part II – Life After College

Chapter 1 – Catching Up

The trip to Europe turned into a wonderful few months. Europe's cities and cultures offered many pleasurable distractions. I also found the time to come to some unexpected personal clarity—I decided that once I returned to the United States, I would pursue a career in journalism.

*****

Within days of my flight landing at the Minneapolis-Saint Paul Airport, I had picked up my Mercedes roaster in Northfield and rented an apartment on the top floor of an old Victorian home in Saint Paul.

That week, I went into *The Saint Paul Daily Journal*'s offices to inquire about being hired as an entry-level reporter. I was brimming with optimism until the human resources assistant informed me that instead of adding new staff, the paper was laying them off. The following day, The Minneapolis *News Chronicle*'s human resource staffer gave me a similar answer.

I had confirmed what I should have already known. The newspaper industry was shrinking. Advertising dollars that had once funded hometown newspapers were now flowing to billionaires who owned internet companies.

While my financial position didn't force me to find a job immediately, my question was if I wasn't working, what would I do? I spent a couple of weeks applying for assorted management trainee positions throughout the Twin Cities without any success.

*****

My landlady asked me how my job search was going. I told her. She told me that her son had run into a similar challenge and decided to take a job as a janitor at Saint Paul's Children's Hospital. She added that the hospital currently had another opening.

Without a good alternative and needing some sort of daily routine, I applied for the position and was hired. While the work was mindless and the pay quite low, the people I worked with were pleasant and the convalescing children who I came into contact with in the hospital wards were extraordinarily sweet.

What hadn't changed in any regard was my fundamental question: *What was I going to do with the rest of my life?*

*****

One snowy Friday night in early October, I ventured out to the Triangle Bar, a university-area tavern that always had good live music and catered to hip young people. I was sitting at its bar, drinking a Guinness and listening to some guy singing folk songs when a woman sat down next to me. She ordered a whiskey sour.

She turned to me and said, "Hi. My name's Jenny."

"My name is Paul," I responded. "Do you come here often?"

"Sometimes, after an intense workweek, I like to have a drink with some good old-time rock and roll."

She gave me a funny look and said, "You look worried. What's up, Doc?"

I smiled as I realized that I must be wearing my feelings on my sleeve.

"I just graduated from college last spring," I started out. "But I have no clue what I should do with my life. I'm working as a janitor right now. That's OK. But I need to figure out what I'm going to do. I want something satisfying, something worthwhile. I had hoped to become a journalist until I found out the newspapers are laying off reporters rather than hiring new ones. My dad wanted me to become an attorney. I told him I couldn't stand it. I thought I might copy my college professor who went to grad school, got a PhD and taught at a university—but somehow that just didn't seem right. I just don't know."

"OK Paul," she said. "I'll offer you a deal. You buy me a second whiskey sour. In exchange, I'll solve your problem."

I laughed and told her, "Sister, you've got a deal."

A couple of minutes later, the bartender had placed a second whiskey sour in front of Jenny and handed me another Guinness.

"OK," Jenny said, "here you go. First of all, you need to know my bias—what I do for a living. I'm a kindergarten teacher. It's my second year. Kindergarten teachers are used to telling people who don't know what they're doing what they should be doing. And we expect them to listen. I tell you this so you'll understand my expectation—no, my requirement."

I laughed again and said, "OK. I'm ready to take your direction. But it had better make some sense."

Jenny all of a sudden began to speak with passion. "Young people are the future, Paul. Do you want to do something satisfying, something valuable? I'll tell you what it is. Help young people! Your college teacher's path wasn't totally wrong. But teaching at a university is the wrong place. High school students are going to be running this country in a few years. I'm telling you, Paul, teach high school students! That can be your mission. Tons of PhDs are competing to teach in universities. But public schools need good teachers—they need 'em badly. Enroll at the University of Minnesota. Get yourself a master's in education and a teaching certificate. Go for it, Paul. Change the future—for a few young people."

I was taken aback by the zeal with which she had delivered her message. And I was interested—in her as well as in her message.

"OK," I said. "I listened to you. I'll seriously consider what you recommended. In exchange, you need to give me your phone number."

She gave me a big, beautiful smile and said, "You're pretty cute, bub. But I just don't think my boyfriend would approve. Sorry."

*****

I never saw Jenny again. But she changed my life. During the winter term, I enrolled at the University of Minnesota, beginning a master's in education program with an emphasis on history. I decided that I may not become the next Edward R. Murrow, but I could teach young people about who he was—about his heroism.

*****

I finished my master's. Teaching young people turned into my labor of love. Maybe I never accomplished the fabulous things that Edward R. Murrow achieved. But I have been telling young people about his noble accomplishments and about a myriad of other worthwhile lessons of history—heroic stories about brave people upon whom my students can choose to pattern their lives.

Yes. Jenny was right. I am making a difference in some young people's lives.

Chapter 2 – One More Life Decision

When I enrolled at the University of Minnesota, it was the beginning of winter term in the year 2000. I was beginning the Millennium with a plan for my future.

I was excited about my newfound mission and felt a strong need to tell others about it. I visited Louise Pedersen. Louise praised my career choice. She wished me nothing but the best. I drove down to Carleton to let Dr. Harris know. As I had anticipated, she was thrilled and complimented me on a successful conclusion to my search for a personal mission.

I felt so damn good.

*****

Later that afternoon, I ran into Kathy.

Well, I guess that's a lie. I didn't just run into Kathy. I phoned her after I met with Dr. Harris. I was lucky to catch her in her dorm room. She was in between classes. Kathy was surprised to hear from me. We hadn't spoken since before I graduated.

Once she had answered my call, I hemmed and hawed and then decided to go ahead and ask her if she wanted to have dinner with me—I had news to share.

Kathy seemed a little taken aback by the invitation, but said, "Sure. When?"

I explained that I was on campus. I had just visited Dr. Harris—and hoped Kathy could go to dinner that evening.

"The only problem," she said, "is that I have a seminar that goes until seven. I could meet you after that."

I looked at my watch. It was 3:30 and while the sun was still shining, January in Minnesota is cold—very cold. I would have to figure out something to do for the next three and a half hours to avoid freezing.

It had been sort of a spur-of-the-moment decision to call her—I guess. But I began to feel like I wanted to tell her about my plans. So, we agreed that I would meet her in front of the student union a little after seven. We would go to my car and I would drive us to a restaurant.

I went to the roadster and grabbed my new textbook, *The Psychology of Being an Excellent Teacher,* and spent the next few hours in the Carleton College library trying to focus on the book.

*****

I was standing in front of the student union at seven, waiting for Kathy. It was cold and I'd only worn a light jacket. But I was looking forward to dinner and waited with enthusiasm. Around 7:15, Kathy showed up. She apologized for being late. The seminar had dragged on for a few extra minutes.

We went to the roadster and headed off to a restaurant in a nearby town. I wanted to impress Kathy with a nice dinner.

As soon as we were on the road, Kathy said, "I saw your car a couple of times last year. But I've never ridden in it. It is nice. Do you have snow tires on it?"

I had no idea what sort of tires I had on it. But I slowed down. The roads did look a little shiny. Half an hour later, we were seated at the Don Juan Cantina & Grill in Owatonna. We ordered steak fajitas and margaritas.

I enthusiastically told Kathy about my entry into the University of Minnesota master's in education program and about my intent to teach high school history. She responded warmly. It felt like old times. She told me that she had continued to focus her studies on French with the intent of teaching it at the high school level.

I said, "We can talk more about teaching as my courses progress. Would you like to come up to the Twin Cities sometime and maybe we could talk over dinner?

Kathy took a shallow breath, made a funny face and said, "Oh Paul. That's such a nice offer. But I don't think my boyfriend would approve."

The wind had suddenly disappeared from my sails.

We chit-chatted throughout the rest of dinner. Afterward, I drove her back to campus.

As I drove her back to her dormitory, I tried to come up with things to say that were both lighthearted and expressed my sincere interest in her. As she got out of the car, I laughed and said, "If that boyfriend of yours ever up and disappears, call me."

She promised she would do just that.

My drive back to The Twin Cities was full of quiet embarrassment, loneliness and lots of regret. I believe I may have sworn at myself several times—out loud—for my stupidity, my arrogance and my bad luck.

*****

However, about a month later, I received a call from Kathy.

She began the call by saying, "Paul. Did you know something I didn't? About a week after you took me out for dinner, the boyfriend did, in fact, do it—the son of a bitch dumped me. And Paul, if the invitation is still open, I would love it if you would take me out on a date in the Twin Cities."

*****

I don't want to go on and on about the courtship of Kathy. Even that description sounds like the title of a television sitcom. Suffice it to say that we saw a lot of one another and enjoyed it. When Kathy graduated a year and a half later, she enrolled at the University of Minnesota in their master's in education program. And of course, Kathy needed an apartment. And well, I had space for a roommate. In any case, we did pretty well together.

And we continue to do pretty well together. Now, more than twenty years later, we have two wonderful children, a fourteen-year-old girl, Ingrid, and a twelve-year-old boy, Webster. I love teaching history at the high school and Kathy has graduated from being an outstanding high school French teacher to becoming the capable vice-principal of our school.

Chapter 3 – One More Goodbye

In 2010, I got a call from Louise. She wanted to let me know that Sharon Harris had passed away. Louise asked if I could drive her to the funeral which was being held in Northfield.

"Of course," I told her.

The two of us drove down to Carleton together. On the way, Louise let me know that she and Sharon had become even closer over the last few years. I told Louise I felt guilty because I had sort of forgotten to stay in contact with Dr. Harris. Dr. Harris had done so much for me at a time when I needed it badly. I told Louise I felt I had deserted her.

But in her typical thoughtful manner, Louise corrected me. "You know, Paul, Sharon never married. She never had children of her own. Her adult life was spent as a teacher. But she never felt that she lost out because of that. You weren't the only young person whose life she helped steer toward a meaningful path. But she always asked how you were doing when we got together and was so pleased to hear that you stayed with the ambition of teaching—that you are so passionate about it and that you do it so well. Sharon took personal pride in your success."

*****

Still, I've always felt that I failed by not staying in touch with Dr. Harris. However, Dr. Harris has remained an inspiration for me as a teacher even after her death as I work with young people who need direction in their lives.

Chapter 4 – Time Flies

Louise Pedersen died early in 2022, twenty-three years after I graduated from Carleton. During Louise's last decade, Kathy and I had her over to our home almost weekly. She was as close to a grandparent as our son and daughter had ever known. When Louise passed, our whole family grieved.

*****

Louise's funeral service was held in the same church in which Webster had been memorialized more than two decades before. As I walked into the sanctuary, I couldn't avoid being overcome by the powerful memories of attending Webster's funeral service. It seemed so strange to be saying goodbye now to his dear wife in that same place.

There were a couple dozen people at the service. When Kathy and I entered the sanctuary, the first person I saw was Jeff Washington. Jeff had aged a lot—I guess we all had. His powerful frame now seemed frail. Where he once had towered over me, we were about the same height. But his sincere smile and cordial demeanor had not lost a beat. I introduced him to Kathy. Jeff was gracious as ever. With a wink, he asked me if I had ever solved the case of the missing mayor. I laughed and responded, "That's the one success that has unfortunately eluded me."

The only other person I recognized there was Miki Oleson. When Miki saw me, she rushed up and gave me a warm hug. Her husband, whom I had met briefly at Webster's funeral, was with her. When I introduced Kathy to them, Miki clarified that her last name was no longer

Oleson, it was now Jenson. She and her husband sat next to us during the service.

I hadn't seen Miki in two decades. Her hair was no longer jet black. It was now streaked with silver. Still, she moved with as much style and elegance as I remembered from our first meeting.

Once the service began, my attention was focused on the words of those who spoke. Each speaker offered a unique set of circumstances that had been the basis for their appreciation of Louise's grace and kindness. As I listened, it was hard for me not to reminisce about that first meal I had with Louise after Webster had brought me home to dinner during my internship.

After the service was over, Miki, her husband, Kathy and I went down to a reception in the church's basement. The four of us made the small talk that old friends have when they introduce one another to their spouses. Miki's husband took Kathy's arm saying, "Let's go grab a cup of tea and give Paul and Miki a chance to chat about some old memories."

As our spouses walked off, Miki turned to me and said, "Over twenty years ago, I read your senior year thesis the moment I received it. Thank you for sending it to me, Paul. I've always felt guilty that I didn't immediately write to let you know how much I appreciated how respectful your paper was regarding my feelings. I had been through so much hell and throughout your senior thesis, while you certainly maintained fairness and objectivity, your words about me were so kind. Thank you."

Then, she carefully looked around the room for a moment and her voice became hushed.

"It seems so long ago that I was the wife of that scheming, ambitious man. Sometimes I shake my head and wonder how I could have been taken in—why I married him? It even seems at times like the whole thing might just have been a dream—one horrendous nightmare."

Miki gave me a serious look as she continued, "But there is something I must share with you, Paul. About a year ago, a woman who worked with Douglas at the state legislature approached me. She had just returned from a trip to France. She told me she had seen him—seen Douglas—in Lyon. She was buying strawberries at Lyon's public market. She looked up and there he was. She told me she was certain it was him. She called out, *Douglas*. He glanced at her, spun around and disappeared in an instant. But this woman told me she was sure—there was no doubt about it. Even the way he turned and moved off into the crowd—she said it was vintage Douglas."

Miki took a deep breath and sighed. "For such a long time, Paul, I'd assumed the bastard was dead. I asked the woman, *What did he look like?* She told me, *He was still handsome as hell; he had grown a goatee, had a lot of wrinkles on his face and while his hair was still thick, its once black color had turned almost white.* But she had no doubt it was Douglas Oleson."

After hearing this from Miki, I was taken aback. The only thing that occurred to me to ask was, "Did he know how to speak French?"

She laughed. "Yes, Douglas spoke French quite well. He was so proud of that skill. Whenever we went to a French restaurant or met someone from France, he couldn't resist showing off his French language skills."

Just then, Miki's husband and Kathy rejoined us. We stopped speaking about Miki's ex-husband and chatted for a few minutes about sundry unimportant items.

Suddenly, Miki looked at her watch and said, "Oh, God, we need to run. Douglas Jr. is going to visit us this afternoon—with his new girlfriend! I can't miss that."

The goodbyes were warm. Promises were made to stay in touch—promises that like so many similar commitments are often forgotten.

*****

The instant Miki shared the story about the Douglas Oleson sighting, I knew I had to find him, to meet him and ask the questions I had carried around for almost a quarter of a century. As Kathy and I walked away from the church, I am ashamed to share I wasn't thinking about Louise Pedersen. I was thinking about Douglas Oleson. I was thinking that I could hire some sort of private detective to find out if Oleson really had been in Lyon.

Regardless of whether it turned out that the man that woman had seen really was Oleson or not, I knew I needed to find out if Douglas Oleson was alive. If he was alive, where was he living? And if I found him, I needed to go to him and ask him those questions.

That day, as I drove home from Louise's funeral in my still beautiful, but almost forty-year-old, blue Mercedes roadster, I repeated to Kathy every detail that Miki had shared about the Douglas sighting. Then, I told Kathy about my idea of hiring a private detective.

Because Kathy and I each had inherited large sums from our folks, we could afford to be extravagant.

Kathy softly put her hand on my arm and said, "Go for it, Paul. Just go for it."

Chapter 5 – Initial Conclusions

Two months after hiring a private investigator, I sat in my study and listened to a voicemail on my iPhone. "Paul Newton, this is Bill Amoth here. I'm calling from *Twin City Investigations.* We've located your guy, Douglas Oleson. Come on into the office and I'll give you the report and the bill."

I called Twin City Investigations and set up a time to meet with Amoth for the following afternoon.

*****

The furniture in Bill Amoth's Twin City Investigations office wasn't at all different from what you would have expected to see in a detective's office in a Dashiell Hammett novel. The inconsistency from that comparison was that the building in which the office was located was a new, glass-walled, modern structure. Amoth was sitting in a leather office chair in front of a big old nicked-up wooden desk. I sat down across from him on an equally old oak and leather captain's chair.

After a little chitchat about the weather and the Minnesota Twins, Amoth slid a yellow folder over to me. "There it is, Newton, Your guy's still in France. Been there for over twenty years—in one city or another. He's a French citizen now; retired; living in Bordeaux. In addition to collecting his French pension, Oleson started collecting his US Social Security a few months ago. His current address and phone number are in the report. Any questions?"

I opened the investigation report and skimmed through it. There wasn't too much more in the report than what Amoth had just shared.

"How long has he lived in Bordeaux?" I asked.

"He moved there less than a year ago. His prior address was Lyon. So, whoever told your friend that he had been there was correct."

"Do you think he has any idea that anyone is investigating him?"

"The way I work, he doesn't have a fucking clue."

"Is he married?"

"Don't know. You didn't ask. But for another fifteen hundred buckaroos, I am certain I could find out."

I asked several other questions including what sort of work Oleson had done in France. The responses were similar to those he gave me when I asked if Oleson was married.

I thanked Amoth, pulled out my checkbook, wrote the check and left his office.

*****

As I drove home, I asked myself, *What would I say to Oleson when I faced him? Which question would I ask first?*

There was an empty moment when it occurred to me that this whole search might have been a foolish waste of money. Then I realized that I would never forgive myself if I didn't follow up. My curiosity was too great.

I told Kathy about the meeting with Amoth. I concluded by saying, "I'm going to Bordeaux. Will you come along?"

"No, Paul," she said. "I just can't go. The kids have too many plans to drag them along to Europe and I'm not about to leave them here by themselves. Anyway, this is the one thing you need to do by yourself. Of course, I want to hear every detail of what happens. I've heard too much about Oleson over the years not to be totally interested in whatever you learn."

I went into my study and Googled Bordeaux. There it was, in southwest France, just above Spain. That evening, I headed over to *Moon Palace Books* and bought a couple of guidebooks about Bordeaux. When I returned home, I went onto *Expedia.com* and made my flight reservations.

As I lay in bed that night, waiting to fall asleep, I couldn't stop thinking about the whole curious adventure. This project had been going on forever. Now, I was finally about to complete it. I needed to structure my approach and write out my questions the same way I had for my first internship interviews a quarter of a century before.

That night, I dreamt about Webster Pedersen, Douglas Oleson and Bordeaux, France.

*****

Over the years, I'd often wondered what happened to Olesen. I'd analyze him in my mind's eye, getting confused as to whether he was a good man who was dumb or an evil man who almost succeeded in pulling the wool over everyone's eyes.

There were times I'd be listening to a news item about local politics or speaking to my students about American politicians when the similarities between Douglas Oleson and other politicians would strike me out of the blue.

The most obvious parallel was ex-President Bill Clinton. Clinton was in office during Oleson's first term. Both men were bright, intelligent policy wonks who came from poor backgrounds. They were both skilled at telling their stories. They knew who they were trying to sell themselves to and what sort of policy compromises would be required to make those sales. Both were raised without fathers by mothers who taught them to be aggressive. They each had smart, attractive wives, but each had difficulty managing their zippers.

That last feature got both of them into trouble.

*****

I was thinking about those similarities as my Delta Airlines flight circled Charles De Gaulle Airport. My exact thought was, *Why did Clinton get away with all of his shenanigans, while Oleson ended up in France?*

*****

A few hours later, I was traveling at one hundred and eighty miles per hour on a high-speed train that was headed to Bordeaux from Paris. As the train pulled into the Bordeaux Saint-Jean station, I reviewed—for the umpteenth time—the questions I planned on asking Oleson.

I had decided not to approach him that day. I would check into my hotel and be a tourist for the afternoon, soaking up the atmosphere and getting a feel for the city.

It was a nice afternoon and was topped off that evening at the restaurant next door to my hotel. I enjoyed a wonderful dinner of calamars à la basquaise, a French Basque combination of squid, tomatoes, bell peppers and pieces of chorizo sausage. After a half bottle of Basque white wine, I wobbled back to my hotel room and slept like a baby.

*****

The following morning, after a café au lait and croissant, I walked to Oleson's home.

I had given a lot of thought as to what would be my best approach. If I phoned him first, he might go out of his way to avoid me, possibly leaving town for a few days. If I just knocked on his apartment door, he might slam the door in my face. But after a lot of back-and-forth considerations, I decided the best bet would be to risk having the slammed door. Once Oleson answered my knock, I would tell him who I was and why I was there. If it was somebody else, I would tell them I was Doug's old friend.

*****

Oleson's home was near *Le Jardin Public*, a spacious park located just north of the city's center. I walked through a corner of *Le Jardin Public* to get to Oleson's neighborhood. Oleson's street was narrow and lined with three and four-story buildings that looked like old mansions converted into apartments. As I walked up his front steps, I admired the home's elegant but very old wooden door.

I rang Olesen's doorbell and waited.

A couple of minutes later, that grand wooden door swung open. There, standing in front of me in a brown silk robe, was an older version of the Douglas Oleson I had seen so often in photographs.

Oleson said, *"Bonjour, comment puis-je vous aider?"*

While I didn't speak French, I realized I'd just been asked what I was doing there.

I took a deep breath and said, "Mr. Oleson, my name is Paul Newton."

Then, I froze for a moment—forgetting everything I had planned to say.

A moment later I got back on plan. "In 1997, I was a student at Carleton College and..."

But Oleson scowled, said *Merde* as he slammed the door shut. The action was so quick, I wasn't able to say anything in response. I didn't know what to do. I just stood there in shock; trying to figure out my next step.

However, a moment later, I heard the door unlock, then it partially opened and Oleson's face peaked out.

"What did you say your name was?" Oleson asked with a puzzled look on his face.

By now, I was totally confused, but I was able to say, "I said my name is Paul Newton."

By this point, I didn't have a clue what the hell was happening because Oleson slowly opened the door the rest of the way.

Then he smiled and said, "Hey Paul, I just made a pot of coffee. Why don't you come on in and have a cup with me. Then you can ask me as many questions as you want. I may even choose to answer a few of them. Only one thing Paul, please call me Doug."

Then Olesen began to laugh. My head was spinning. What the hell was going on? How did I get from a slammed door to a fresh cup of coffee? Despite my confusion, I stepped into his apartment.

Oleson's grand room was quite elegant. In addition to a living room area, it included an extremely well-equipped kitchen and a dining area. The living room portion was furnished with elegant brightly colored European furniture and its walls featured a couple of powerful surrealist posters.

Oleson led me to the room's intensely yellow couch. "Have a seat," he said. "I'll be back in just a flash with the coffee. Do you take cream or sugar?"

I passed on the cream and sugar and sat down on the couch. All context was gone. I felt like I did a quarter of a century before—as if I were nineteen again—waiting for my first interview. Oleson disappeared for a moment and came back carrying a tray with a glass press-pot of coffee and several clear glass mugs.

He sat down on the couch next to me, poured coffee into three mugs, handed me a cup and, as I tasted it, he looked across the grand room and hollered, "*Nous avons un visiteur, ma chérie.*"

Then he asked, "Do you like the coffee?"

I said, still totally confused, "Yes—uhm—it's—uh—really good."

Oleson said, "I'm glad."

I was pressing myself to try to figure out what was happening; but with no luck. It felt as if I had fallen down Alice's rabbit hole and met the white rabbit's best friend, Douglas Oleson. At that moment, the door across the room from me opened and through it, dressed in a white silk nightgown with her gray hair tied in a ponytail, walked Sandy Benoit. Except for the gray hair, she didn't look a day older than the last time I saw her in 1998.

As she walked up to me, she had that large, off-center smirk. She stopped about a yard in front of me, leaned her head back at an angle and said, "Hey Slim. How're we doing?"

Douglas Oleson and Sandy began to roar with laughter as I remained speechless. I am sure that my face turned a deep shade of crimson.

"Maybe, I need to help you out a little," Sandy said while retaining the smirk. "I know everybody in Minneapolis pronounced my name as *ben-oyt*. Like it was supposed to rhyme with Detroit. But that just reflected their ignorance. The correct pronunciation of my last name is *ben-wah*. My parents are from Dijon France. And that, abracadabra-alakazam, makes me a French citizen. Part of the reason Doug and I liked talking together so much was that he loved to speak French—and so do I."

She paused, winked at me and said, "But you didn't come to see me—did you? No, you came to see Dougie. So, I'll just let the two of you boys have your chat."

Douglas Oleson took over. "OK Paul," he said. "We can do this one of two ways. Based on what Sandy has told me, I am willing to bet a vintage bottle of Château Lafite Rothschild, 1961 that you have a list of questions. I've been waiting a decade for you to show up with that list. I begin by telling you about the last few years and then respond to any additional questions or," he looked at Sandy and smiled at her (and she grinned back), "or we can just go down your typewritten list. I'm gonna let you choose. What's your preference?"

By now, I had partially collected my wits and responded, "First of all, Sandy appears to know me better than I know myself. But go for it, Doug. Tell me about the years after you left Saint Paul. What happened? After that, I'll ask my questions."

Olesen grinned and said, "I have to admit, Paul, Sandy knows most of us better than we know ourselves. That was something that required me to make a bunch of adjustments. Sandy told me all about your project. And since you met with everybody and their cousin, you probably know more about me before 1996 than I do. I've been curious about what everyone said and would love to read your senior thesis. I hope you brought me a copy of it as a gift."

"I have it right here."

And I handed him the large envelope I had carried to France for that purpose. Oleson took the envelope. But he didn't open it.

Instead, he drained his cup of coffee and began to tell his tale. "When I first dreamed about going into political office, it seemed like an opportunity to accomplish so much and to validate my worth—all at the same time."

He was quiet for a while. I think he was thinking things through for himself before he shared them with me.

After a couple of minutes, he looked up, sighed and said, "Before I ran for office, I was told a political candidate must be able to absorb criticism. I was warned by a guy who had served in the State House for a couple of decades. He told me that if I was lucky enough to get elected, everybody else would always know more than me about everything. They will always second-guess me and, in doing so, they will use the harshest terms to describe whatever I did. *Whenever you do anything wrong*, he said *—they will come after you. And, if things go well—they will come after you with even more venom.* The guy who told me this added that if that bothered me, then I shouldn't go into politics. Well, I figured I could deal with all of that. God knows I'd had the opportunity to deal with a lot of crap while growing up."

Oleson refilled his coffee cup, took a sip and continued. "Now, I will admit that I deserved some of the criticism that was thrown my way. Sometimes I behaved sort of like an asshole."

Sandy interrupted him, "What do you mean *sometimes* and *sort of*?"

"OK. I admit it. I often was an asshole—but not all the time. In any case, I quickly figured out that I had to have thick skin to survive."

He stopped again. For a moment I wondered if for some reason he just wasn't going to say anything else.

But after a moment, he continued. "You know, I haven't talked to anybody about this stuff in a long time. I've tried not to even think about it too much. So, for a lot of what I'm going to be saying to you, I may be the most interested listener."

He stood up and started to walk around the room as he spoke. "Hindsight is twenty-twenty. You can look back a decade or two and see the things you did that were wrong. But you can't go back and change what you did. I had a pretty tough childhood—that's no excuse, but it's the truth. I decided I was going to be successful despite the challenges I faced as a kid. I was going to be tougher, smarter and work harder than the next guy. And, you know what? I did." He sighed. "But that wasn't enough."

He chuckled and added, "I imagine you'll have more questions about that later."

Oleson returned to the couch and sat down. His shoulders were slumped. Sandy reached out and squeezed his hand. He looked up at her and smiled.

"After it all fell apart—you know—everything had just turned into shit, I came to Paris. I had been to Paris once before—on a political junket. I'd learned back then, that Paris—well, the whole damn country of France—is as wonderful as people always say. Anyway, I had a little money with me and took six months spending it, screwing around, traveling across France and drinking a whole lot of wine."

Oleson looked across at Sandy who nodded, encouraging him to continue.

"I'll admit it," he said. "I was damned bitter. I felt I had worked so hard to be a good mayor for the City of Saint Paul. In exchange for my blood, sweat and tears, they treated me like crap. It just didn't seem fair—not fair at all."

He chuckled before saying, "I once saw a quote: *It's hard to remember that your plan was to drain the swamp when you're up to your ass in alligators.* I felt I had done everything I could to drain that damn swamp—but it hadn't worked. Again and again, good ideas had been quashed by some little bureaucrat or know-it-all because of their personal biases or jealousy. It was disgusting."

Oleson turned to Sandy. "Heh, Sweetie, could you get out three wine glasses and pull out one of those 2013 Nebbiolos?"

Sandy got up and left the room. Douglas stopped speaking and waited for her to return.

She was back several minutes later with the wine and the glasses. After she sat down, Oleson continued with his story.

"But the truth is, I was like every other jerk politician. First, I wanted to be a state legislator, then I went for mayor. After that, I had dreams of becoming governor and finally, I wanted to be president of the whole Goddamned country."

Sandy had opened the bottle and was pouring each of us a glass of a deep red wine. Oleson stopped speaking and watched her pour. Then he took a sip, closed his eyes and smiled.

I tasted the wine. It was full-bodied and smooth.

"This Nebbiolo is really good stuff," I said.

"You better believe it," responded Sandy.

Oleson looked off across the room as he said, "I was in Nice when my money ran out. I was flat broke and had no work permit. But I could speak French pretty well and the woman who managed the restaurant where I had been hanging out finagled a work visa for me. Then she hired me as a waiter. After a career of being a big shot who gave all the orders, I started taking them. Waiting on tables may have been the only thing for which I had the right set of skills. I knew how to make those I served feel important. That woman—she owned the restaurant—later helped me begin my pursuit of French citizenship."

Oleson looked at Sandy—evidently for confirmation of the direction he was going with what he was saying. Sandy nodded and Oleson continued.

"I gotta admit it. I was still a jerk. I used her. I took advantage of her. Chalk that up to one more person for whom I'll always feel guilt."

He gave a big sigh. "I worked in French restaurants for two decades—a third of that time as a waiter, a third as a chef and the rest as manager, chef and part-owner—with Sandy. We ran a small bistro in Lyon. Six months ago, we sold it."

He lifted his glass as if to propose a toast and said, "Now I am retired and ready to respond to any questions you have."

While he talked, Sandy had refilled our glasses with the intense wine.

I said, "You were right about my list of questions. But this meeting is going a lot differently than I ever imagined. I'd like a couple of minutes to go through my list. I think I won't need to ask half of them."

"Go for it," Douglas said.

While I reviewed my list of questions, the two of them chatted gaily in French. I couldn't understand anything they were saying. I had made the mistake of studying Spanish in high school and Russian at Carleton—two languages that I had never mastered and which were certainly of no use on that particular day.

****

When I looked up, Sandy said, "It's almost lunchtime. Doug and I haven't eaten anything yet today. Why don't you and I let the Dougster fix us a nice omelet? We can hit your questions afterward."

I told her, "That would be neat."

Sandy gave a sly smile and said, "Doug's been pretty honest with you about his life. It's your turn now. While he makes us lunch, how about you telling us a little about how your life turned out, Slim? Are you working for the *New York Times* yet? Did the NBC News team steal you away? Are you the new Edward R. Murrow?"

"OK," I said, "I know my dream was to go into journalism and I took that plan seriously. After I graduated, I applied at *The News Chronicle* and *The Daily Journal.*"

Oleson had moved into the kitchen and was busily chopping onions, pulling down pans, shredding cheese and cracking eggs. He looked up when I commented on the Twin Cities newspapers and said, "Boo, hiss."

I looked up at him. He was smiling. I continued with my response to Sandy. "But getting into journalism just sort of seemed like I would be going uphill—uphill on ice with bald tires. The industry was facing so many challenges and was letting go of really skilled reporters. However, I still wanted to do something meaningful, something satisfying—something that would make a difference."

I told them about my running into the kindergarten teacher at the *Triangle Bar*. Sandy and Doug both knew the *Triangle* and complimented me on my good taste in taverns. I told them that after speaking with Jenny, I had enrolled in the University's master's in education program."

Sandy was delighted and laughed even harder when I shared how I went back to Carleton to brag about having found a solution and ran into Kathy.

"Oh yes," said Sandy. "Falling in love with and marrying your old college sweetheart. I've heard that story before."

She looked over her shoulder at Oleson who rolled his eyes as she laughed.

"Anyway," I concluded, "I became a high school history teacher. When I was an intern, working on my Douglas Oleson paper—you are right—I did have dreams of becoming the next Edward R. Murrow. Now, instead of being Murrow, I teach young people about Murrow's courage, his integrity and his wisdom."

It seemed they both approved.

*****

Then I turned to Sandy and said, "And now it is your turn. Tell me about how you ended up in France and what you've been doing here."

"Hey man," she said, "I thought we were here to interview the Dougster, not me. I should get a free pass!"

I responded, "Your living circumstances and partnership in the restaurant qualify as guilt by association."

She laughed and said, "OK. I enjoyed my job working with Chuck Persons in commercial real estate. But I happened to be in love with some fool who was becoming a Frenchy. I decided I needed to go over and make sure he was using all the correct French declensions—and absolutely confirm that he was not using them on any unsuspecting French virgins."

As he cooked, Doug yelled out something in French that I didn't understand. They both laughed.

"Anyway, the Dougster had sent me a postcard from some dive he was working at in Marseilles. I showed up. He told me he wasn't too surprised. And I moved in."

Doug stopped chopping and looked up, obviously listening closely.

"But unfortunately, it seemed like Doug liked the idea of loving one woman and sleeping with others. I didn't think that approach was as cool as he did. I believe your name may have come up in a few of our discussions. I told him about our little tryst. Dougie was furious. *What the hell*, he said. *Don't you love me?* I told him straight out, what is good for the goose in this nest is sure as hell gonna be good for the gander. If Doug wanted to sleep around, there were going to be two of us showing off that behavior."

She took a sip of wine, then gave me the sideways smile again and said, "We had a couple of—uhm—let's call them *loud debates* during those first few months. They resulted in several noise complaints to the local *gens d'armes* from other building tenants. The Dougster and I have since ironed out those nuances. But that should give you some insight into why he quickly recognized your name."

Sandy gave Doug a mildly wild-eyed look and Doug shrugged his shoulder, then grinned.

"Anyway, in addition to working in restaurants, I needed to do something useful with my time. So, I started taking classes at Marseille University. I finished up my law degree in Lyon a few years ago. So, Mr. Newton, you are looking at a French licensed real estate attorney. Should you ever decide to buy a house here in Bordeaux, I can assist you—for a small fee."

"Congratulations," I said. "I guarantee that when I buy that elegant chateau in the countryside, you will be at my side. That's assuming Doug allows us to be together. Sorry Doug for cheating on you."

Doug said, "Absolutely. You are forgiven. But only after lunch. Come on—both of you— to the table. *On mange maintenant.* "

The lunch that Doug had prepared proved his skill as a chef beyond any doubt. The meal began with a simple butter lettuce salad with a delicate orange blossom vinaigrette dressing. That was followed by an omelet with minced and sauteed shallots, finely sliced shiitake mushrooms and gruyere cheese. Doug topped the omelet with a sprinkling of chopped parsley. We washed the meal down with a sparkling Perrier.

After Sandy had cleared the table and we had returned to the living room, I turned to my questions.

"So," I said, "in the spirit of Edward R. Murrow, please excuse the journalistic directness of this interrogation."

Sandy made a cross in the air and said, "You are formally absolved of the sins that you are about to commit."

"My first question is this, did you accomplish what you wanted to get done as mayor?"

Sandy looked inquiringly at Doug.

He took a deep breath, exhaled with some force and said, "What did I accomplish? I don't know, Paul. Maybe I added a few parks. Maybe I promoted a couple of young people who would have been ignored otherwise. I certainly got rid of some dead wood—people who just didn't want to leave their jobs but who didn't do them well at all. They hated me for it. I created some much-needed accountability in departments and strengthened financial management across the city. In that regard, I changed the city government's culture. But no, I didn't accomplish what I wanted."

Sandy had brought a bottle of Perrier and three glasses to the coffee table. She poured each of us some sparkling water. Douglas immediately took his glass and drained it.

As he set the glass down, he continued. "I wanted Saint Paul to be such a well-run city. I wanted it to be nationally recognized as the standard of excellence in city management. I wanted Saint Paul to be a place where poor kids had noticeably more advantages than they would have otherwise had. I know I accomplished a little of that—but not a lot. I was young and ambitious. I wanted to be famous. I wanted to show people they were wrong about me. That I— well, that I was someone who could not be cast aside—could not be thrown on the dung heap of life. I clearly didn't pull that one off."

Douglas Oleson sighed. Sandy looked at him with a furrowed brow. Her eyes expressed caring.

Then Olesen chuckled again and said, "OK, what else do you wanna know?"

I look down at my list and read the next question. "There were rumors that you took bribes when you were a mayor. Do you want to comment on that?"

Doug gave a hearty laugh. "You know, citizens who don't understand anything about government, will accuse whoever is in power of being a thief whenever their government doesn't do whatever they want. Before I was elected, people and organizations that felt they would benefit from my election contributed to my campaign. But it was done openly. Nothing under the table. The people who accused me of stealing or taking bribes; well, I just don't have much use for them. But for the record, the only funds I had when I left town were what I had saved from my official salary that was not awarded to Miki as a part of our divorce settlement. That's it. Zippo. There was nothing else."

"Speaking of Miki," I asked, "did you love her? If so, why the affairs? Do you want to send any sort of a message back to her?"

"Hmph." He took a deep breath, looked down and shook his head from side to side. "You're taking this reporter thing seriously, aren't you? This is a pretty hard-hitting set of questions."

He paused, then added, "Still, I'm glad you asked. They're questions I need to answer. Yes, I want to send a message back to Miki. I realize now that I was a pretty horrid egotist. When I managed the city—and even before that— everything was always about me. The one person who believed in me—who was always supportive of me—was Miki. I was a little like a drug addict—only my disease was intense egotism. Sleeping with other women had more to do with how lost I was then with any lack of affection for Miki. I hurt Miki—a lot. I was wrong. And I'll always have to live with that. Please tell her that."

This was getting a whole lot more open than I had anticipated. What had begun as an intellectual pursuit related to an incomplete college paper had somehow turned into something quite personal. But I felt I had a responsibility—I don't know to whom or why—I just had to continue.

"Do you want to know what's happening with your son Douglas Jr.? What are your feelings about disappearing from his life?"

Douglas Oleson stood up, walked across the room and looked out a window down onto the street below. He took a deep breath and exhaled. Then he shook his head from side to side again as he stood there, his back to me. I waited, unsure of what was next.

After about five minutes of intense silence, Oleson returned to his seat.

"Sandy told me that someday you'd show up. She said you were a really sweet kid and that I shouldn't be hard on you. I trust Sandy. She has seen me through a lot of shit and has always been honest with me. Sandy has criticized me for being hurtful to other people when I deserved the criticism. And yes. My son, my son."

Oleson took another deep breath and let it out slowly. He looked down. When he looked up, he looked directly into my eyes.

"I was raised in a home without a father. I was raised by an abusive woman. My son certainly didn't have an abusive mother. If I had stayed there," he paused, "if I had stayed there, my son might well have had an abusive father. I was carrying too much pain inside me—too much pain which I did not know how to manage. That's no excuse, I know. Asking about Douglas Jr. is the toughest question, Paul; the toughest question. Abandoning my son is something I don't like to think about. But it's something I need to think about. I haven't figured it out yet. But I know I need to."

I looked at Sandy. Her face told me that this whole dialog was painful for her to hear. She was watching Douglas closely but did nothing to stop me.

I kept going. "Do you have any regrets about dropping out of politics?"

Oleson roared with laughter. "No, I don't. Next question."

*****

We took a break. Each of us used the bathroom.

It had been intense and taking a few minutes off seemed like a good idea. As I waited for Sandy to return from the bathroom, I thought about how the whole thing was going. I was feeling unkind—like I was just beating Oleson up for no real purpose. I decided I needed to say something to that effect.

When they had both returned, I apologized. "I'm sorry Doug. This is not going at all like I thought it would. Somehow, I didn't expect to run into a human being. You've thrown me off. I have only one more set of difficult questions—really difficult questions."

He nodded at me, signaling me to go ahead.

"Were you aware that your mom passed away? Why did you disappear from her life?"

"You asked the toughest questions already, Paul. This one, I can deal with. Sandy wrote me when my mom passed away. Ma was a troubled person who had had a hard life. People who were abused when they were young often abuse the young people for whom they are responsible. I'm not angry at Ma. I once was. But as I've gotten older, I've come to understand that the pain she inflicted on me was an expression of the pain inside her. Why did I disappear from her life? I think that the hurt in me at that point was greater than the love I had for her. As we grow older, hopefully," he sighed, "hopefully we become wiser. I think I have. But who knows?"

Then a question from left field popped into my head. Even though it had nothing to do with what we had been talking about, I couldn't resist asking it. "What do you think of Trump?"

Oleson gave a hearty laugh. "He's an idiot. He's a serial abuser and a son of a bitch. But he is an excellent politician. The Donald tells lies to people who shouldn't believe him—but they do. But then we're talking about the psychology of the masses. Why did the Germans follow Hitler? The Italians, Mussolini? The Russians—well, take your pick: Lenin, Stalin or Putin? You explain humanity to me and I'll explain the Donald's successes to you."

I was in an impromptu role. "What do you think of the American political system?"

"That's a question I've thought a lot about. America is the Mecca of democracy—the capitol of capitalism. And the American political system—it is an amazing merger of democracy and capitalism. When I was mayor, I came to hate reporters. I felt they were always trying to bite at my back, to find fault whenever and wherever I succeeded. But in retrospect, I now know that democracy depends upon journalism. Democracy requires the Fourth Estate to keep it honest. That's why the first thing that a prospective autocrat or dictator does is to try to tear away the independence of the press—and the people's respect for news organizations. The wannabe tyrants always try to destroy the free press."

Douglas stopped speaking for a moment. I thought he had completed his response and was ready to move on.

But he held up his hand stopping me; then expanded on his understanding. "The reason I said our political system is a merger of democracy and capitalism is that elections are basically retail purchases by the electorate. Politicians are a product. A candidate has been designed to appeal to certain segments of the population the same as a shiny fast car or a quiet washing machine or any other product a retailer might try to sell. My job as a candidate, my campaign's responsibility, was to make me appear to be what the voters wanted to buy. That is what Trump does so well. He convinces people that he is what they need. And the only ones who have called him out on it are the journalists. If you write this up, if you add our meeting to your paper, you need to apologize to all of those journalists I maligned. I attacked them and I was wrong. I was really, really, really wrong."

I asked, "Has anybody else found you since you left Saint Paul?"

"Well, in addition to Sandy," he looked at her and they both laughed, "in addition to Sandy there was one lady in Lyon, a woman who I had known in the legislature. She spotted me. I quickly lost her. But I've been surprised. You're the first person to make an organized effort to find me. Maybe that's because people were so glad to have me out of their lives, they saw no purpose in chasing after me."

"Is there anything in your life that you regret?"

Douglas Oleson took on a furrowed look. "There is so much, Paul, so much I regret. I didn't have a whole lot of wisdom back then—and I'm not sure I have that much more now. I could make a list of the people I allowed myself to hurt because I was so self-centered. I regret hurting them. I regret that I didn't have the largeness in me to deal with my mother. I regret hurting Miki and Douglas Jr. They top my list. And I want you to give them my apologies. I will also write each of them a letter. I'd like to meet Douglas Jr. someday. I don't expect him to feel warm toward me. But I owe him a huge and humble apology. And I will do it. I've also hurt Sandy. I regret that a lot."

His last statement was said slowly. There were tears in his eyes. I noticed that there were tears in hers as well.

I wasn't sure where to take the conversation. It seemed to be coming to closure. It was my turn to take a deep breath.

After exhaling, I said, "I guess I lied before. I do have one more question. I'm very uncomfortable about this one. But I have a responsibility to ask it on behalf of somebody else who I cared for."

Oleson waited and I paused and took a deep breath before asking, "Do you know who your father was?"

Douglas was silent. He looked down. A moment later, he looked up and in a very soft voice said, "When I was young, it hurt me that I didn't have a father. When my teachers asked what our fathers did, I was always so ashamed. When I was little, I used to imagine who my father was—what he was like. My mother never told me anything. One time, I asked her who my father was and she just said, *That son of a bitch is enjoying his own life. He doesn't care about you.* That hurt."

I sat there, absorbing the candor Douglas Oleson was allowing himself. Sometimes you struggle with things and you just don't know what the right thing to do is. I had wondered if I would say anything—or not—about his father.

Finally, I went ahead and said, "I learned who your father was after his passing. Your dad was a good man. He was also extraordinarily proud of you. When I decided I wanted to become a journalist, a teacher of mine at Carleton touched bases with a friend of hers who ran a small paper in Bloomington and...."

"*The Weekly Dispatch*?" Oleson interrupted me and his jaw dropped. Then he said with a look of shock, "You got to be kidding me. Webster Pedersen? Webster's my dad?"

"Yes. When I started the internship, I needed a project that I could turn into a senior thesis. Webster handed me a manila folder full of clippings. He told me to review them and see if the subject of the clippings would work for my project. The clippings were all about you. Webster told me you were a young politician who had begun a stellar career and then disappeared. He told me that trying to document what happened to you would make a great project. Webster followed your career the whole way from when you ran for the state house until you disappeared. After he passed away, Louise, his wife, told me how proud he was of you. She told me that as soon as he had learned that your mother had a child, he went to her and asked if he could help support you financially—if he could get to know you. He made this offer to your mother more than once. Each time she angrily told him to get out of her life."

Douglas Oleson was silent.

Sandy brought over another bottle of wine and poured a glass for each of us.

He took a sip, then a deep breath and said, "Wow."

A couple of minutes later, Douglas Oleson said, "I knew Webster. He interviewed me a few times. He was a nice man. His..."

Oleson stopped speaking. He was choked up. He just sat there. I didn't know what to say or do. A moment later, quiet tears were running down Oleson's cheeks.

Sandy took over the conversation. She glanced at Oleson who nodded at her.

Then she said, "Look, Paul. This has been pretty intense. But it also has been meaningful. I know I speak for Doug when I say we don't want to say goodbye right now. We were planning on going out to dinner this evening at a neighborhood bistro where we often dine. I think you would enjoy it. Why don't you plan on joining us? Come back around seven and we'll go out for dinner."

Chapter 6 – Going for a Walk

I was surprised at how emotionally drained I was. This project that I had taken on almost a quarter of a century before had become fundamental to who I was. Today, the cast of characters that I had interviewed when I was young had come together (in my mind's eye at least) with the person in whom they all had an interest. I had been transformed into an unusual sort of messenger. In some regards, I felt good about having channeled their feelings—in other regards, not so good. But for certain, I was drained.

I spent the next hour walking through the magnificent park near Douglas and Sandy's apartment. *Le Jardin Public* was so peaceful. I watched kids playing, lovers walking hand in hand and parents riding with a child or two in small rented boats that graced the park's elegant lake.

As I walked, I thought of a couple of things that I should have said to Douglas—things that were in my notes, but I had been too distracted by the intensity of our conversation to share. I would bring them up that evening.

It was 4 o'clock when I got back to my hotel room. I set my phone alarm for 6:15, closed my eyes and was immediately asleep.

*****

I had a dream about Webster and Louise. I was enjoying dinner in their home. In the dream, I noted that Webster was smoking cigarettes at home. He held his cigarette in his classic ash-balancing maneuver while blowing smoke toward the ceiling. And, in the dream, Louise just watched and smiled.

I was sitting at the table with Louise and Webster, waiting for Louise to serve dinner. However, for some reason, she just delayed bringing the food out. It was then that I looked around the table and noticed that there were five other place settings. I realized we were waiting for five more people to arrive, to join us for dinner.

In the dream, Webster was speaking about the empty farmhouse that he and Louise had found in a field in Nebraska. Webster told us he had found the couple who had lived there. "I apologized to them for entering their home. The husband did not respond to me but his wife did. She said, *We're glad you enjoyed our home. It meant so much to us. We are gratified that our home also had meaning for you and your wife.*"

At that point in the dream, I heard a knock at the front door. Webster left the table and returned a moment later. He was with Douglas Oleson and Sandy. Louise stood up and gave each of them a hug which they warmly returned. Everyone sat down at the table.

In the dream, Oleson said to Webster, "Sorry we were late, dad. Traffic was horrible."

A moment later, there was another knock at the front door. This time, I got up and went to the door. It was Kathy. I hugged her and brought her into the dining room, introducing her to the others.

Kathy said, "Webster and Louise, if there was one single meal in the world that I could be invited to enjoy, this would be it. Paul is always talking about your chicken fricassee. And today, I'm going to eat two helpings."

But there were still two unoccupied place settings.

I heard another knock at the door. This time Louise got up and went to answer it. When she returned, she was leading my mother and father. They were holding hands. Introductions were made around the table and kind things were said by all.

Webster raised his wineglass. Everyone else at the table followed suit.

"To the good things in life," he said. "There is so much misery in this world, so much pain and we struggle to understand it all. But there are so many good things as well. Let's drink to the good things in life."

We all repeated, *to the good things in life* and we drank to Webster's toast.

Then Louise stood up and said, "And now for some of my chicken fricassee."

*****

I was awakened by the alarm on my phone. For a moment, I was totally confused. What was going on? Then I realized that the dinner party I had been enjoying so much had only been a dream.

*****

Three-quarters of an hour later, Douglas and Sandy welcomed me as an old friend. They opened an excellent bottle of Champagne. Douglas was about to propose a toast, but I asked if I could make the toast instead.

He was a little taken aback, but said, "Sure."

"To the good things in life," I said. "There is so much misery in this world, so much pain and we struggle to understand it all. But there are so many good things as well. Let's drink to the good things in life."

*****

As we walked to the restaurant, Douglas Oleson walked ahead of Sandy and me. In a hushed voice, Sandy said to me, "Today was the first time I saw Douglas cry. This visit has been pretty incredible. I think it has given me as much new insight into the Dougster as it has given you."

"I sincerely doubt that," I responded.

*****

An hour later we were enjoying a wonderful dinner at an outdoor table a couple of blocks from the Bordeaux Opera House.

We each ordered poulet à la moutarde, pan-fried chicken thighs braised in a white wine cream sauce spiked with Dijon mustard—a meal inspired by my having told Doug and Sandy about my meal with Webster and Louise. Having heard a description of my meal with Louise after Webster's passing, Douglas ordered an excellent bottle of *Pouilly Fuissé* to accompany our dinner.

*****

After the intensity of our earlier meeting, the evening's lighthearted conversation was a relief. I told Douglas stories about his father. He and Sandy laughed when I described Webster's ceremony of smoking a cigarette. I described the man's kindness, his love for his wife, his sadness at losing his daughter Ingrid in a car accident and his desire to learn as much as he could about his only son.

Douglas had read my senior thesis that afternoon and shared a funny story or two about each of the people I had interviewed.

I repeated one story I had neglected to share earlier in the day. "Miss Hanson, your fourth-grade teacher, told me if I ever saw you, I should tell you that she often thought about you. She told me that you were one of the sweetest kids she'd ever known. She asked me to tell you that she hoped you were doing well."

"You know something," said Douglas. "That lady, Miss Hanson, she was so nice to me. Oftentimes, when I was feeling sad and lonely in the school years that followed, I would think of some of the special things she had said to me. They would lift me. Boy, was she ever a special person."

I also remembered to repeat Millie Oleson's words from her deathbed. "Your mom told me, Doug, she said, *tell him his mother does love him. Tell him I'm sorry about the things I did wrong, I'm sorry for anything bad that I said. Tell him I wished I'd gotten him that dog. Tell him...tell him I'm sorry.*"

After I repeated that story, Doug's jaw tightened. Then tears emerged again. Sandy reached out and put her hand on his shoulder, but said nothing. We waited. A minute later, Douglas Oleson composed himself, gave a smile and suggested we finish up our meal with a bottle of Sauterne.

After the half-liter bottle of chilled dessert wine came to our table, and once our small dessert wine glasses had been filled, Douglas lifted his glass and said, "To Ma. I don't think there was any way I could have understood the pain in your life, Ma. But if you're listening, know that I love you." He paused and added, "And I forgive you."

*****

Very little was said after that. We each had an espresso. Douglas insisted on paying for dinner and I was wise enough to accept his generosity and just say *thanks*.

Sandy hugged me. "Thank you for coming Paul. I was right. You were a sweetheart when I met you two decades ago and you were a sweetheart today. I'm really glad you visited us. I wish you a rich and happy life."

*****

I stayed several more days in Bordeaux taking a day trip to the nearby village of Saint Émilion to buy gifts for Kathy and the kids and to taste the village's fine Bordeaux.

Then I headed home, taking that TGV bullet train back to Paris' Charles de Gaulle Airport.

After what seemed like just a short nap on the Boeing 787, I was greeted by Kathy and the kids at the Minneapolis-Saint Paul Airport.

Chapter 7 – Following Through on Commitments

A couple weeks after I returned to the Twin Cities, I received a note from Miki. Douglas Oleson had reached out to her saying some of the things that needed to be said. He also had invited Douglas Jr. to visit Sandy and him in Bordeaux.

*****

So, I had kept my promise to Louise. I had not disclosed her secret about who was Douglas' father until after she had passed.

And I am also keeping my commitment to Dr. Harris—to complete my senior thesis. While I graduated from Carleton more than two decades ago, I'd always felt I'd cheated a little by not responding to the unanswered questions that were asked in that paper.

This book provides a necessary closure.

Roger Neumaier's Previously Published Titles:

Imprints from an Odyssey
The Cuban Girl
Alex in Deutschland
A Home in the Bitterroot
Joseph Imagines God
Poetry and Reflection